AGNARR'S TEACHER

ABANDONED ON NIFLHEIM

JENIFER WOOD

AGNARR'S TEACHER

ABANDONED ON NIFLHEIM BOOK ONE

JENIFER WOOD

Cover art by Rowan Woodcock.

Cover design by Ash Raven.

Editing by Lavender Prose.

Piracy is a serious concern for small indie authors like me, who have poured many hours into our books. Piracy prevents us from being able to support ourselves and continue to write more.

If you know someone who might enjoy this book, but cannot obtain a copy legally, please reach out to me at authorjeniferwood@gmail.com.

If you are reading a pirated copy of the book right now, please also get in touch with me. I want to work with you to get my book into readers' hands legally. Thank you for understanding.

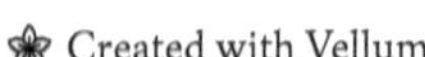 Created with Vellum

For Carlotta, who told me to just start.

For Rob, who knew all along.

A NOTE ABOUT CONTENT

While there has been debate about the necessity of content warnings in books, I, as an anxious person, am firmly in the pro-content warnings camp. If you do not want any part of *Agnarr's Teacher* spoiled for you, feel free to skip ahead.

Agnarr's Teacher falls on the lighter side of sci-fi and fantasy romance, but there are certain aspects readers may want to know about in advance.

- Alien Abduction
- Drugging
- Anxiety/Mental Illness
- Mentioned parental neglect
- Near drowning
- Explicit sexual scenes
- Mentioned death of parents
- Dangerous encounters with flora and fauna
- Knotting
- Stretching and stuffing

CHAPTER 1

PIPER

*J*erked awake with a gasp, blinking rapidly, trying to figure out what woke me up. As I tried to shake off the confusion of sleep, I rolled over. I nearly toppled out of bed when what I was seeing came into focus. I was eye to eye, almost nose to nose, with a child, who was staring at me in surprise.

The feeling of being watched must have been what pulled me to consciousness. But what was I actually looking at? I felt like my brain was short-circuiting. It was the right size to be a child, its eyes equal level to mine where I lay in bed. Yet, this child was unlike any child I had ever seen. Standing before me was… well, if I had to put a name on him I would say it was an orc. An orc child. He looked like the orcs I'd seen in one of my high school boyfriend's *Dungeons and Dragons* books, just child-sized.

He was roughly the height of an average eight-year-old, but much stockier in build. His skin was a dusky green, almost the same color as pine needles. Black toenails and fingernails tipped both his fingers and toes. It didn't seem to be because of dirt or uncleanliness, but the natural color of his nails. He was wearing pants and a vest that looked as if they were made of woven fabric, neatly made and with decorative stitching down the seams. He was well cared for, this orc child.

Examining his face, his startled eyes had light gold sclera, and brown irises rimmed in black. His mouth hung open to reveal teeny tusks jutting up from his lower lip, and elongated canines peeking out from his top lip. He had a shock of black hair and delicately pointed ears, and he looked absolutely horrified. Tears were leaking out of his eyes and his lip wobbled as he realized he'd been caught. I kicked into teacher mode immediately.

"I'm okay. You just startled me. There's no need to cry," I whispered. Why was I whispering?

"I just wanted to meet our new visitors. You won't tell my mamma, will you?" he asked, his face full of concern. He met my gaze, then looked down, clearly ashamed to have been caught in my room. I grabbed the edge of my blanket and wiped his eyes, hoping to provide a small comfort.

I took more of him in, noticing a leather belt that carried two small hunting knives, not much bigger than butter knives, really, and a small bag of some variety. He had a necklace of brightly colored beads around his neck, and one of his pointed ears had a small hoop earring.

He glanced back at me, meeting my eyes. A child was a child, no matter what species. Being a teacher, I had a soft spot for little ones and the somewhat misguided decisions they made. I grinned at him, and he hesitantly grinned back.

Years of teaching had taught me to keep it together on the outside, even if I was losing it on the inside. Despite my friendly and calming demeanor with this orc child, on the inside, I was absolutely freaking out. My eyes darted away from his face, and I realized not only was an orc staring at me in bed, I wasn't in my room. My ability to keep myself calm was deteriorating rapidly.

"What is your name?" I asked in my sweetest teacher voice.

"My name is Odin. You won't tell Mamma that I woke you up, will you?" He looked at me hopefully.

I had to make some quick decisions. Would I be safer if I kept Odin with me or if I somehow sent him away? I was about five seconds away from a full-blown panic attack. It was probably for the best if I sent Odin on some sort of errand while I tried to get my bearings.

"Odin, why don't we do this? Why don't we tell Mamma that I opened the door and you happened to be walking by? I won't tell her you came into my room if you won't tell. Deal?" I whispered conspiratorially.

Odin smiled at me hesitantly. Thank the universe I was good with children—apparently, regardless of their species.

"You're sure?" Odin asked.

"Absolutely. Actually, I think I would like to meet Mamma. Do you think you could tell her I'm awake? Is she far from here?" I was trying to get a minute to collect myself while getting as many details as possible.

"Oh, our cabin is all the way across the village from here, but if I run, I can be right back." He said this all very quickly, enthusiastic at the prospect of running through the village with news.

If I had Odin go get his mom, I'd get time to figure out where I was. However, I would also alert others to my presence. I tried to think as quickly as I could while keeping my teacher smile on my face. My pounding heart and racing thoughts made the decision easy. Yes, I would take the risk of sending Odin to get his mom. I needed the time.

"That sounds great. I would be so happy to meet her," I said, enthusiastic teacher voice in full force. I gave him my most encouraging smile. Without any hesitation, Odin took off running for the door, opening it quietly but then slamming it behind him as he darted off.

I was alone. My inner introvert unclenched—time to figure out where I was. I let my teacher's facade fall and blinked several times as I took in my surroundings. I was definitely not in my room. That was not my nightstand. Odin had been standing in front of what appeared to be the interior portion of a log cabin wall, the kind where the bark had been meticulously stripped so you could see all the knots in the wood. It looked like pine, but it had more of an orange tint to it. And the knots in the wood were smaller, more evenly spaced out. There was an open window on the opposite wall with crisp white curtains that fluttered in the breeze. I could feel the fresh air on my face, but I couldn't see out the window from where I was in bed.

The clean wooden floor gleamed in the morning sunlight that spilled in from the window. There was a woven rug in front of the window made with a pretty mix of red and yellow fabric. On the windowsill was a tiny bud vase holding a type of flower I had never seen before. Almost like a peony but much studier looking.

Okay, this place seemed somewhat... welcoming? Yet, the panic I had pushed aside for Odin's sake was creeping back in.

After a few moments of breathing exercises, I calmed enough to take in more details of the space. Seeing more of it definitely reinforced the woodsy cabin vibes I was already getting. I sat up to get a better look around and gather more information about where I was.

The bed I was in was made of logs similar to those that made the walls, bark scraped free, and wood shiny with varnish. Blankets that appeared to be made of a loosely woven material I didn't recognize covered me. Maybe wool?

Next to me was a wooden chest of drawers with a pitcher and a cup sitting atop it, made of some sort of dark metal. Across from me was a fireplace, with a fire cheerfully crackling in the hearth. Next to the fireplace was a large rocking chair with a blanket that looked similar to the one on my bed, neatly folded.

I was comfortable under the blanket. Someone had tucked me into the bed. Someone had stoked the fire throughout the night or lit it early this morning. The thought that a stranger had been in here while I slept was creepy, no matter how comforting the space seemed.

It was all very homey. My panic was receding because, wherever I was, I didn't seem to be in imminent danger. Yet, I couldn't for the life of me figure out where I could be. How had I even gotten here? I started wracking my brain to think of the last things I could remember.

Was that nightmare I had woken up from actually a nightmare?

It had been a Thursday night after an incredibly long day of teaching. The kids were amped because the next day was a half day and Monday was a holiday. It was almost impossible to get anything done before a three-day weekend. Never mind that I taught seventeen-year-olds. The idea of an extra day of freedom had them bouncing off the walls. By the last period, I was over trying to wrangle them into writing their essays on the foundations of American government. Being the "fun" teacher, I had given in and let them watch an episode of *Parks and Recreation* and called it a day. *Parks and Rec* counted as government content as far as I was concerned.

After work, my commute felt like it had crawled by. I was eager to have some time to myself. Managing a classroom all day had me tapped out. I decided that two frozen waffles and string cheese counted as dinner and crashed on the couch with a new book.

Fuck.

It all came flooding back to me. It wasn't a nightmare.

There had been a knock on my apartment door around nine p.m. Being the true crime aficionado and millennial I was, I had no intention of answering. It was probably an Amazon delivery. I was expecting more toothbrush heads. Thrilling.

But the knock was persistent, which seemed odd. The Amazon driver usually dropped the packages and was gone before I even had time to get to the door. Finally, as the knocking continued, I quietly looked through the peephole only to see no one there.

Yep, definitely not opening the door. I looked again just in time to hear a thundering crash come from the kitchen. The lights flickered out.

Heart hammering in my chest, I attempted to find something to defend myself. With the lights out, I relied on the ambient light from the street lamps outside to see. I found a heavy candle, of all things, and palmed it, figuring I could at least throw it at someone.

I was trying to decide if I should stay where I was or run out my front door, screaming my head off to alert my neighbors, when a figure appeared in the entry to the kitchen. Tall and slender, with an abnormally large head, the figure took up most of the doorway. I couldn't make out much more in the relative darkness. Between fight or flight, I was definitely a flight kind of girl, so I backed up, trying to find the doorknob to the front door behind me. I'd take my chances outside.

But it had been too dark, and the thing had been too fast. It was upon me before I'd even grabbed the doorknob. I felt something cool and metal press against my neck, then a prick of a needle, and everything went dark.

Feeling suddenly cold in the warm cabin, I reached up and touched my neck. The skin where I remembered the metal being pressed against my neck was tender. Oh fuck. Definitely not a nightmare.

The memories of the prior night had my panic creeping back up to dizzying heights. Whoever or whatever had arrived at my house had taken me. But the eerie creature who had clearly knocked me out with some sort of drug did not fit the vibes of this cozy cabin bedroom I was in. What the hell had happened?

I realized I was not in the pajamas I'd had on when I was knocked out in my living room. I was wearing a soft shift dress with short sleeves. While comfortable, the fact that I was wearing it definitely did not bring me comfort. Someone had taken my clothes. Someone had seen me naked. They had dressed me while I was unconscious, like a doll.

Well, that made me incredibly weirded out. When was the last time I'd washed my bra? Yeesh. Now I didn't have a bra on.

Unsure of how much time I had until Odin returned, it was time to figure out where I was. Had the stranger driven me to some remote cabin in the woods? Was I involuntarily joining a commune? Were they going to shave my head? I had definitely watched too many cult documentaries.

However, a cult didn't explain Odin. I could not ignore that, no matter how harmless Odin seemed, he was definitely not human.

Maybe it was less nefarious. My principal was all about team building, and we'd been on many trips as a staff. Maybe this was some sort of bonding exercise to make us break down our walls and share our feelings. I had never had problems with any of those exercises. Thanks to years of therapy,

I had plenty of feelings to share. But this seemed a bit extreme. Being kidnapped and forced to go camping? No thanks. Also, forced work bonding still didn't address the presence of an orc child. I was losing my mind, grasping at straws, trying to make any sense of my current situation.

I swung my legs out of the bed and stepped onto the floor. Surprised to find my feet not on the wooden floor, but on a plush rug that appeared to be made of some sort of animal fur. Add that to the list of things that pointed toward me being a guest, not a prisoner.

There were homemade slippers next to the rug that appeared to be made of leather and lined with the same sort of fur as the rug. I slipped them on and snorted immediately; they were at least five sizes too big. Wherever I was, they were used to giant visitors. I wasn't dainty by any means, with a size-nine feet, but these slippers were gargantuan. That worried me a bit, but I decided all the other welcoming parts of the room outweighed the giant slippers.

I tiptoed to the open window, wanting to gain more information about my surroundings but definitely not ready to meet anyone else. The curtains were partially open, but I pushed them wide, trying to see out. The cabin appeared to be at the edge of a forest. Trees, taller than any I had ever seen, started only about ten feet from my window. They soared up so high that they disappeared into the mist that seemed to sit over the land like low-lying fog.

The trees resembled pine, but again, were more orangey in hue. The forest floor was littered with pine-like needles, and I could hear birds chirping in the distance. It really felt like I was in some sort of cabin in the woods, peaceful and serene. Yet, it was bringing me anything but serenity.

Having a minute to myself let me slowly add everything up.

The shadowy figure and the shot to the neck.

The orc child.

The cabin that definitely wasn't designed for a human.

The plants that were similar yet different to plants from home.

Then the realization came crashing down upon me. I hadn't just been kidnapped. I'd been abducted by aliens.

CHAPTER 2

I had no idea how long it would be until Odin came back, but if he knew I was here, others would too. I sifted through all the information I had, trying to make sense of it. But with my anxiety riding high, it felt like trying to untangle a giant wad of jewelry.

Odin did not seem to be the same species as whatever had taken me. The alien from my living room had been tall and slender. Odin, even at his young age, was built solidly, nothing slender about him. This had to mean that the aliens that had taken me weren't orcs.

I was in Odin's home village. I was in a cabin, tucked nicely into bed. Someone had put me in comfortable clothes. Heck, they'd even left me slippers, even if they were several sizes too large. They wouldn't care for me in this way if they had nefarious plans for me, right? Right?! What could the orcs possibly want with me?

Then I thought about Odin's little tusks. Orcs didn't eat

people, did they? Oh, how I wished I had paid attention when my high school boyfriend made me watch all of those *Lord of the Rings* movies. I knew literally nothing about orcs other than their general appearance. The ones from *Dungeons and Dragons* seemed okay, if not a little violent, but the ones from *Lord of the Rings* seemed like the type that might eat a human.

That thought had me laughing to myself. Here I was, abducted by aliens, likely no longer on Earth, in clothes that weren't my own, and I was berating myself for not paying attention to *The Lord of the Rings* in high school. It was so ridiculous that I couldn't help but laugh even harder. Perhaps I was a *teensy bit* hysterical.

The sound of metal against metal outside pulled me out of my internal hysteria. I dropped to my knees, afraid of being seen, and peered over the top of my bed to attempt to see out the window. I could see nothing from where I knelt. As the clashes and clangs got louder, I could hear voices interspersed.

"Is that the best you've got? You're getting weak as a mated male!" The voice was friendly. It sounded more like good-natured ribbing between friends than an actual insult. A pause, then more sounds of metal upon metal before a second voice responded.

"Já, ever since Saela and I accepted our bond, I have found better ways to spend my time than practicing sparring with you." The second voice was good-natured and full of innuendo. I had no doubt what he and Saela were doing with their free time.

"Must you remind me? It is enough that I can hear the sounds of your mating whenever I walk by your cabin. Have some pity on your brother," the first voice bemoaned. Another loud clash of metal followed.

I crept closer to the window, feeling safer. It was clear

these two were friends and not attempting to kill each other, regardless of what sounds their weapons made. Reaching the windowsill, I hesitated for only a moment, my curiosity getting the better of me. I peered outside. Luckily, the two swords struck each other right as I gasped.

Two fully grown orcs were engaged in a sword fight outside my window. It was clear from their features that they were the same species as little Odin. Both males were green, though in different shades. The one to my left was duskier than even Odin, more of an olive-green shade. The orc to my right was a brighter green, with less brown mixed in. They continued to fight, grunting with exertion.

"Your time will come, Agnarr. You are young to be losing hope of finding a mate," he said amiably. The orc to my right was the one speaking, the one that was a brighter green. Looking at him more closely, I realized he looked a bit older than the orc to my left, who I now knew was Agnarr.

"I am thirty-two árs this winter solstice. How is that young, Brandr? In times that have come before, a male would have sired three to four orklings by my age," Agnarr complained. He ratcheted up his swordplay, clearly taking out his frustration on his fighting partner.

Both orcs were oblivious to their audience, so I did what my anxious brain knew how to do best—gather more information. Now that I had names, it was a bit easier. Maybe Brandr looked a bit older than Agnarr, or maybe it was that he had the scruff of a five o'clock shadow and Agnarr was clean-shaven. I knew Agnarr was thirty-two, at least by this planet's years, if that's what *árs* meant. They were orcs in their prime, if the way they looked and fought was any indication.

Agnarr and Brandr did not look like orcs from the Tolkien movies at all. If I was remembering correctly, Tolkien orcs were covered in slime. Agnarr and Brandr looked more similar to the orcs from Dungeons and Dragons. I was never really a D&D player, but my nerdy boyfriend had been hardcore into it. While still fearsome, they were less disturbing than the orcs of the Tolkien world. At least based on my hazy memories. I had never paid as much attention as Brian had hoped during D&D, focusing more on the snacks than the gameplay.

Refocusing on the practice battle in front of me, I continued to analyze the two orcs. For science. They were definitely humanoid, yet both of them were absolutely enormous. I was never good at judging height, but if I had to guess, they were at least seven feet, easily basketball-player sized. Agnarr was thicker than Brandr, appearing like a solid wall of muscle. Brandr looked no less deadly, being taller and leaner. Both orcs had long black hair. Brandr had his woven in two intricate braids down his back, whereas Agnarr's hair was in a messy bun. Maybe because he didn't have a mate to braid it for him? I felt a sudden rush of sympathy for Agnarr.

It was too hard to keep switching back and forth as they circled each other, so I focused my observations on Agnarr. He had rough-hewn features, with a heavy brow ridge and a square jaw. From where I crouched, I could see the sweat glistening on his forehead. He had thick black eyebrows that arched expressively. The sclera of his eyes matched the light gold of Odin's, but his irises were a much darker brown, almost black. Wide cheekbones tapered down to full lips, a shade slightly darker green than the rest of him. Fearsome-looking tusks protruded from his lower lip, almost reaching his prominent nose, his mouth was set in a frown of concentration as he fought Brandr. If I weren't still undecided on whether orcs ate people, I would definitely say he was attractive in an otherworldly sort of way.

The two orcs continued to circle each other, swords clashing. I knew nothing of sword fighting, but the two appeared evenly matched. They deflected each other's advances with effortless grace, both holding their weapons with the confidence that came with years of practice. Agnarr was scowling, but Brandr seemed almost bored. It did not appear that this fight was taxing either of them.

"Do you want to call it an even match and head to the baths?" Brandr shouted over the sound of the swords.

"Absolutely not, Brandr. You know I can beat you. I know you'd rather be elsewhere with Saela, but we both know we need to stay in peak condition, all things considered." Agnarr launched himself forward, sword outstretched, coming down hard on Brandr's weapon as if to prove his point.

As Agnarr lunged and parried, I left my analysis of his face and dropped my eyes down the rest of his body. Agnarr was wearing a tunic that hit mid-thigh; it bunched and pulled as he moved his muscles in battle. Jesus Christ, he was the orc equivalent of a stacked dude in a white t-shirt.

His arms were corded in muscles, veins prominent enough that I could see them from my hiding place. His broad hands had black fingernails, just like Odin's. He held his sword easily as he continued to fight. Both orcs wore soft-looking pants tucked into knee-high leather boots. I couldn't help but notice how snugly Agnarr's pants fit over his muscled ass and thick thighs.

Was I ogling an alien? Maybe.

Discarding the fact that neither males were human, they both were handsome in a monstrous sort of way. The tusks were a bit shocking and their eye coloring was definitely alien, but once you got used to the differences, they weren't all that jarring. Both orcs were immaculately clean and well-dressed, something you couldn't say for a majority of men on Earth.

I found myself continually drawn back to Agnarr's face. Maybe it was that I knew he was unattached, or maybe it was just that he was physically a bit closer to me, but if I had to take my pick, Agnarr would be it.

As I admired their muscles, I wondered about Agnarr's comment. Why did they need to stay in peak physical condition? They were clearly skilled in battle. Were they at war? That thought completely derailed my comparison of Agnarr to some sort of lumbersnack and ramped my anxiety back up.

Intrusive thoughts about being traded to an enemy or used as some sort of hostage flooded my brain. Maybe they would trade me to some species even more fearsome. Maybe they needed me as bait.

My therapist called this catastrophic thinking. Yet, given I was on an alien planet apparently inhabited by warrior orcs and had no idea what they planned to do with me, I allowed myself to catastrophize for a minute.

I wasn't creating worst-case scenarios; I was in a worst-case scenario.

It was really only my anxiety that had allowed me to detach from my panic for a moment to take in the details of Agnarr and Brandr, needing to gather all the information I could about my surroundings in order to self-soothe. Now my panic was back in full force. I needed answers to my questions, and I needed them now.

Just as I was readying myself to stand up and announce my presence, a knock sounded on my door.

Startled, I stood up and rushed to answer it, trying to stay out of the line of the window so the males couldn't see me. I was in blind need of comfort. From what I had seen of the orcs so far, I wasn't afraid of one being at my door. I pulled the door open to be greeted by a beautiful orc female, holding hands with little Odin.

"Hello! I am so happy Odin brought you to see me. My name is Piper. I have about five hundred questions that I hope you'd be willing to answer." I said this all with cheery overconfidence, very aware that I was expressing a bizarre amount of enthusiasm. The female in front of me looked startled at first, but then gave me a warm smile.

"Good morning, Piper. I'm Tora. I'm Odin's mamma. I'll try to answer as many questions as I can." She continued to smile at me, clearly seeing my panic and attempting to put me at ease.

I took a deep breath. This orc woman was the comfort I needed. She stepped into my room, followed by Odin. She squatted down to eye level with him.

"Odin, baby, I am sure that Piper is pretty hungry, considering the journey she's had. Could you go to the kitchens and get her some breakfast?" She smiled sweetly at him and stroked his black hair.

"But I wanted to stay here and meet her too!" Odin pushed out his lower lip petulantly.

"I know, baby, but she's hungry and we need some time, just us females. Please? I promise you can spend some time with her when you get back. And hey, I bet Cook would be willing to give you a second breakfast while you're there."

"Second breakfast?!" And with that, Odin was off running without a backward glance.

"Somehow, I knew that would give him the motivation he needed," Tora said with a laugh. "Now then, let's get you off your feet and see what I can do to put your mind at ease."

She led me to the rocking chair. I sat down on it while she lowered herself onto the three-legged footstool next to it. My mind suddenly blanked. I had no idea what question to start with. There were far too many. I just sort of stared at Tora, slack-jawed.

I knew I felt safe, but I needed to know if these aliens were the reason I'd been drugged and taken from my living room. Otherwise, all that feeling of safety was a lie. The first question was definitely going to be the most uncomfortable, but I had to know.

"Did your people… I mean, did the orcs…" I hesitated, frowning, and attempted to try again. "I remember someone breaking into my house, drugging me, and then waking up here. I need to know if the aliens that live here had any part in my abduction." I clasped my hands together in front of me, squeezing them together so tightly I could feel my nails digging into my skin. It felt as if my entire fate hinged on the answer to this question.

Tora took my hands out of my lap and held both of them. Her hands were much larger than mine and calloused from some sort of manual labor. I looked down. She had long, slender fingers and black nails. She was another, different shade of green. Her green was similar to that of Odin's, but a bit brighter. I was starting to realize the greens were very similar to the wide range of skin tones back on Earth. I looked into her eyes and they were the exact same color as her son's.

"Well, I am glad I can ease at least one of your fears immediately. We had no part in your abduction. We don't abduct humans—or anyone, for that matter. We don't even have the technology to travel to Midgard. And yes, you guessed correctly, we're orkin." She smiled as my system flooded with relief.

Okay, so I was definitely on an alien planet, but I was not in the hands of my abductors. That had to be good news, right? Yet, the way that Tora looked at me, I knew there was bad news she was waiting to share.

"You can rest assured you'll be safe and taken care of. But I have other news that you might not find as reassuring."

"Tell me. I need to know." I looked Tora square in the eye, steeling myself for the hard truth.

"You can't go home. Ever." She said it quietly, as if it would lessen the blow.

Well, shit. I was so worried about making sure I was safe in the here and now that I hadn't even considered getting home. I was too busy ensuring I lived through the present. Never go home? Ever?

No. Hell no. Nope.

"What do you mean, I can't go home? I have to go home! I have a life. I have a job. I have two cats!" My breathing came in short pants and my chest constricted. I felt like I couldn't get enough oxygen to my brain. I tried to slow down my breathing, but it was too late. My vision blurred and darkened around the edges.

Oh no, I was going under. The panic was going to win this time.

CHAPTER 3

When I came to, I was back in the bed. Tora was still with me. She was looking out my window. I couldn't hear swords clashing anymore. I tried to sit up. She must have heard my movement because she rushed to my side. The three-legged stool that used to be by the rocking chair was now next to my bed. Had Tora been watching over me? She sat down on the stool and took my hands in hers again. This must be an orkin way of providing comfort. I must say, I didn't hate it.

"I'm so glad you're awake. You scared all of us." Her face was etched with concern.

"Us?" I whispered, alarmed.

"Já, when you collapsed, I called for two of our male orcs to help get you back in bed. They had been practicing sparring outside. I shooed them away so you wouldn't wake up with male orcs you didn't know standing over you." She said this with a smile, probably trying to comfort me. Clearly, she was worried I'd pass out again.

"The two orcs that were sparring outside put me back in bed? Agnarr and Brandr?" I questioned, mortified.

"How'd you know their names?" Tora looked at me quizzically.

Uh oh. Now I had to think fast or it would be clear I had spent a good chunk of time ogling them while they practiced. It was plausible that I just heard what was going on outside and hadn't spent time getting a good look at them, right?

"I heard them outside my room. At first, I thought there was an honest to gods sword fight happening, but as I kept listening, I realized they were practicing. They addressed each other by name," I explained, as if it made perfect sense and wasn't a cobbled-together lie. I was currently on an alien planet with a brief explanation of what was happening. I'd just been informed I had no way back to Earth. Now was not the time to admit I was ogling an orc. We needed to get back to the matter at hand. I needed to get back to Earth. I had students. I had cats. I had houseplants that were mostly dead.

"I'm sorry, but there must be some sort of mistake. I can't stay here forever. My home is on Earth," I said, hoping against hope that she was mistaken that there was no way off this planet. Yet, the look on her face told me everything I needed to know. I couldn't help it. Tears started welling in my eyes. How could I never be going home? Surely, if I got here to this strange orkin planet, there had to be a way back, right?

"I'm sorry, Piper, but it's true. You won't be able to get home. We barely know any information about how you arrived. Our tribe had never even seen humans before you and the other females arrived. We knew that Midgard—or Earth—and humans existed, but only through stories passed down from generations and stories from other tribes. It was only our elders and the little information that was left with you that helped us to piece together where you came from." She said this all very cautiously, clearly aware that the news permanently affected the trajectory of my life.

"Okay, so, if you don't have the technology to travel to Earth, how did I get here?" My heart hammered in my chest. If they didn't take me, how the hell was I here? I was trying to remain as calm as I could so I didn't pass out again. I needed answers.

"We don't have very much information at all. Only the sentries we keep on duty overnight saw what happened. Three dagrs ago, a strange disc-like object landed in a clearing near our village in the dead of night. The sentries said it was almost as large as our meeting house, where we have village gatherings. Our sentries are armed and trained to protect our home, but no one ever approached the village.

"The sentries saw a lower hatch open at the bottom of the disc, and tall, slender beings cast in shadow exited. Each of them dragged a heavy burden behind them. Each *alien* left whatever they were carrying in the grass of the clearing, then reentered the silver disc. After all the aliens were aboard, the hatch closed and the silver disk silently lifted off the ground. The sentries said it hovered for just a few seconds before it disappeared into the sky." Tora said this all delicately, as if acutely aware of the gut-churning emotions that were now roiling through me.

My head was spinning. I could not decide if the information she was giving me made my situation better or worse.

"Okay, I need to get this straight. You didn't abduct me, you didn't even know about aliens until I arrived, and humans and Earth were only a myth on your planet up until three days ago? Wait. And I've been asleep for three days?" I asked, unable to keep the panic out of my voice.

Tora looked at me sadly. I could tell she truly empathized

with the conga line of panic that was currently taking over my brain.

"Unfortunately, yes. There were stories of something similar happening many árs ago, in the Snaerfírar tribe that is far north of here, but only our elders remember. Our tribes don't interact regularly, especially not with the Snaerfírar tribe, so it was something we knew few details about. We knew non-orkin females from a foreign land had arrived, but not much more than that."

Something was starting to click together in my mind. Tora had said multiple aliens had deposited multiple heavy burdens in the clearing. "Tora, how many females did the aliens leave behind?" I asked, a forced calm in my voice.

"Twelve females. You are the first to wake up." She seemed pleased about this. Maybe she thought I would find comfort in not being left alone. Maybe she thought I would be proud to be the first to come to? I did not feel like this was going particularly well. I was more horrified that eleven other women were going to wake up soon to find out they were left on an alien planet with no way home.

"You said you have very little to go on other than stories from faraway tribes. What else do you know?" I asked shrewdly. She used the words *human* and *Earth* with confidence. She had to have some other information.

Tora looked hesitant.

"Well, when the sentries found you in the field, you all had a tag attached to your clothes somewhere. The aliens that left you decided you were undesirable for one reason or another. Your basic information and reason for being left behind were on your tag."

I went from being distraught that I was abducted to pissed that some creepy race of aliens found me "undesirable." What about me was undesirable? I wasn't a supermodel or anything, but I wasn't ugly. I had a cute face, and big butts were totally on trend right now.

Get it together, Piper; you probably didn't want to be kept by the creepy aliens, anyway. They were abducting human women. Why was I offended that the aliens that abducted me didn't find me desirable? I blamed the patriarchy for instilling in me a need to feel wanted. But I had to know.

"Do you know why they found me undesirable?"

Tora pulled something out of her pocket. It looked almost like a folded piece of receipt paper. She unfolded it so I could see the typed script. It was in a language I didn't recognize.

"Every human female they left behind had a note like this attached to her clothes. At first, we didn't know what to make of them, since we don't speak or read their language. But some of our elders have been able to translate the meaning of many of them. Yours was easy for us to understand because there are multiple females that have the same cause." She held it up for me to see. I couldn't make sense of the words or letters. They were very blocky, and I wasn't even sure which direction I should read them from.

"What does it say?" I whispered.

"It says, '*Human female. Age: twenty-eight Earth years. Category: undesirable. Cause: system compromised by illicit substances.*' We assumed this meant you had fermented drinks the night you were abducted?"

I couldn't help but snort. They'd taken me on a Thursday night. I rarely drank and definitely not on a school night. I didn't do drugs either. I had never really experimented with any in high school. I ran with a pretty straight-laced nerd crowd. In college, I had been tempted because everyone was smoking weed, but I didn't think any sort of drug would mix well with my anxiety.

Then it hit me. *My anxiety.* I was on two different medications for generalized anxiety disorder. Illicit substances. I actually started to laugh, whole body laughter. Tora looked at me, alarmed. Apparently, this was not a normal reaction. This made me laugh even harder. Tears streamed down my face. Oh, the thought that my anxiety meds took me out of the hands of the "bad" aliens and into the hands of the "good" aliens was too much.

"I *definitely* was not drinking the night I was taken. I am on medication for anxiety." As I wiped tears from my eyes, I chuckled. I'd been on medication for anxiety for years. I had no shame in discussing it openly with anyone, alien or human. Actually, my years of therapy made me the go-to person in my circle of friends when someone needed help with mental health resources. Need a therapist, psychiatrist, counselor? Go to Piper, she's got you.

A new thought entered my head. How was I going to manage my anxiety on an alien planet? I was sure as hell they didn't have prescription medications here.

"Do you know what anxiety is?" I asked Tora, suddenly worried about her response. I relied very heavily on therapy and medication to keep my anxiety and depression at bay.

"Of course. We have had orcs that have struggled with anxiety in the past in our tribe. We may treat it differently than you do on Midgard, but here we accept that not every-one's mind works in the same way." She clearly didn't think any less of me due to my mental health. Yet, I was still concerned. What if they treated it with crystals or prayer? I didn't know what gods they had on this planet, but I was an atheist. Then again, I hadn't believed in aliens up to this point either, so what did I know?

"How exactly do you treat anxiety?" I asked, hopeful that it wasn't praying to some god I'd never heard of.

"We have herbs that have medicinal qualities that help calm the mind. We make them into a tea that is drunk daily or even more often if the orc needs it. Then most of our orcs that deal with anxiety also see a healer regularly to help them sort through things. I don't think we currently deal with anxiety, but Emla would know." The matter-of-fact way she explained this told me they at least had some understanding of mental health. They had meds, and they had therapy. Even if I was on some alien planet, at least I had access to mental health care, something that definitely wasn't true for all Americans.

"Okay, I am not going to pretend that I am ready to accept that I will be here forever, but I am going to need some time to process that. In the meantime, can I ask some more questions?" I needed to move on to some of my other questions before I lost it.

"Of course. I will answer everything I can." She smiled so genuinely at me that I felt better even though I was currently in a scenario not even my anxiety-ridden mind had ever come up with.

"You said there are twelve of us? And I am the first one to wake up?" Knowing that I had other humans to be with would make this significantly easier to accept.

"Já. We gave you each your own room. We weren't sure if you were from rival tribes or if you would find it scary to wake up with a stranger. I don't know if it was the best call, we debated about it quite a bit with the elders and our jarlin. Some thought you might find comfort in waking up with other humans."

"And I have been out for three days?" That part still horrified me. It felt like they had knocked me out for a few hours at most.

"Yes. Our healer was starting to worry that you were never going to wake up," Tora replied, studying my face with concern.

Three days. I had been out for three days. How had I gone three days without eating? As if on cue, my stomach gave a loud rumble. Yep, I was definitely hungry. Tora heard the noise and stood up immediately. I blushed to my roots. How embarrassing.

"While you were out, Odin came back with some food. I hurried him back to the village square with the promise I would get him when you woke up. But given that he selected the foods, I am afraid it consists of what a five ár old would eat." She stood up and looked at the tray on the dresser.

It was filled with foods I had never seen before. There was a bowl of what looked like grits, a piece of fruit that looked like a cross between a pear and an apple, and a pastry that had an intricately woven top. Tora brought me the tray and set it on my knees in my bed. I picked up a spoon made of dark metal and scooped up some of the grit-like mixture. I was hesitant, but also very hungry. Taking a small bite, just in case, I was pleasantly surprised. It definitely had the texture of grits, but it was sweet. Less nervous, I took another bite. This time, I got multiple textures. If I had to guess, it was a combination of dried fruit and nuts along with the grain. It was sweetened with something that tasted like sugar but had a hint of spice to it. I must be eating the orkin equivalent of oatmeal. Probably a good idea for a very empty stomach. I looked up to find Tora looking at me uncertainly.

"Do you like it?" she asked. Since I was the first human awake, I was obviously the first human they'd fed.

"It's delicious. And I didn't realize until now how hungry I was. I guess not eating for three days will do that to you. What is it called?" I said through a second mouthful of orkin oatmeal, civility be damned. Now that I realized I was hungry, I was starving.

"It's called grautr. It has grains and nuts and is sweetened with fruit and syrup. It's Odin's favorite. We'll have to make sure he knows you enjoyed it." She laughed at my enthusiastic eating.

We sat in companionable silence for a few moments while I ate. I was still processing all of the information she'd given me. I felt like I would be processing everything for weeks, if not months. Never going home? The news still felt like a sledgehammer to my mind. But even if I wasn't ready to deal with never going home, curling up into a ball and pretending not to exist wasn't going to do me any good.

I continued to eat. The pastry was also delicious. I saved the fruit for last; I wasn't sure if it was an eat the peel or don't eat the peel situation. But by the time I got to it, I found I was no longer hungry. My poor stomach was probably shocked to get food for the first time in such a long while. Tora noticed me slowing down and stood. She picked up the pitcher sitting on the chest of drawers next to my bed and poured what looked like water into the cup next to it.

"It's just water. We wanted you to have it in case you woke when no one was around." She handed me the dark metal cup. It looked to be made of the same material as the spoon I'd eaten the grautr with. I took a cautious sip. Would water still be water on an alien planet?

Turned out, yes. It tasted cold and crisp, exactly like chilled Earth water. Well, at least that was something familiar. I took another sip and continued to gather my thoughts. What next? I looked at Tora. Did their tribe have plans for the human women? She'd said we'd be taken care of and kept safe. Surely, we would have to work for our keep. I knew how to teach, but I doubted my knowledge of the complexities and failures of the American government would be much appreciated in any sort of schooling system they had. I was wondering if I could teach reading and writing to younger orkin when a thought slammed into the back of my head.

I understood Tora perfectly. I understood Odin. I even understood Agnarr and Brandr. They didn't even seem to have accents. Were they speaking English? I looked at Tora, who was gathering up my breakfast dishes.

"Tora, do you speak English?" I asked.

"No, we speak Kveoja here. You have been speaking it this entire time." She looked alarmed.

"I'm not speaking English?" Just when I thought my brain couldn't break any more...

"No, everything has been in Kveoja," Tora said, obviously just as puzzled as I was.

I thought about it. If there was a species advanced enough to come to Earth and abduct people, probably on more than one occasion, they definitely had sophisticated technology. I had seen sci-fi movies where characters were just able to download a language directly into their brains. Perhaps the bad aliens had been kind enough to give us some sort of language download? I couldn't think of any other explanation. I ran my theory by Tora.

"Well, that's beyond any technology we have here, but it's possible. I can't think of any other way you would speak Kveoja fluently." She seemed to accept my theory, but that was all that it was—a theory. However, since we didn't have anyone to ask, it was the theory we were going to have to go with. The lack of explanation brought back my unease.

"Tora, what am I going to be expected to do now that I am here? How will I earn money? I teach high school back home," I asked, concerned.

"I know that all the human females will probably have the same concern you have. It is something our jarlin and elders discussed. We want you to be given time to settle here. Then, if you want to work or have experience that you feel would be helpful, we would welcome that. Otherwise, the tribe will care for you, unless you choose to take a mate or find an elska mate."

Hold the phone. A what?

"An elska mate?" I sputtered. "What do you mean by elska mate?" This word had to have no translation in English because I had no idea what she was talking about.

"An elska mate. Fated. Bound for life. Not everyone finds their elska mate, but many orcs put great value in finding their one true partner." Tora looked blissful as if she were imagining someone dear to her.

"Do you have an elska mate?"

"Já, I do. He's everything I ever hoped." She beamed.

"Is he Odin's father?"

"Of course!" She laughed.

How was I to know? We didn't have fated mates on Earth. We had marriage. And divorce. My parents divorced when I was young, and they definitely weren't fated mates. Fated mates sounded like something that came from a fairy tale. I had never bought into the idea of soul mates or one true love. I wasn't even sure I believed in souls.

I wasn't ready to get into mates and elska mates or whether I believed in them. I needed to figure out how to survive here first. I had been single plenty back on Earth. Few men wanted to date a woman who went to bed at nine thirty every night. A teacher's schedule wasn't very adventurous.

So what next? I was on an alien planet with orkin that were willing to accept me. I knew as much as I could digest at the moment about what my new life was going to be. I needed some time to process it. Tora had just provided information overload, and I definitely felt like I needed some of their calming tea.

"Tora, what are the plans for the humans now?" I asked, formulating some plans for myself.

"Well, we're still waiting for the other humans to wake up. It could still be some time. We don't know what they gave you to knock you out," she explained.

And I bet none of them woke up face-to-face with Odin. That had to have contributed to my startling awakening. I wanted to be there when the other women woke up, but I also wanted some time to mull over everything Tora had told me.

"Tora, this has all been a lot to take in. Is there somewhere I could go for a walk to think about everything?" I looked at her hopefully but fully expecting her to say no. I needed to get out of this room, get some fresh air, and try to calm my racing thoughts.

"Of course. There's a path that runs around the edge of the village that many orkin use to go for walks. It is close enough to the town square that you will be safe. I can't promise that you won't run into any orkin, but it should be relatively peaceful. There's even a stream you can sit beside if you'd like."

That sounded perfect. I looked down at the shift dress I was wearing, then to Tora's outfit. She was in an embroidered tunic, soft-looking leggings, and leather boots.

"Um, am I in pajamas?" I asked.

"Já, the female orcs put you all in sleep clothes. The clothes you arrived in were dirty from your being left in the field. I have some clothes that you can wear here." She indicated the chest of drawers beside my bed.

She pulled open the top drawer and pulled out a pair of leggings and a tunic. I remembered that I no longer had my bra on and I realized didn't have underwear on either.

"Um, Tora, do orcs wear underwear?" I asked, wondering about my translator download's abilities.

"Under clothes? Humans wear clothes under clothes?" She looked confused.

"Never mind." I turned away for a bit of privacy and pulled on the leggings before taking off the nightshirt and putting on the tunic. I did not love the feeling of my boobs bouncing freely. If I was staying here long term, we were going to have to come up with a solution. However, the clothes seemed to fit surprisingly well. The leggings were a dark brown and the tunic a creamy white with decorative embroidery at the hem. It was snug over my chest, the v of the neckline definitely revealing more than I was used to in the classroom.

"Tora, who do these clothes belong to?" I asked. Seeing how Tora was almost a foot taller than me, I couldn't be wearing hand-me-downs from an adult orc. "Some of our female orcs who have yet to come of age donated them." She looked embarrassed.

"How old was the girl who wore these clothes before me?" I smiled, knowing I was about to get a shock.

"Twelve árs." She grinned at me.

"Ha! Adult females are the same size as your pre-teens? That is… wild." I laughed. It was all too much. Tora looked pleased that it did not offend me to be wearing a child's clothes.

"There seem to be some particular differences in the way you are built," she said, her eyes straying to my boobs that were busting out the top of the tunic. Tora seemed to be much more flat-chested, muscular and willowy. Thankfully, my tunic covered my generous ass. Otherwise, she might realize that was also definitely not orkin. She turned and grabbed me a pair of boots that were tucked next to the chest of drawers and handed them to me.

"They're lined, so your feet should be warm even though the cold season approaches. You're sure you want to go on a walk alone?" she asked.

"Yes, as long as it won't cause a bother. I need to wrap my mind around everything."

"Well, I will make sure our sentries know you are out for a walk. Make sure you don't stray from the path. You will be plenty safe. We don't have any predators that come close to the village, but I don't want you getting lost." She headed toward the door. I followed.

"I promise I will stay on the path. Scout's honor," I said. Tora just looked confused again. American slang definitely would not translate here.

CHAPTER 4

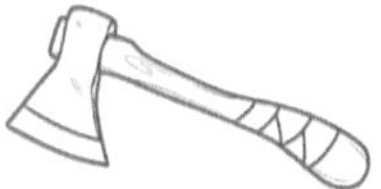

AGNARR

It was quiet in the forest, except for the rhythmic *thwack* of my axe into the furutré's flesh and my labored breathing. I had been working on the same giant tree for quite a while. It did not want to fall. I took another calculated swing and slammed my axe into the deep groove I had already created. It was going to be some time yet before I felled the giant.

I'd headed out to the woods at the edge of the village to fell trees alone even though it was time for the midday meal. I could not get my mind off the events of the last few days. Twelve human females had essentially fallen out of the sky at the edge of our village. We'd spent two days debating what to do with them. Many of the elders hadn't wanted to take them in, worrying they would upset the balance of our village. However, many of the unmated males were quite interested in the prospect of new females. Would these females be compatible mates? Maybe even elska mates?

The female elders had shot this down as a reason for giving the females shelter. They argued it would be unfair to wake the humans and tell them we only gave them refuge because our males were interested in the possibility of mates. I agreed with this even though I felt my time was running out to find a mate. I doubted we'd even be compatible with humans. If what the sentries said was true, the humans were no larger than orklings.

The female elders had insisted we take in all the humans and place no demands on them until we learned more of their ways. They argued that many of the females came with heavy burdens, as was indicated on the notes left with them by the "bad aliens," as everyone had taken to calling them. They needed time. The male elders had begrudgingly accepted, making it very clear that they hoped that the women would be able and willing to take on mates immediately.

In the last twenty-five árs, our population had become skewed. Our orkin females started giving birth to males at twice the rate they gave birth to females. We had dozens of males that were of age or about to come of age, but very few females. We were on the brink of reaching out to other tribes to see about finding compatible mates for our males and to find out if they were experiencing the same skewed birth ratios. We had no idea why our females weren't giving birth to more female orkin, but it was a continuing problem.

Luckily for the new humans, our jarlin was a fierce female, Astrid. She was the elska mate of our prior jarl, Ulf, who had died many seasons ago. Her position as jarlin in our tribe was unquestioned. Her pairing with Ulf had been one of the last elska mates we'd had in many árs. Astrid refused to back down in her protection of the human females. The women would be given a chance and a choice, in all respects. While many males were desperate for a chance to find their mate, myself included, we agreed that all we could do was wait and see how the humans settled into life in our forest tribe of Fýrifírar.

I had accepted this plan as well-thought-out and measured, but I couldn't deny that the human females had created a small glimmer of hope in the back of my mind. I was on the older side of being of age and had yet to find a mate. It wasn't for lack of trying, either. I had been with some females that were of age, but I felt nothing more than friendship toward them. We always ended up parting ways and wishing each other the best. I didn't want to admit that I was holding out hope for an elska mate, as they were so rare, but some small part of me wanted it so badly it hurt. The idea of finding an elska mate nagged at me, but I tried to put it out of my mind. There were several males in my position. It didn't matter that I was the most fearsome fighter or that I provided the most for the tribe. Elska matehood was fated, and if I was honest with myself, that is what I was hoping for.

The sentries that had found the humans had described them as small, no larger than females who had not come of age. If anything, that gave me less hope. I was a hulking male, one of the largest in our tribe since Ulf. It was unlikely that I would be a suitable mate for a delicate female. I tried to put the humans out of my mind and continue my training and providing for the tribe. I tried to smother any small spark of hope the human women brought.

That was until this morning. This morning changed everything.

* * *

I WAS SPARRING with Brandr near the edge of the village when Tora called to us from an open window. She was in the building where we'd housed the humans and sounded panicked. We rushed to her to find one human female out cold in the rocking chair in her room. I looked down at the human slumped in the rocking chair, my first time seeing one of them up close. The sentries weren't wrong. She was so small. She looked delicate slumped over in the rocking chair. Her tiny feet didn't even reach the floor. Her toenails were bright red. At first, I thought that was the color they naturally were, but I realized they were painted when I saw chips on her largest toe. How odd.

I looked up at her body. She had pale peach skin that appeared thin in the morning light. Her veins showed through, a light bluish color on her legs. She was wearing a child's nightshirt; it reached the middle of her thigh. I couldn't help but notice that though she was small, her thighs were plump, filling out the nightshirt.. I reminded myself I was there to help, not gawk like a male barely past his first mating season. I looked at Tora.

"Do you want me to put her back in the bed?" I asked, barely above a whisper. I didn't want her to wake while Brandr and I were there. If she had already passed out, she definitely wouldn't respond well to waking up to two orc males in her room.

"Her name is Piper. Do you think you can move her without waking her?" Tora whispered back.

I merely nodded, then looked to Brandr. She was so small that this really was only the work of one orc. He strode to the bed and pulled back the covers. I bent to scoop her up, one arm behind her knees, the other around her shoulders. *Pfft.* This female weighed nothing. Tora probably could have lifted her without us. When she was in the chair, her valhnot colored hair had hung forward and covered her face. As I hoisted her up, her head lolled back, revealing it.

And that was it. I knew. She was mine. I looked at her

face. I felt her skin against mine and fire shot through my veins—that fire that had always been lacking when I was with females of my tribe.

Piper's face was pale and wan. The skin underneath her eyes looked bruised and tender, probably because of multiple days without food or water I mused. But beneath the damage her rough arrival on my planet had caused, she was stunning. Completely otherworldly to me, but stunning. Her face was pale, a light peach, like the rest of her. It was a color I'd never seen on orkin skin. Her cheeks held a faint pink, with her thick lashes fanning out below her closed eyes. Her nose was adorable and pert—tiny, like the rest of her. Her lips were full and upturned, a slightly darker pink than her cheeks. Her mouth parted slightly as she took steady breaths. I longed to look into her eyes, but she remained blissfully unaware of her surroundings. I tried to absorb every detail of her face as I carried her from the rocking chair to her bed. From the way her eyes fluttered back and forth nervously under their lids to the smattering of small freckles that adorned her one cheekbone, she mesmerized me.

I gently placed her on the bed, admiring her soft curves. Brandr stepped in to pull up her covers. He looked from her to me. I immediately tried to mask the hungry look in my eyes and attempted to feign a look of concern. Based on the look on Brandr's face, I hadn't been quick enough. He was on to me. I looked away from Piper and to where Tora stood. I needed to get out of this room.

"If you think she'll be all right, I will head out. I have matters to attend to," I said brusquely. Without waiting to hear Tora's response, I turned and walked out of Piper's room.

* * *

AND NOW I WAS HERE, cutting down a tree for no particular reason. There was always a need for log felling in our village, whether it be for building or firewood, but it wasn't part of my duties in the tribe. I hadn't used an axe since before I came of age. But I needed a distraction. Something, anything, to get my mind off of the dainty human female. I swung the axe again and again, jumbled thoughts sifting through my mind.

How could I be so infatuated with her? I knew nothing about her. Yes, she was beautiful, otherworldly. But the orkin females I had been with had also been beautiful. It couldn't be just her looks that had me driven to distraction. I had never felt my skin light up how it had when I picked her up. I wanted to crush her into me. I wanted to bury my nose in her hair and take in deep breaths of the scent that clung to her. I couldn't quite place it, but it was intoxicating, spicy with a citrus undertone. But she was so small and looked so frail.

I continued chopping, putting as much physical exertion as I could into felling the tree. I paused only to remove my tunic and hang it on a low branch nearby. I was dripping with sweat and still couldn't get the tiny human off my mind. The same thought kept cropping up, over and over. Could she be my elska mate? Is this what it felt like? Tora and her mate, Rune, were the only elska mates near my age. I had tried to ask Rune on multiple occasions how he knew Tora was his before their marks appeared, but he would only tell me it was "all consuming" and that I would "simply know." We, neither Rune nor I, had taken into consideration the arrival of an entirely different species. How could I simply know?

I was torn between wanting to actually meet Piper and wanting to stay as far away as possible. If I felt this way for her already, having only seen and touched her, surely, meeting her would drive me mad with longing and lust. Just remembering her pale, rounded thighs had my erection straining painfully against my pants. How could I possibly give her the time and space to adjust to Fýrifírar when I couldn't even seem to form coherent thoughts? I adjusted my leggings and went back to work on the tree, doubling my efforts. I was determined to clear my head. On the off chance I saw Piper again soon, I would greet her as a new member of the tribe, not an obsessed male unable to contain himself.

PIPER

The walk around the village was exactly what I needed to clear my head. I had received so much overwhelming information. Focusing on putting one foot in front of the other was grounding. I stayed on the cobblestone path, as Tora had warned, and walked for quite some time. Thankfully, it was far enough away from the village that I wasn't getting any attention from my new...family? On the side of the path closest to the village, the trees had been cleared, leaving room for what honestly looked like normal Earth grass to pop up. On the other side of the path, the grass continued for several yards until it broke off into dirt and moss, shifting from a clearing to a forest. Giant trees, the same orangey ones that I had seen out my window, disappeared up into the mist. They seemed to circle the entire village. The orcs must have cleared the space for the village, leaving the surrounding trees.

As I walked, my mind whirled, trying to hold on to different bits of the conversation I'd had with Tora. There was so much left unanswered. I was stressing the most about the lack of meds. Even if I could get to the tribe in the north in record time, it was likely that my meds would be well out of my system by then, leaving me with the threat of unchecked anxiety on an alien planet. What could go wrong?

I continued along the path, lost in thought, when I realized there was a methodical noise slowly getting louder and louder. It sounded like the swing of an axe against a tree. The *thwack, thwack, thwack* intesified as I rounded the large curve of the walkway. I looked toward the forest and saw Agnarr, the orc from that morning, methodically chopping into a tree at the edge of the forest. He was about twenty-five yards away, bare from the waist up, aggressively swinging his axe into the trunk of the tree before him. He was well past halfway through, the tree shaking dangerously each time the axe bit into the wood. With a few more swings, a crack split through the air and the tree started to fall.

Directly toward me.

AGNARR

I was dripping with sweat, but satisfied, as the tree finally fell. The air was filled with the snaps and cracks of branches as the tree hurtled toward the earth. As I admired my handiwork, I heard a scream rip through the sky. I looked to where the very top of the tree was rapidly approaching the ground only to see Piper standing directly in its path. Dropping my axe and ran to her, hoping I could reach her in time. I wasn't quick enough. I watched in horror as the tree slammed to the ground. Her scream ended, and a deafening silence filled the air.

I ran back for my axe. I started hacking away at the branches where Piper had stood just moments before. Maybe if the trunk hadn't hit her, she would be trapped under all the branches, but unharmed. I couldn't see her at all through the limbs and needles. I was swinging wildly at the upper branches when I paused suddenly. In between the branches, I could see a pale arm poking out. It was flailing wildly and trying to grasp at the branches. Well, all signs pointed to her still being alive. I grabbed my blade from my belt. If I was this close to uncovering her, an axe could cause serious injury. Starting from where her arm was pinned, I tried to pull and cut away branch after branch. As I cut and tore away branches, a muffled voice came from under the tree.

"Don't you know you shouldn't fell a tree toward a path?" Piper demanded.

I grimaced. I knew little about felling trees; my tribe had trained me as a warrior. But having already sparred with Brandr this morning, I'd been looking for another way to get my mind off of the humans' arrival—specifically, this human's arrival. I'd seen many of my orkin tribe mates who were woodworkers and loggers cut down trees. I'd assumed, as a trained warrior, I was more than capable of felling a tree. Apparently, I was wrong. I continued to pull branches and limbs away from Piper. As embarrassed as I was, I couldn't help but smile at the bite in the human's voice.

"I don't actually know how to chop down a tree." I tried to say casually as I continued my attempts to free her.

"Then what the fuck were you doing out here looking like a lumbersnack from *Ax Men* chopping one down?" she challenged.

None of that made sense. Did she just call me a *lumbersnack?* I wasn't sure if that was an insult or a swear word—or both. I had no idea what she meant by "ax men," but she sounded outraged that I'd accidentally dropped a tree on her.

"Uh, I needed to get my mind off some things, and tree chopping seemed like a good way to clear my head?" Saying it out loud made me realize the plan was even more ill conceived than I'd first thought.

"Tree chopping seemed like a good way to clear your

head? You couldn't pick something less dangerous, like yoga?" she yelled.

I was equally amused and embarrassed. She clearly wasn't seriously injured if she was able to shout at me with such aggression, which I found delightful. This tiny human had claws. Yet, I was to blame for her current situation. And I still only understood about half of what she was saying.

"What is yoga? Also, what is a *lumbersnack?*"

I could hear an irritated huff. I definitely was getting closer to freeing her.

"What do you mean *what is yoga?* Okay, sir, we seem to be having difficulty communicating. Do you think you could finish freeing me from this tree that you just dropped on me?"

Sir. I had no idea what that meant either, but she said it with such disdain I assumed it was another insult. However, she did have a point. I went back to work. I continued to cut away branches and limbs, able to see much of her body but still unable to free her. Finally, I reached a branch that was pinning most of her torso and ripped it away. With the sound of splintering wood came the sound of ripping fabric, and the upper half of Piper came into view.

I had just ripped her tunic in half.

One of her breasts was exposed completely. It was unlike any female orkin breast I'd seen. It was full and round, tipped with a light brown nipple that pebbled in the cool air. Orkin weren't shy about their nudity and I had seen plenty of naked females, but the differences between Piper's breast and an orkin female's were definitely. . . appealing. I was staring openly when Piper used her free arm to snap her fingers in my face, drawing my attention away from her chest.

"Um, hello? I'm still trapped here. Can you take your eyes off my boobs and free my other arm? I don't know what's normal for orcs, but for humans, it's rude to stare at some-one's boobs."

My eyes snapped to her face. Her cheeks were pink, much pinker than they had been earlier. My own cheeks were growing hot. She was scowling at me, but I could finally look her in the eyes. She had white sclera, unlike the orkin, and irises the color of the needles on the furutré, a sharp green. Her brow was furrowed as she continued to stare me down. She was definitely not pleased. This tiny human was fierce.

"Sorry, sorry. Of course. Let me get your other arm free."

The last tree limb pinning her arm was large. I was going to need to use my axe to cut through it.

"Let me use my axe for this last limb."

"Should we really be trusting you with an axe at this point? Last time you used it, it didn't go particularly well."

I sighed. She had a point. I would never live this down if my other tribe mates found out about me felling a tree on one of the humans. "I promise to use the utmost care."

She continued to scowl at me. Honestly, it was adorable. This tiny creature was clearly not afraid of me.

"Fine. But try to keep your eyes in your head while you free me. It's clear you haven't seen boobs in a while." Her tone was defiant, but her cheeks were even pinker. I wasn't sure what she meant by "keep my eyes in my head." They were definitely still in my head.

Maybe by asking me to keep my eyes in my head, she meant I should stop staring at her exposed chest. As I turned to pick up my axe, I saw my tunic hanging nearby and an idea formed. Hopefully, she wouldn't be as irritated with me dropping a tree on her if I provided her with another shirt. I rose to fetch it wordlessly.

I returned to find her trying to squirm out from under the branch that still pinned her right arm, using her left arm to hold her tunic together. There was no way she was going to get herself free.

"Let me help. I brought you my tunic to use while I finish getting you free."

"Well, that was considerate," she said dryly.

She took my tunic and held it to her chest. I looked at the branch pinning her arm, trying to assess how best to cut her free without causing her injury.

"I am going to cut the branch off where it meets the trunk," I said. "This way, the axe is nowhere near your arm."

"Given your history with axes, that is probably for the best."

This human did not hold back. I grinned. She had no problem giving me a piece of her mind. If I wasn't so busy being embarrassed, I would find her fire delightful. It was going to take me a few minutes to cut through the branch; I could at least try to make conversation with her while I freed her. I was dying to know more about this fierce female.

"Can I ask you some questions while I chop you free?"

"Well, I guess. It's not like I can go anywhere else," she groused.

I picked up my axe and started chopping at the branch.

"What is 'axe men?'" I asked.

"It is a reality TV show about loggers. Do you have television here?"

"Mmm, we do not have tee-vee. What is tee-vee?"

"Well, it is a way to watch entertainment. It is like a flat box that you can watch a pre-recorded play on. Do you have plays?"

"Já, we do have plays. So it is like a play that you can watch in your own house?" I swung the axe again and again. The sound of it made it hard to continue our conversation, but I was so curious I couldn't help but continue with questioning.

"So you would watch a tee-vee play about human men chopping down trees?"

"Yes, it is called reality TV. You are watching a show about someone else's life."

"And what is a '*lumbersnack?*'"

At this question, Piper's cheeks were no longer tinged with pink; her entire face turned red. This was definitely a sign of embarrassment. I loved it. She could needle me, and I was going to needle her right back.

She looked away and tried to focus on pulling her arm free. I could still see her bright red cheeks even though she didn't want to make eye contact. Whatever a *lumbersnack* was, she was embarrassed to have called me one. I repeated the question, "What exactly is a *lumbersnack?*"

"It's… well… um… well… Okay, so on TV, there are shows about loggers and men who chop down trees. The men are corded in muscle but *thick*. They are stacked and powerful. They look like they could rip a tree out of the ground. Sometimes, they post videos of them crushing watermelons with their thighs or ripping logs in half with their bare hands. They are…delicious." She said this all very quickly and then looked up at me defiantly, as if challenging me to question her further.

I grinned at her, my thoughts turning wicked. She compared me to these human men, these *lumbersnacks,* who she clearly found appealing. Judging by Piper's size, I was at least a head taller than most human men and definitely much thicker. My muscles were defined and hulking from árs of training to protect our tribe. Maybe I didn't know the technique of chopping down a tree, but I knew I could rip a trunk in half with my bare hands. I stopped my attempts to free her, causing her to look up at me, face still aflame.

"So what you're saying is, you find me delicious, like these *lumbersnacks?"* I paused to emphasize the word. "Would you like to find out if I am?" I said, looking her square in the eyes.

Piper's smell suddenly flooded my nostrils. I had caught it before when I lifted her from the chair to the bed, but it suddenly took on a heady quality. She smelled of spice and the fruit of the plomme trees that hung heavy in late summer. The spicy undertones of her scent were over-whelming me. There was no misreading this shift and spike in her scent. She was aroused.

CHAPTER 5

PIPER

*A*s Agnarr stared at me, heat wafted off my face. I had to be blushing to my roots. I'd inadvertently told him I found him *delicious.* I was mortified. But the way he was looking down at me had my thoughts scattering alto-gether. He wasn't embarrassed in the slightest that I had, in my rage at having a damn tree dropped on me, told him I found him attractive. His wolfish smile told me that there was nothing to be embarrassed about.

If I had thought he was attractive before, seeing him smile was devastating. It revealed his perfect white teeth, including two tiny tusks that mirrored the much larger tusks of his bottom teeth. Instead of finding the tusks alarming, I wondered what they would feel like against my skin. He had dimples on each cheek, and the corners of his eyes crinkled as his grin broadened. He could tell I was flustered. Seeing him grin lit me up in a way that had nothing to do with embarrassment.

Setting the axe aside, he bent close to me, trying to remove the last branch trapping me. I caught a whiff of his scent. He smelled salty and musky, like sweat. Underneath the smell of his sweat was a hint of the trees that surrounded us, almost as if he used soap made of it. I had never been a scent girl before, mainly because my prior boyfriends had always smelled of the deodorant a teenaged boy would use rather than any sort of man. But the way this orc smelled had me wanting to put my nose to his neck and inhale deeply. Just the thought of it made me break out in goosebumps.

Agnarr continued to keep working at the branch that pinned my arm, acting unaffected by our proximity. Yet, having him this close to me and being enveloped by his scent was having a dizzying effect. I felt my pulse pick up and my breath quicken. Agnarr finally looked me in the face again.

"If you could keep it together for just a few moments longer, I can free you and we can see to your needs," he said, giving me a heated smile.

"See to my what?" I said faintly, completely distracted by his grin.

"I can smell the change in your scent. Are you aroused by me? Or merely the thought of the *lumbersnacks* you watched on tee-vee?" he asked smoothly, his eyes returning to the branch he was working on.

He could *smell* my arousal? Jesus Christ, I was fucked. I had grown up in a "good Christian home;" I was used to pushing aside my sexual arousal and desires, pretending they weren't there so that I could be *chaste*. Yet, if he could smell whenever I was aroused, there was no lying about it. No pushing it aside. I shook myself, looking back at him to find him gazing at me.

"So is it me that arouses you?"

The look he gave me made my pulse race. I felt my stomach tighten and clenched my legs together, a throbbing beat between my thighs. I lost all sense of embarrassment. I reached out with my free arm and wrapped it around his neck, pulling him to me. He planted his right hand on the ground next to my head as my lips met his. I went in for a full open-mouthed kiss and was met with a completely non-responsive mouth. Nothing. Like kissing a statue. Oh God, had I misread what I thought were very clear signals? I leaned back to look him in the eye and he looked dumbfounded. Confusion replaced shame.

I asked, "Do orcs not kiss?"

"Is that what that was?" Agnarr asked.

Oh boy. I was going to have to explain kissing to an orc. With tusks. Maybe that was why they didn't kiss. Too many tusks?

"Yes, that was an attempt at a kiss. But it takes two people, or rather, two um…beings?"

"And you just press your lips together?" he asked, clearly confused.

At this, I blushed again. "Well, it is usually more than just lips. You use your tongues and lips. Sometimes even teeth," I said as I looked at his mouth, again noting his large tusks. "You use your teeth gently," I clarified. I was still very much interested in kissing him, even considering his lack of experience and the tusks. My own first kiss had been terrible; the guy had just eaten a hotdog. I'd nearly barfed into his mouth. I wanted to make this a better experience than *that* for Agnarr. Given the delicious way Agnar smelled, I sincerely doubted that he would taste like a hotdog.

His look went from confused to heated as everything clicked together. He slammed his mouth into mine. What he lacked in skill, he made up for enthusiasm. I pulled back and slowly placed gentle kisses along his jaw. Before I asked him to take part, I would show him. I pressed small but deliberate kisses up from his firm jaw to his mouth. I kissed him on the mouth, slipping my tongue out and dragging it along his lower lip. He groaned at the feel of my tongue on his skin. He parted for me and I hesitantly brushed my tongue inside, dragging it across his. His tongue was rougher and felt much larger than mine. I felt his uncertainty dissolve as I explored his mouth, taking my time to slide my tongue across his. His stiffness disappeared, and he thrust his tongue to meet mine. He licked along my tongue, dragging his across my teeth, my lips, learning my mouth as he went. I swiped my tongue against his again, loving the difference in texture. He was still holding himself up with one arm, and he moved the other from the branch he'd been trying to remove to my hip.

We tangled together, lips and tongues. As he gained confidence, he began an all-out onslaught of me, practically fucking my mouth with his tongue. I moaned into his mouth and shifted, using my free arm to pull him closer to me, wishing I could use both arms to wrap myself around him. I sucked on his tongue and dragged my own across his tusks. We kissed like teenagers, sloppy and with too much tongue, devouring each other. Agnarr slid his hand up to my neck and threaded his fingers through my hair, tugging gently.

I pulled back, taking a breath. Agnarr was looking down at me with a hungry expression, looking almost upset that I had pulled away.

"Are you okay to continue? I mean, do you want to continue?" he asked, voice low and gravelly.

Did I want to continue? I wanted to climb this orc like a tree. That he legitimately asked if I was interested in continuing even though I was already physically giving him enthusiastic "yes!" cues was just icing on the cake. There was only one minor problem. One of my arms was still trapped under a tree.

"I would love to continue, but I would really like to use

both of my arms. Could you finish freeing me from this stupid tree first?" I asked.

Agnarr looked almost ashamed, clearly having forgotten that I was still trapped under a tree. He looked over at the last branch that pinned my right arm thoughtfully. He took his hand out of my hair and reached over to grasp the branch. With a swift tug, it snapped, freeing me completely. I pulled my arm out. No damage.

"Why didn't you do that before?" I demanded, pressing my hand to his enormous chest, preventing him from leaning in again.

"I was almost finished when you distracted me with this...? What is it you called this?" he asked.

"Kissing. We're kissing."

"Can we go back to that? I felt like I was just figuring it out." He grinned at me. That was a tough request to resist. I removed my hand from his chest and slid it back to the nape of his neck, pulling him toward me once more. However, this time, instead of going directly for his mouth, I decided to do a little exploring. I buried my nose in his neck, inhaling his intoxicating scent deeply before beginning a series of open-mouthed kisses up toward his ear. His skin was soft and so much warmer than mine. I used my teeth to nip at his lobe gently before dragging my tongue all the way to the tip of his pointed ear. He shuddered at this, and I felt him stop breathing. I leaned back to look into his eyes.

"Was that okay?" I asked. Maybe ear licking was not appropriate for someone who had never kissed before.

He didn't even answer. He dropped his weight down on me and began kissing and sucking the sensitive skin of my neck. I was now pinned to the ground by his massive form, both of us surrounded by the remnants of the fallen tree. I would take pinned to the ground by a giant delicious orc over a tree any day.

"You're a quick learner," I whispered.

"Am I?" He chuckled darkly. "Now that I see what makes you aroused, it seems pretty self explanatory."

He didn't even bother to look up, continuing his ministrations of my neck and slowly making his way up to my ear. He licked and bit the lobe, sending shivers down my spine.

"I can smell you. You are absolutely drenched for your own personal *lumbersnack*," he growled in my ear.

I was going to come apart at the seams. I needed to be touching more of him. All of him. My hands went to my tunic, ready to rip what remained of it off. Agnarr got there first. With one quick swipe, the tunic split completely in half, revealing my breasts. Agnarr looked down at my chest for so long that I felt uncomfortable. Yes, my boobs were big, but they definitely couldn't be described as perky. I usually wore a bra with a decent amount of support in order to haul them up. I moved my arm to cover myself and he grabbed my wrist, pinning it over my head.

"You…um," he rasped, seemingly at a loss for words. He shifted over me, and the firm bar of him pressed into my thigh. "You look absolutely delectable," he said. Agnarr's nostrils flared as he surveyed me. He palmed one of my breasts as if trying to judge the weight of it in his hand.

"These are magnificent. Like nothing I've ever seen," he said.

He stroked the delicate skin of the underside of my breast almost lazily, with a calloused thumb. I moaned breathlessly. I arched into his touch, wanting more—more of everything. He lowered his head and pulled my nipple into his mouth, sucking hard. I grasped his head, pulling him in closer to me as he dragged his gloriously rough tongue over my sensitive nipple. He took it between his teeth and gently tugged, causing the pleasure to shoot straight to my core.

I couldn't take it anymore. I needed him. I wanted him to

fuck me until I couldn't see straight. He already had his tunic off, giving me a glorious view of his thick, roped muscles. My hands went to his pants only to find a complicated belt situation unlike any man's belt I'd encountered. There were far too many clasps and buckles; it seemed designed to hold his multitude of weapons. I attempted to unbuckle the main buckle only to be met with more buckles. I let out an annoyed sigh and felt him chuckle against my breast.

"Would you like some help?" I could hear the smile in his voice as he returned to teasing and flicking my nipple with his tongue.

"How the hell do you get this blasted thing off?" I whined. I was full of need and beyond caring.

Agnarr sat so that he was sitting with one knee on either side of my waist. His giant fingers nimbly undid the multitude of buckles and tossed aside not only a belt, but some sort of weapon-carrying contraption that looked straight out of a medieval museum. Didn't care. I reached out and stroked the length of him that was clearly visible underneath his woven pants. He was hot to the touch and thick. He was physically larger than any human man I had encountered, so him having a larger cock would be logical, but I was definitely not expecting the girth. I used the heel of my palm to slide up and down his considerable length again and felt him shudder underneath me.

I propped myself up on my elbows and looked up into his dark brown eyes, hooded with want.

"Well, big guy, are we stopping at the belt?" I asked as I continued to stroke up and down the length of him with the heel of my hand.

"Mm, not if you don't want to," he murmured.

Such a gentleman. As if I hadn't made my intentions perfectly clear. I reached up and undid the laces on his pants, now that his complicated belt was gone. I slipped my hand into his pants and grasped him. Oh Lord, I was not wrong about the girth. Not only was he thick, but his skin was also so much warmer than mine. It felt like it was radiating heat, definitely hotter than any human cock I had come into contact with. I stroked up and down his shaft. The skin was soft but textured.

"May I?" I asked coyly.

Agnarr didn't even respond. He merely bucked his hips forward, pushing my hand further down his shaft. I leaned forward, using my other hand to pull down the front of his pants, drawing his cock and balls out. I was expecting a large penis, green but essentially humanoid. But as I pulled Agnarr's erection free from his pants, I noticed some very significant differences.

His shaft was a deeper shade of green than the rest of his body. It was ridged in almost a braided pattern on both the top and bottom. There was a knot-like protrusion halfway down that also had the braided texture. I clenched my thighs together just thinking of what the ridges and knot would feel like. At the end of his shaft, the head of his cock flared out past his uncut foreskin with a deep divot in the head which pooled with pre-cum. I felt my mouth flood with saliva. It was a closely guarded secret, but I loved a good blow job. Seeing a man come completely undone by my mouth and tongue? Yes, please. And this cock, with all of its extra bells and whistles, was begging to be licked from top to bottom.

Eying his balls, I noted they seemed very similar to a human man's, if significantly larger, darker green than his shaft and dusted with silky black hair that mirrored the hair on his head. The hair tapered off toward his navel, giving him a delicious happy trail that I couldn't wait to lick. Reverting my attention to his cock, I was drawn to it like a moth to a flame.

I leaned in and looked up, meeting his hooded gaze and

locking in on his brown eyes. "Mind if I have a taste?" I whispered.

He raised his eyebrows. Oh, was this another first for him? *Yes, please.* I could get used to introducing this orc to the particulars of human pleasure seeking. I leaned in further and licked him from root to delicious tip, swirling my tongue in the divot of the head. His cum tasted as he smelled, salty and musky and all male. I looked up to gauge his reaction while still swirling my tongue around the head of his cock.

"*Unhg...*" he ground out through clenched teeth. "Is this...is this something human women do?" he said, clearly trying to maintain some semblance of control. He stared down at me in wonder.

"I can't speak for all human women, but it is definitely something *I* do. May I continue?" I looked up at him through my lashes as I took another long lick of him from his balls to his tip, laving my tongue in the deep divot of his crown again. If I was going to get to give this lumbersnack of an orc his first blow job, I was going to make it a good one.

"Já, já, já, definitely. I mean, only if you want to. But yes, I mean. Yes, I am interested," Agnarr rushed out in a heated jumble.

I grinned. I could feel myself dripping between my thighs. Seeing this giant orc completely undone was making me ache with need. I wanted to see him completely shatter at my ministrations. The pleasure that I was giving him was so intense that I could see it bringing me to my own orgasm. I shifted my weight, leaning in to focus on the beautiful alien cock in front of me. There was no way I could fit the entire thing in my mouth, but I was going to try my damndest.

I scooted back so I was leaning in front of him as he was on his knees. Using my one hand, I stroked his cock up and down. I pumped him again, knowing there was no way I would fit the entirety of him into my mouth. That didn't mean I wasn't going to try. I grasped the base of him with one hand and rested my other hand on his thigh. I lapped at the divot of his crown before giving attention to his corona, something I'd learned that men enjoyed. It was incredibly sensitive and just begging to be licked. I dragged my tongue all along where Agnarr's crown met his shaft, all the while pumping below his knot steadily with my hand.

His cock jumped, and he groaned in response. I could tell he was unsure of what to do with his hands, having never had a female give him oral before. His need provided a heady feeling. I wanted to touch myself while still pleasuring him.

I paused and looked up at him. "Feel free to grab my hair. You can set the pace."

He lifted his hands hesitantly, and instead of fisting my hair, he cupped my face, looking into my eyes. "Is this something that you want to do?" he whispered.

This giant orc, taken to his knees—literally—by a blow job…

"I assure you, I wouldn't be on my knees in front of you if I didn't want to be," I replied.

At that, I leaned forward and took the entire head of his cock into my mouth, forcing his hands to shift from my face to my hair. I sucked his crown, only getting partially down his shaft. I used my tongue on his ridged underside, flicking along his frenulum. As hot pre-cum continued to spill in my mouth, Agnarr shuddered under me. I couldn't help but moan as I continued to work him up and down with both my mouth and my hand. Agnarr's hands clenched on either side of my head. I could tell he was attempting to stop himself from grabbing my head and pushing me further down his cock. Adorable. I let my mouth fill with saliva so I could slide up and down easier, widening my jaw as far as it could go.

My lips brushed the knot halfway down his cock before the tip of him bumped the back of my throat. I used my hand

and my mouth to pump him up and down in a steady rhythm. Agnarr made a throaty, strangled noise above me, causing me to look up at him. His jaw was clenched, eyes hooded in lust. He was close but trying desperately to keep a hold of himself. I hollowed my cheeks and tightened my grip, wanting to see his resolve shatter as I continued to work him. He groaned.

"Piper, if you don't stop, I am going to explode in your mouth," he ground out through his clenched jaw.

I looked up at him, the tendons in his neck taut. Using my free hand, I reached out and stroked his thigh, letting him know it was all right. I moved my hand up the base of him to feel the knot at the middle of his cock that I was most curious about. His knot was much firmer, bulging out from the rest of his shaft. He jerked as I brushed my fingers over it, letting loose a string of unintelligible noises. Spurred on by his reaction, I gripped the knot, my fingers not even coming close to reaching all the way around, and pumped it up and down as I had his shaft. Agnarr shuddered as I squeezed down on his knot and took him as deep into my mouth as I could. With a roar that I felt to my core, hot cum hit the back of my throat. I continued to pump his knot and pull him deeper down, swallowing and gulping him down. As he pulsed to finish, I pulled off of him, slowly licking him from bottom to top one last time. I looked up at him through my lashes.

"Piper," he growled.

"Mm?" I looked up at him, dazed with lust.

"Now it's my turn," he snarled, gripping my thighs with his enormous hands.

AGNARR

Piper looked up at me, surprised. "Wh...what?" she stammered.

I shifted back, dragging her thighs with me. This human thought she could suck and pump my cock with her delicious mouth and her tiny soft hands and I wouldn't want to spread her wide like a feast? It had me questioning the intelligence of human men. As I pulled her to me, she lay back, propped on her elbows, looking at me uncertainly. This human had shattered my world in one afternoon. I had never experienced this *kissing* she referred to; now I couldn't imagine a day going by without pressing my lips to hers, nibbling at her soft lips, and sliding my tongue across her tiny smooth one. And then, not only did she suck on my cock until I exploded in her mouth, the act of it had *aroused* her. Her arousal perfumed the air, making it impossible for me to go a moment longer without another taste of her.

I leaned over her, planting each hand on either side of her, and brushed my lips against hers. How had orkin gone so long without kissing? I pressed soft kisses from her lip to the shell of her ear.

"I want to taste you, Piper. From top to bottom," I whispered, my voice ragged.

Her breath hitched as I trailed open-mouthed kisses down the column of her throat, stopping to suck on the sensitive skin where her neck met her shoulder. I could feel her pulse fluttering beneath me as I suckled her neck. I moved further, taking one of her nipples between my teeth and flicking my tongue against it. She fell back and moaned, moving her arms from where she'd propped herself up to grasp either side of my head, pulling me closer to her breast. I continued to toy with one nipple with my tongue and teeth before kissing my way across her chest to the other. I clamped down on it, causing her to yank at my hair and mumble something that sounded very close to "oh fuck, yes." I lapped at her other nipple, sucking it into my mouth, loving the way it pebbled at my touch. The smell of her arousal filled my nostrils, making me want to rut her into the soft forest floor beneath us. I left her nipples, kissing my way down her soft stomach. She was so soft. Her pale skin was delicious. I wanted to kiss and lick it until the end of time. I kissed and licked my way down her torso, noting scars and marks as I went. A question for another time. This female was mine; I would have a lifetime to learn every inch of her body.

As I kissed down her stomach, making my way to her cunt, saliva filled my mouth at her smell and the thought of licking her until she shattered. I kissed across her hip bone, right above the waist of her leggings. Just as I was moving to pull them down, she snapped her thighs shut, blocking my path. I let out a grumble of disapproval and looked up at her. She looked at me hesitantly. I could tell she was aching with want. Why would she stop me from devouring her like the feast that she was? "I know where you're headed, and I'm not ready for that," she said, her voice hesitant.

I was stunned. This beautiful female had provided me pleasure beyond what I had ever experienced and now was denying what was natural. I leaned back on my heels, studying her. She was clearly aroused; her skin was flushed all over and her nipples hardened points. I cocked my head.

"Do you want to stop?" I breathed, unable to hide the desire in my voice.

"No, no. Definitely not," she said. "I just, I don't have a lot of experience with..." She waved her hand toward the apex of her thighs. She trailed off, looking embarrassed.

Ah, understood.

"You don't have a lot of experience with males licking your cunt?" I said bluntly.

Her face was no longer red with arousal; it was red with shame. "No. No. Definitely not. The human men I have been with have not made it an...enjoyable experience," she said matter-of-factly.

"Tell me more," I growled.

"Well, on Earth, it is common for a man to treat oral sex as a chore. Or maybe not even a chore, but as something they have to get through in order to get what they want," she said.

I was perplexed. She just provided what I would call spectacular "oral sex" for me, but she was unused to and unwilling to receive it? It didn't add up. Then again, for orkin, "oral sex" was common for males to perform, but I had never experienced it in the reverse. I couldn't say why. Maybe we'd never considered it? Our elders taught us the ways of female pleasure. Males yearned to devour their female's cunts with their long tongues. Piper was clearly soaked for me but didn't want me to lay her out before me so I could taste every drop of her juices. I wasn't really sure how to proceed. Maybe she wanted to stop altogether?

"Do you want to stop?" I asked, my voice low and husky.

Piper reached up and grasped me by both of my ears, yanking me down to her face. She kissed me fervently on the mouth before whispering in my ear, "Just because I am not ready for that doesn't mean I am not ready for other things. I want your cock. Now."

I pulled back, looking Piper in the face. "You aren't ready for my mouth, but you want my cock?" I questioned, astonished. This was not how orcs went about things.

"Agnarr, perhaps if we get to know each other better, we can discuss the ins and outs of human lovemaking, but for now, I'd really love it if you just railed me," she said.

I didn't even know what *love making* meant. I had to

assume she was referring to mating. But as I looked down at this gorgeous creature, I didn't want to just give her my cock. Hadn't I just been hoping that the arrival of the human females might mean something more for me? If my first reaction to her was any sign, this tiny human could be so much more than a fuck in the middle of the woods. I reached down and stroked her cheek, looking into her eyes.

"Piper. If the first hours of knowing you are any indication of what lies ahead, I want this to be more than me *railing you* in the woods. If you aren't comfortable with me yet, we can take this one step at a time," I said, running my fingers along her jawline.

Piper looked at me, uncertain. "Are you saying you want to stop after I've just given you what was very clearly your first blow job?" she said, clearly irked.

Oh, no. Definitely not the message I was looking to send. Shit.

"No, no, no. I am just saying that I want you to feel comfortable with me seeing, touching, and *licking* all of you. If you aren't comfortable with me laying you out before me and worshiping you like the goddess you are, we can slow down," I said.

I wanted to fuck Piper until she couldn't see straight, but I wanted to find out if she could be more than that. I looked at her, still stroking her cheek. She turned her face and took my thumb into her mouth, sucking on it the way she had my cock. Gods, this woman would be the death of me. I was trying to be a good male here. If we were to have any chance at being elska mates, I wanted her to feel secure and safe with me. I wanted her to know me. But she was making it more difficult with each passing moment. My cock was already hard again, ready to rut her into the forest floor. Piper looked at me as if trying to really see me.

"So, you want to slow down because you think this could be more than just sex?" she asked, studying me.

"Já. I want it to be more than just sex," I said with no hesitation.

She drew me to her, kissing me again. I slid my hands up her body until my fingers tangled in her hair, my lips meeting hers again and again. I kissed from her lips to her ear, using my teeth to grasp at the lobe.

"If you aren't ready for all I can give you, the least I can do is satisfy you with my hands. Is that something you'd welcome? I don't want to treat you as a random fuck in the woods. I want to exceed your needs and wants in every way you will accept," I whispered against the shell of her ear.

There was a long pause before she gave me the smallest of nods, the silent permission I needed. I licked the shell of her ear from top to bottom before moving down to kiss and lick her neck. I trailed my kisses down to her chest. She moaned and arched into me, feeding me one of her breasts. I licked and suckled her nipple, drawing it into my mouth. She grabbed my head and pulled me closer to her. I took her nipple gently between my teeth while flicking the tip with my tongue.

"Oh fuck, Agnarr, don't stop," she moaned.

I took my hand from her hair and slid it over the soft skin of her stomach to the waistband of her pants. Her breathing hitched as I slipped my hand inside, stroking downward. I continued to kiss her, listening to her breathing. She stiffened under me. This made her nervous.

"Is this okay?" I whispered into her mouth. I would stop if she asked, even if it killed me.

She nodded vigorously and continued to kiss me.

I skated my hand further down, finally reaching the apex of her thighs, delighted to find a thatch of hair covering her. I stroked into her curls. Different. Female orcs didn't have hair on their cunts. I loved it. I wanted to see all of her, but in time. Right now, this is what she was comfortable with. I stroked along her seam, finding her already wet. I slid my fingers up and down, allowing her to adjust to my touch, the force with which she'd slammed her knees together earlier still fresh in my mind. I sucked her lower lip into my mouth as I used my fingers to spread her folds, dipping my fingers into her wet cunt. Gods, she was dripping for me. I continued to slide my finger up and down, finding a small bead of flesh at the apex of her folds. I stroked it, curious. Piper gasped and jerked in my arms. Oh, she liked this. I continued to stroke the bud, gauging her reaction.

As I stroked and circled the tiny bead of flesh, Piper's kisses became more urgent and hungry. She grabbed me by the shoulders, pulling me closer to her as I continued to learn what she liked. I traced small circles around the nub of flesh with the pad of my thumb. Piper moaned into our kiss. Continuing with the circles with my thumb, I used my index finger to dip into her core. She was impossibly warm and tight. It was probably for the best that we didn't go straight to sex; I would definitely have to prepare her for the size of my cock. I continued to pump in and out of her heat with my finger while circling her nub with my thumb. Piper quivered under me. She ground her hips against my hand, her movements becoming more erratic as I continued.

"More," she breathed.

"More?" I questioned.

"More pressure. More pressure on my clit," she said.

Well, at least I had a name for it now. I increased the pressure I was using on her *clit* all while thrusting in and out of her with my finger. Piper trembled and moaned, using her hips to ride my hand. Her tiny fingers dug into my shoulders as she gripped me harder. Adding a second finger, I pumped in and out of her faster as she thrust against my hand.

"Agnarr," she said my name as a high-pitched, breathy moan before she threw her head back and jerked all at once.

She flooded my hand with her juices as she rode her release, shuddering. She gave a final twitch before her arms and legs fell limply at her sides. She looked up at me with hooded eyes, a small grin on her face. I slid my hand out of her pants and drew it up to my mouth and licked her juices from my fingers while I looked at her. She tasted delicious.

"Agnarr! That's…" she exclaimed.

She looked shocked at me licking her off of my hand.

"This is what?" I asked, switching to licking my thumb.

"Well, I was going to say that's weird. But it's actually really hot," she said.

"I want nothing more than to lick your pretty little cunt until you come on my face. But until you are ready, I will settle for licking your taste off my fingers. You are absolutely delicious," I said, grinning at her.

"Well...well... That is...well that is..." Piper seemed at a loss for words.

"That is?" I questioned, smirking at her.

"That is an idea for the future," she said looking up at me with a hesitant smile.

CHAPTER 6

PIPER

My arms and legs felt like Jell-O. I had never come so hard in my life. Not with my other boyfriends, not with my plethora of toys, not on my own. As I floated back to reality, Agnarr was still beaming down at me. I smiled back at him. This was the orc I'd been ogling from the morning and now here he was, licking my taste off his fingers. I should have found this horrifying, but it was strangely erotic. Every guy I had ever dated treated oral like something to get through, something that they had to do in order to get to their final goal. Agnarr acted like I had denied a starving man a feast. Not only was I startled by his interest, but I definitely wasn't ready for it. Having someone go down on me felt much more intimate than a blow job or sex. I was definitely attracted to Agnarr, but I wasn't ready for his face in my lap. Yet, based on what he could do with his hands alone, I had no doubt that he'd eat pussy like a rockstar.

I looked up at him, still dazed and smiling, "we should get

out of here. We're right off the main road around the village, I wouldn't be surprised if someone walks by."

Agnarr looked up at the sky. The mist was so thick overhead the sun was obscured—that was, if this planet had a sun. Or multiple suns? Because of the mist, I still wasn't sure. Whatever Agnarr was looking at told him what he needed to know. He smiled back at me.

"It's about time for the midday meal, I'd say we're safe for a little bit yet," he said.

As much as I would love to stay in the soft grass, partially hidden by a felled tree, Tora probably assumed I had died at this point. I needed to get out from underneath Agnarr, no matter how regrettable it might be. I also needed to make sense of Agnarr. I'd been on an alien planet for less than a week, awake for less than a day, and I'd already given a relative stranger a blow job. To be fair, that kind of checked out for me. Growing up in a repressed Christian household meant that when I was finally out on my own, I let no one but me decide my sexual boundaries. I had no regrets about Agnarr; both his cock and the orgasm were exquisite. I was dying to find out what that knot would feel like. But if fated mates were part of this society, I should probably find out more about what I was signing up for.

"We probably should still get back; I know Tora will be worried after me. I told her I was going on a walk to clear my head," I said.

"Funny, I was chopping trees to clear my head. Were you successful? I know I was," Agnarr said as his eyes dipped down to my still-exposed breasts.

"I'm not sure the walk is what helped, but I can definitely say my mind is less jumbled than it was before," I replied dryly.

I grabbed my shredded tunic and pulled it together to cover myself. Not only had the moment passed, I was getting cold. As I put my boobs away, Agnarr started looking at the rest of me. I had minor cuts on my arms and torso. Given that a giant tree had fallen on me, I had no complaints.

"We should get you checked out by the healer before we join the others for the midday meal," he said, voice full of concern.

"It's nothing. They'll heal on their own," I replied.

"Do humans possess exceptional healing capabilities?" he asked.

"Um...no, just normal healing capabilities. These all seem relatively minor."

"We're taking you to the healer," he said firmly.

Well then, I guess we were going to the healer.

"You don't happen to have an extra tunic I can wear, do you?" I asked, looking down at my barely covered torso. The tunic was shredded beyond repair.

"Here, wear mine," he said.

"So you expect me to go to the healer wearing your tunic and you shirtless? Won't the healer make some pretty signifi-cant assumptions?" I asked.

"Would they be false assumptions?"

He did have a point. He'd just finger fucked me within an inch of my life, and I had absolutely no regrets. My only concern would be if this sort of sexual encounter meant we were fated mates or the equivalent of married.

"Agnarr, us fooling around doesn't mean anything to your tribe, does it?" I asked.

"What do you mean?" He looked confused.

"Your tribe won't assume we are permanently together?" I clarified.

"No, orcs are free with their physical affection. As we haven't mated fully, no one will assume I have claimed you as my own," he said.

Uh oh. Jealousy mixed with anxiety led to insanity. Before I could stop myself, the words were out of my mouth.

"So, how many orcs have you been 'free with your affection' with?" I asked, trying and failing to sound casual.

I had no claim over Agnarr. We had gone to third base in the woods. I knew nothing about him other than he had no idea how to chop down a tree. Yet, the idea of him with other women was like a punch to the gut. I wanted this sexy lumbersnack to be mine and mine alone. It had always been this way. Once I made up my mind about something, there was no convincing me otherwise. I definitely wasn't ready to believe in mates, but if Agnarr wanted more than a fuck in the woods, I sure as hell wasn't sharing. No thank you. This was a one human, one orc situation. I looked at Agnarr hesitantly.

"I've mated several of the female orcs of our tribe, but there were none that I wished to take as a mate," Agnarr said.

Not a great answer, but not exactly a bad answer either. Not a virgin, obviously, but unmated. I hadn't just sucked off a married man—bullet dodged. Yet, Agnarr wasn't done talking.

"I've never touched a human woman, though. You are much more..." Agnarr trailed off.

I let him sit in silence for a moment, then prompted him, "Human women are much more?"

"Well, if all human women are like you, you are much more responsive to touch than orkin females. Orkin females don't have what you call a 'clit' at the peak of their folds. Their pleasure center is in their core, harder to reach without the right angle," he explained.

"You think a woman's clit is easy to find?" I snorted.

Agnarr needed to give lessons to all the human men back on Earth if that was truly his first experience with a clitoris.

"Your reaction was immediate when I so much as grazed

it. Are human men not able to tell when you're aroused?" he asked, looking confused.

"I'm not sure if it is so much that they can't tell but more like they don't care. They are way more focused on the actual sex, not anything that leads up to it. Once they get to fucking a woman, for a lot of them, what the woman wants or needs kind of goes out the window. Or, at least, that has been my experience," I explained.

Agnarr looked shocked.

"You mean human males don't care if their partner orgasms?"

"Again, I can't really speak for all human males, but the ones I have been with didn't particularly care about how I felt. One time, I gave a hand job in a movie theater, then when I tried to insist my boyfriend reciprocate, he dumped me. When that happened, I was fourteen. I learned pretty early that a man is going to put his needs first," I said matter-of-factly.

Here I was, oversharing again. I did that when I got nervous. Like when I had an important meeting with my boss and got so nervous, I started talking about decomposing bodies.

Strangely, I wasn't nervous with Agnarr. His confusion about human men was charming. To meet a male that had never even considered leaving his partner hanging was dumbfounding. If this *something* with him was the start of anything, he was definitely going to need to know about my hangups regarding sexuality and sex—and where they came from. Agnarr was still staring at me like I had grown two heads. I guess orc males cared a bit more about getting their partners off than the cishet white dudes I'd fooled around with in high school and Christian college. I looked at Agnarr, trying to make sense of him. I had a feeling sex with him would differ greatly from the sex I had experienced before.

"What does dumped mean?" he asked.

"Oh boy, there's going to be a lot that doesn't translate. I was with a male partner and when I insisted that pleasure go both ways, he decided he didn't want to be with me anymore."

"He didn't want to be your mate anymore because you asked for your needs to be met?" He looked outraged.

"Yep."

"That would not happen here. Our males value our females," he said fiercely.

"Well, that will definitely be a new experience for me. But is one way you value your females dropping trees on them?" I asked.

Agnarr's cheeks shifted to a darker shade of green, probably the orkin equivalent of blushing.

"Ah. Well. Like I said, that was an accident. I am not the most skilled at chopping down trees. Like I said, I was trying to clear my mind," he explained.

"And what had gotten you so flustered that you needed to take to the woods to clear your mind?" I asked, looking up at him beneath my lashes.

At this, Agnarr's cheeks and neck turned an even darker shade of green. It turned out, my conclusions about him placing me back into bed after I'd passed out weren't far off the mark. It seems we'd both been ogling each other. He rubbed the back of his neck with one giant hand and looked at me sheepishly.

"When you passed out earlier, Tora asked me to help put you back in your bed. While I was carrying you, I couldn't help but notice your..." He trailed off.

"My what?" I prompted, grinning at him. I definitely wasn't letting him off the hook. He'd literally dropped a tree on me.

Just when I didn't think Agnarr could blush any more

deeply, I noticed the tips of his pointed ears take on a darker shade of green. He was definitely averting his gaze.

"When I was lifting you from the chair to your bed, I couldn't help but notice how creamy your skin looked. Or how delicious you smelled. Like spice and plommes," he said, still not meeting my eyes.

"So you were checking me out while I was unconscious?" I asked, a wicked grin spreading across my face.

It didn't really bother me he checked me out while I was unconscious, but needling him was delightful fun. I was just as guilty of ogling him while he practiced sparring with Brandr, but he didn't know that. Agnarr looked even more abashed.

"I wasn't *trying* to notice how you looked and smelled, but you were in my bloody arms!" he said in a strangled voice.

Oh, I was getting under Agnarr's skin—and loving every minute.

"Well, do I look and smell as good as I did earlier?" I asked.

Agnarr took his time studying me. His eyes dipped over every part of my exposed flesh. His eyes lingered on the minor scratches and cuts I'd received when the tree landed on me. I wasn't really worse for wear, but it was evident that I'd had a minor accident.

"You smell and look even better than earlier. Now that I know the scent of your arousal mixed with my scent on you, I doubt I will ever tire of it. And now that I have seen your breasts, they will be all I see every time I close my eyes," he said. "But we definitely need to get you to the healer."

Well, holy fuck, the man knew how to sweet talk a girl. Not that I had ever been complimented on the scent of my arousal before, but I'd take it. I didn't really feel the need to see a healer, but if it would make Agnarr happy, I would gladly do so. I looked down at his oversized tunic.

"Well, as long as me wearing your tunic doesn't announce marriage or that we're mates or whatever, we can go to the healer," I said.

"I'll quietly hope she assumes we're mates," Agnarr said, smile wicked.

Well, then. Agnarr was laying claim to me. I couldn't bring myself to mind. I'd only seen two male orcs so far, but I was ready to shack up with Agnarr, no questions asked. He made all the human men I'd been with look like sniveling, uncooked shrimps.

"I look forward to explaining how you felled a tree on me," I said, grinning mischievously.

"We can tell the healer you were in the wrong place at the wrong time," he said, placating me.

"Or we can tell the healer that you do not know how to cut down a tree, so it landed in the middle of the path."

"Or we could tell the healer you were wandering the edge of the village unescorted?" he parried easily.

"Let's just go to the healer. They can make their own assumptions," I said.

AGNARR

Piper was still flushed from coming, but I couldn't ignore the cuts and scratches I had caused by felling the furutré on her. It was my fault for attempting to chop down a tree without knowing how, but I wouldn't admit that to her. Now that I'd seen her fierce spirit, I wouldn't give her the satisfaction. Yet, I wanted to get her seen by our healer. I had no idea how a human would heal, and I didn't want to cause Piper more damage by not getting her injuries seen to. I stood and helped Piper up.

"Let's get you to the healer. It is only a short walk from here," I said.

I offered my arm, and she ignored it.

"Where to?" she said as she straightened my tunic.

My tunic reached almost to her knees, dwarfing her small frame. Seeing her wearing my clothing made me want to bury my face in her neck once more and smell our combined scents. My eyes roved over her again, taking in all of her delightful curves and pale skin before looking up to her face. She had one eyebrow raised at me.

"Well, are we going to head to the healer or are you going to stand there gawping at me?" she asked, running her fingers through her mussed hair.

"To the healer, of course. Though you can't blame me for admiring the view as we go."

"I will be doing the same," she quipped, staring at my bare chest. "Which way?"

I again offered her my hand, if only to help her climb through the branches that still partially blocked the path. This time, she took it as she carefully stepped out of the fallen tree. My pulse quickened at her touch and the warmth of her tiny hand. I led her away from the tree and back onto the path that curved around the entirety of the village.

"It is just a short walk to the healer's cabin. Are you sure you are okay to walk? I would gladly carry you," I said.

"I think if I can get on my knees and suck your cock, I can make a short walk, but thanks for the offer," she said, giving me a rueful look.

As we walked toward the healer's cabin in companionable silence, I replayed the events of the morning in my mind. This woman was going to be the death of me. Between her fiery snark and our obvious physical attraction, I was done for.

I had been with several of the female orcs of our village. They were in short supply and had their choice of mates. Some of them had wanted more than just a casual mating, but I knew deep in my bones that I wanted an elska mate more than anything. I had enjoyed my time with them but always ended things feeling like I hadn't found what I was looking for.

I looked over at Piper. She was unaware of my gaze, instead taking in all of her surroundings. This tiny human set my blood on fire in a way that no one had previously. In the small time I had known her, she had gone toe to toe with me with witty remarks, unafraid to mock me. She'd shown me vulnerability in being upfront with me about the damage caused by her previous partners and her inexperience with things. As if that weren't enough, she'd taken my cock into her tiny, soft mouth and sucked it like it was the most delicious treat she'd ever experienced.

Piper had to be my elska mate. There was no doubt in my mind. I'd never reacted to a female in such a way. She was like a drug I couldn't get enough of. Yet, I had no way of knowing if humans could be elska mates with orcs. I knew humans had arrived in other villages in the past and taken mates, but I didn't know if they were capable of the elska bond. The Snaerfírar village in the north, over the Fjall Mountains, had the most information about human females. They'd had a human female left behind more than three áratugur ago if the word that traveled through our tradelines could be trusted. They would know more about elska mates and the ways of humans.

I mused about what it would take to visit the Snaerfírar tribe village as we continued to walk. It was probably a two-dagr journey if the weather held and I took my hestr. It would be longer if I was trapped by snow or struggled through the Niflfýri. If I went on my own, I could be there and back in less than a vika. I looked over at Piper again. This time she looked at me, meeting my eyes.

"You're thinking awfully hard over there. Worried what

the healer is going to think you've done?" she asked, eyebrows raised.

At this I stopped, looking her up and down again. She wasn't just covered in small nicks and scratches from the furutré. She had bruises and marks all down her neck and what was exposed of her chest. I blanched. It was fairly obvious that my mouth and tongue had made those marks. There were even marks where I'd forgotten myself and bruised her delicate skin with my tusks. Gods help me, the healer was going to know exactly what had happened. Harming a female in any way was cause for severe consequences, possibly even exile."Piper, I'm so sorry. I didn't realize my mouth would leave marks on your skin. I've never —what did you call it? Kissed?—before. I must have gotten carried away. And your skin seems much more delicate than orkin skin. We can't take you to the healer this way. She'll think I harmed you on purpose," I said, ashamed of my actions.

Piper grinned at me, placing her hand on her neck and looking down at the marks on her chest.

"I liked it."

"What?"

"I liked it. A lot. I'm used to lovers that are soft. Don't get me wrong, there's a time and place for slow, sensual lovemaking. But after quite a bit of trial and error, I've discovered that I'd rather be railed within an inch of my life than have someone slowly caress my skin. We'll tell the healer that I asked you to make these marks."

I was dumbfounded, my brain a jumble of fuzz. What? What? What.

I looked at Piper, mouth hanging open. I'd never had a female ask me to "rail her." I was much larger than most of the females of my tribe, built thick, with arms and legs like tree trunks. The idea of being less than gentle with a female was something I had always found appealing but never thought possible. And this tiny human was telling me she didn't want to be treated delicately? I had no words.

"Piper, you already have marks all over your skin from my kisses. If I did what you were asking, I could really hurt you," I said, still looking at her, shocked.

Piper cocked an eyebrow and looked me up and down. She was at least two heads shorter than me, barely the size of an orkling. She wasn't rail thin. I'd seen her generous breasts, and the swell of her ass was clear even under my loose-hanging tunic. But she was small. So small. She continued to peruse me from head to toe, stopping to admire the V-cut of my muscles as they dipped into my trousers.

"I think I could manage. I'm up for the challenge," was all she said, looking me in the eye.

She then continued to walk toward the healer's cabin.

I stood there, taking a minute to remember to shut my gaping mouth. This human was unlike any female I had ever experienced. Not only did she know what she wanted, she had no qualms about asking for it.

I sped up to keep walking alongside her. We were walking past the cabin where we held school for our orklings. They learned everything from reading and writing to how to properly sharpen a knife. Our teachers did their best to ensure that every orkling received an education that balanced book learning with practical knowledge. As orklings got older, they picked what they specialized in. Unfortunately for me, I had not chosen logging or wood-working. Perhaps, if I had, I wouldn't have felled a tree on top of Piper. Then again, if I hadn't felled the tree on her, it wouldn't have led to her sucking my cock.

It was probably for the best that I had chosen warrior training.

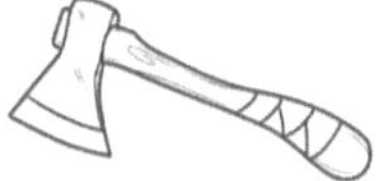

AGNARR

The schoolhouse was now empty, as all the orklings and teachers were at their midday meal in the dining hall. The path surrounding the village and all the communal buildings was essentially deserted. We continued down the path until we reached the small but sturdy hut of our healer, Emla. Emla had been our healer for as long as I could remember. She was currently training an apprentice, as she was carrying on in age, but for now, she was the only capable healer in our tribe.

Walking up to the door, I was hesitant. How was I going to explain Piper's many, albeit minor, injuries? I looked at Piper before I knocked, face scrunched with concern.

"You just let me do the talking, okay?" she said.

"I'm not sure that's the best—"

But before I could even finish my sentence, she rapped smartly on the door three times and gave me a look that told me to hold my tongue. The door opened almost immediately, and Emla stood there with a no-nonsense look on her wrinkled face.

"What brings you here, Agnarr? Another arrow to the arm? A knife wound from an overzealous sparring match with Brandr?"

I was no stranger to Emla's cabin. I had received many injuries as a youth and during my training as a warrior and guard. Piper stepped in front of me.

"Actually, Agnarr is fine. He was kind enough to escort me here after an unfortunate mishap with a tree. I don't have any significant injuries, but he insisted I was seen all the same," Piper said and held out her hand.

Emla looked at her hand, puzzled.

"Well, dear, your hand seems to be free of injuries," she stated, baffled.

"Ah, no. It is a human form of greeting. It is called a handshake," Piper explained.

Piper grasped Emla's hand and moved it up and down while smiling at her.

"Pleased to meet you. I'm Piper," she said.

Emla still looked confused but said, "Good afternoon. I'm Emla."

"Hello! Would you be willing to check me over and give me a clean bill of health so Agnarr here will stop worrying?" She asked, looking back at me, exasperated.

"Of course I will. Let's get you inside and have you take a seat," Emla said, looking at me with an accusatory glare.

It was as if she knew I was the one who had caused Piper's injuries. We walked into her cabin and to the left, toward her examining area. She had Piper sit on the padded bench designated for patients.

"You, stand in the corner and stay out of my way," she said to me gruffly.

I couldn't fathom how Piper was going to smooth this over with Emla, but I sincerely hoped I didn't end up on the receiving end of a tongue lashing. Emla looked back at Piper.

"Okay, dear, how did you get these cuts and bruises?" she asked as she slowly examined each one.

She went to her cupboard to gather her cleaning supplies and healing ointments. I noticed she didn't collect anything she'd need for stitching a wound and let out a quiet sigh of relief. All minor injuries, then.

"I'm the first of the human females to wake up. After Tora explained what life would be like on Fýrifírar and that there was no way for me to return to Earth, I needed some time on my own to gather my thoughts. I went on a walk on the path around the village. About halfway up the path, I heard the noise of someone chopping down a tree. I was curious to see who it was, and I strayed from the path even though Tora told me not to," Piper explained.

She was going to take all the blame for her injuries! I couldn't let her do it. I stepped forward to argue, opening my mouth. Piper shot me a look that would have sent the bravest of orklings shrinking back to their seats in class. I shut my mouth and stepped back. Clearly, she would not let me be the one doing the talking. Emla continued her examination of Piper's injuries. From where I was standing, I could only see minor ones on her arms. Thankfully, her legs were covered by her leggings. She didn't appear to have any cuts on her face. She must have thought to shield it with her arm. Just as I started to relax, I heard Emla tsk.

"And what are these marks all down your neck, my dear?" Emla asked, examining the marks I had left with my mouth. They looked so much worse in the room lit by the large fire in the fireplace. They were purple and red, all somewhat rounded, trailing down her neck and disappearing under the

V of her tunic. I didn't need to guess. I was certain her breasts would be covered in similar marks. I cringed at the thought of the marks I'd left on her nipples, hoping Emla wouldn't ask her to remove her shirt. I could tell Piper was blushing, but she lifted her chin as if challenging the blush to go further.

"Agnarr left those marks with his mouth."

"Agnarr did what with his what?" Emla asked, whipping her head to me with an accusatory glare.

Piper cleared her throat, regaining Emla's attention.

"Once Agnarr saved me from being trapped under the tree, I wanted to express my gratitude. I showed Agnarr the human custom of *kissing,* and we got carried away. I wanted him to leave those marks—encouraged it, actually."

"You are telling me you asked Agnarr to cover your neck in bruises?" Emla asked, clearly skeptical.

"It is a relatively common occurrence amongst younger humans who are intimate with each other," Piper said, not a hint of shame. "It is called a hickey. It is more common with adolescents who aren't as skilled at kissing, but there are plenty of adults that enjoy being marked by their lovers." She looked at me appraisingly.

Was she comparing me to an inexperienced kisser, or was she the type of human that wanted me to leave marks? Definitely not something to be asked in front of the healer. I tried to keep my expression as neutral as possible. Regardless of her meaning, Piper had just referred to me as her *lover.*

Emla looked at me with a furrowed brow, clearly not wanting to accept Piper's explanation of events. Yet, with no reason to doubt Piper, she held her tongue. She looked back to Piper.

"I can clean your cuts and apply a healing salve to them that will speed along the process. As for the *hickeys* left by

Agnarr, I'm afraid they will only heal with time," she said, shooting me another accusatory look.

I did my best to keep my face masked in my most innocent expression, hands clasped in front of me. Piper's plan was going to work. I wouldn't be exiled from the tribe for harming a female. As Emla attended to her scratches, I stayed in the corner and tried to look contrite. I was surprised when Piper spoke up.

"Emla, Tora told me that you have ways of helping those that deal with anxiety?" Emla merely nodded as she continued to put salve on a cut on Piper's shoulder.

"That we do, my dear. We have special herbs that are made into a tea. Orkins that use it to help manage their anxiety usually take it once or twice a day, depending on the severity," Emla explained.

"Do you have any of the tea on hand? I struggle with anxiety, and I don't really know how long I was unconscious. It is possible that I don't have long before my anxiety meds from Earth are completely out of my system."

Piper's hands twisted in her lap, but her gaze remained calm. She looked Emla in the eye as she asked for what she needed. Emla blew out a breath.

"I'm sorry, my dear, but we don't currently have any orcs that take medicinal tea for anxiety, so I don't keep it on hand. Not to worry, though, the Snaerfírar village to the north is where it grows. They are happy to trade with us, and it is only a two-dagr journey on one of our hestrs," Emla explained.

At this response, Piper kept her face calm, but I could see her knuckles go white as she twisted her fingers together. "Do you have a tribe member that would make the journey?"

"We usually only trade with Snaerfírar a few times a season, but if you are in need, I am sure there are many who would volunteer to make the journey. However, it is the cold season, meaning a trip might take even longer than usual."

"I wouldn't want to make anyone go out of their way for me. Unfortunately, I don't know how to ride a hestr. How long would the journey take on foot?"

Emla frowned. "It would be unwise to make the journey on foot, especially for someone who is unfamiliar with our lands. On a hestr it is one dagr of hard travel through the Niflfýri, then a second dagr on the Fjall Mountains. They built their village into the side of the mountains. The baldrian grows only in freezing climates. It snows for at least two full seasons in the Snaerfírar village. They have a significant amount of baldrian prepared and stockpiled. Actually, if I remember correctly, more of their orkin struggle with anxiety than ours. I always thought it might have something to do with the weather they experience," Emla explained.

Emla continued to give Piper far more details than she'd asked for about the Snaerfírar tribe. However, instead of boring Piper to sleep like it would me, Piper paid close attention. Her hands unclasped, and she nodded along as Emla explained more about the orkin of Snaerfírar and their customs.

The tribes of Niflheim avoided each other. All orkin could tend toward violence and aggression, and the intermingling of tribes led to unnecessary warfare. We kept channels of communication and trade open enough that we could exist in semi-isolated harmony, but we didn't encourage any further interaction. Emla, being one of our eldest orkin, knew about the different tribes of Niflheim. Though I was well into my thirty-second ár, I'd only visited the Snaerfírar tribe once, in my youth. Being trained as a warrior, I didn't go on trading expeditions frequently. I didn't remember the trading mission taking an exceptionally long time, but I remembered spending the night in a drafty hunter's cabin on the border of the Niflfýri and the Fjall Mountains.

As Emla continued to talk to Piper, I used the opportunity to straighten my clothes. Emla and Piper were oblivious to me, deep in conversation about the properties of baldrian. I straightened and brushed off my trousers. My long black hair was tangled with small leaves and branches from my encounter with Piper in the woods. My mind wandered back to our entanglement, and I had to stop myself from grinning. Returning my attention to my appearance, I ran my calloused fingers through my hair, then re-knotted it. In our tribe, only mated males wore their hair in plaits. We plaited the manes of our hesrtrs and thus were taught to how to in school, at a young age. However, it was custom for a mated male to have his mate braid his hair as a sign of their partnership. Mine remained in a simple knot—for now. Having straightened myself and fixed my hair, I felt more comfortable approaching the rest of the tribe with Piper, even if she was wearing my tunic and I remained shirtless.

I looked over at Emla and Piper to see they were wrapping up their conversation. Piper had salve on her scratches and looked pleased with whatever information Emla had passed on about the Snaerfírar tribe. She stood from the bench.

"Emla, before we go, do you have a mirror where I could fix my hair?" she asked.

"Of course, dear. There's a washroom down the hall to the left."Piper thanked her and headed down the hall. As soon as Piper was out of sight, Emla looked at me, suspicious.

"Well?" Emla said.

"Well, what?" I asked innocently.

"Well, you bring one of the new humans into my cabin,

covered in scrapes and bruises and what she calls *hickeys. And* you both positively reek of sex. Explain yourself."

What would be the best answer that didn't give away too many details but wasn't an outright lie? I had to think quickly as Emla stared me down. She was a wise old female. She would smell a lie from a mile away.

"I went to the woods to chop down some trees. I heard about the human females arriving and knew that it would lead to disruption in the tribe. I wanted to clear my head, and I had already sparred with Brandr this morning and yesterday," I explained. "However, given that I haven't chopped down a tree since I was an orkling, I forgot to notch the tree in the direction I wanted it to fall. It fell toward the path right as Piper was approaching me."

"Well, that explains the cuts and bruises. What about the hickeys?" she asked.

She was not going to let me get off without a proper explanation. I paused. The elders had agreed that if the human females wanted to take a mate, they would be allowed to do so. So other than leaving marks on Piper's skin, which she didn't seem to mind, I hadn't *technically* done anything wrong other than clearly stake my claim on the first female to wake up. I could give Emla a cleaned-up version of what happened in the woods, for the sake of Piper's dignity. I rubbed the back of my neck with my palm, a nervous habit.

"Well?" she groused.

"*Well...*I used my axe to free her from the branches that entangled her. She was very grateful that I freed her. She taught me the human custom of *kissing* as a means of gratitude. I can't really help that I was over-enthusiastic in my response. And Piper clearly has no complaints about my kissing skills," I said, crossing my arms over my chest and looking down at Emla.

I was trying to look far more confident than I felt. If Emla thought I had taken advantage of Piper, one word to the other elders and I would be banned from talking to her or taking a mate for at least an ár. Emla studied me, clearly unconvinced. A noise from the hall brought us out of our standoff. Piper emerged from the washroom. Her—or my—tunic was straightened and laced up at the top, leaving less of her breasts exposed. She'd washed her face and piled her hair in a large knot at the top of her head, with a few tendrils hanging around her face. She looked from me, trying to look stern and sure of myself, to Emla, scowling at me. She walked toward me and put her hand on the back of my neck, pulling me to her. She wrapped her other hand around my waist and pressed her small body up against mine, kissing me on the mouth in front of Emla. I went for a swift, chaste kiss, thinking Piper's human sensibilities would mean she wouldn't want to fully kiss as we had in the forest, but Piper was having none of it. She dragged her tongue across the seam of my lips, opening my mouth and sliding her tongue in and across mine. I couldn't stop the moan that escaped me as my knees buckled. Piper used her tiny human teeth to nibble on my lower lip as I grasped the back of her head to keep myself steady. Piper pulled away and gave me a wink before turning to Emla.

"Thank you so much for all your help, Emla. All the information you gave me about the Snaerfírar tribe was very useful. I think we should be on our way, though. Agnarr mentioned it is about time for your midday meal and we don't want to keep you," she said with cheery confidence, steering me out of the room.

She linked her arm in mine and walked me out of Emla's cabin. We continued, arm in arm, until we were out of sight of Emla's cabin. When we rounded the bend, the cabin no longer in sight, Piper dropped my arm.

"Have you absolutely lost your mind?" she whisper-shouted at me.

"Me? You're the one who just kissed me in front of Emla. I thought humans were more shy with their affections. What were you thinking?" I whisper-shouted back.

I had no idea why we were whisper-shouting, as Emla was the only one around and we were definitely out of earshot.

"I kissed you because I could tell Emla thought you'd forced yourself on me and I didn't want you to get in trouble! You may have dropped a tree on me, but everything that happened after that was consensual, accidental hickeys aside," Piper whisper-shouted back, putting her hands on her hips as a blush creeped up her neck to her cheeks.

I grinned. She was remembering everything that had happened between us in the woods, just as I had. I took a step toward her when she put her arm out to stop me.

"No, nope. None of that. Weren't you listening when I was talking to Emla?"

"Já, she was explaining to you the baldrian herb we use for anxiety," I said.

"Okay, and did you hear when she said that she doesn't currently have any baldrian in stock and that it was at least a two-day or journey on hestrs to get there?" she asked slowly, as if explaining something to a child.

"I heard her say that we would have to trade for baldrian, yes," I responded.

"So have you ever met someone that has to take medicine for anxiety?"

"No. We don't currently have any orkin with anxiety in our tribe."

"Well, get ready for a quick info dump."

Info…what?

"People that take medicine for anxiety need to keep a

steady supply of it in their system. If they go off of the medicine suddenly, it can lead to withdrawals, their anxiety becoming unmanageable, and their symptoms coming back in a more severe way. At home, I take medicine for my anxiety every morning. The best-case scenario would be that I have gone without it for three days, right? I've been here and asleep for three days?" she asked.

"Well. You arrived at night, so it is possible that if it only took the day to travel here that you'd taken it that morning?" I said.

She looked pensive at this.

"That's a possibility. That would be better, as it would only mean two full days without medicine. However, there's a possibility I was in stasis or some weird shit like that for weeks. Then all of the meds would be completely out of my system. I mean, if that is how stasis works. I don't even know if stasis is a real thing," she said all of this while looking down, as if she was trying to figure it all out in her own head.

The access to baldrian to aid her anxiety was clearly troubling Piper. I should have been paying more attention while she talked to Emla. I could get to the Snaerfírar tribe on my own in maybe a dagr and a half on my own if I took my hestr and pushed her hard. I would go on my own so as not to demand any of our other males from the tribe. We were on the verge of the cold season, and everyone was preparing for snow. Adding in that the other humans could wake up at any time, the timing of an expedition to the Snaerfírar Tribe wasn't the best.

I looked at Piper. She was looking down still, chewing on her lower lip. I didn't know what it was like to experience anxiety, but this was definitely something that was worrying her. Knowing what I knew of her fire already, I had to make decisions quickly before she took matters into her own hands. I didn't want her attempting to make the trek to the Snaerfírar tribe on her own. She'd probably end up as a frozen block of very anxious ice.

"What are you thinking?" I asked.

Piper sighed. "I'm thinking I wish the aliens that had abducted me had at least shown me the kindness of letting me grab some of my things before they changed my life forever. Which is stupid. I'm thinking I need to figure out how to get to the Snaerfírar tribe. I'm thinking I hope the herbs that the orkin use for anxiety work similarly to the medicine I was on at home. Honestly, my brain feels like a jumble of fuzzy string right now. That's what it feels like when I can't get a grasp on the anxiety," she said, looking up at me.

Piper looked into my eyes with a pinched and worried gaze, then reached up to run a hand over her face.

"Do you think you could go a vika without medicine?" I asked. I didn't want her to know what I was considering. She'd stop me. "Have you ever gone off your medicine before?"

"How long is a vika?"

"Seven dagrs."

"Oh, so a dagr is day, vika is week. That makes sense. Yes, I have gone a week without medicine. There were years when, because of moving or other situations, I didn't have access to meds. After about a week, I definitely know that I have nothing in my system anymore. The medicine doesn't make my anxiety disappear, it just makes it manageable. I think about it like a giant boulder that I have to walk around with, worrying me. With medicine and therapy, that boulder becomes more like the size of a...well, I guess you don't have soccer balls here. Um...the size of your head," she explained.

Every day Piper was without medicine was a day her life got harder. That wouldn't do. I would do everything in my power to make sure that the *soccer ball* didn't become a boulder. I studied her. She was looking off to the Niflfýri, contemplative. I knew what she was considering. I'd known her for just a few scant hours, but Piper had a very expressive face when she wasn't bothering to mask it as she had with Emla.

Piper was plotting. She was planning to go on her own. I was going to have to beat her to it.

CHAPTER 8

PIPER

I studied the Niflfýri, wondering how long it would take to reach the other side of it on foot. Emla had said it would take an orc at least a day and a half by foot, but I was no orc. I knew it would take me longer; I didn't even work out back home. I couldn't pretend I was fit enough to match the pace of an orc who lived in the woods and was a good foot and a half taller than me.

If I reached the edge of the woods in two days, then it would be another two to reach the Snaerfírar tribe up in the mountains. This already felt like a stupid plan. Traveling alone on an unknown planet with only a vague sense of where I was headed was ridiculously idiotic. Yet, I knew I didn't want to wait on anyone to help me get the baldrian herbs. I could be waiting even longer if I waited for a good time. Emla had said that the tribe was in a flurry of preparations for the coming cold season, not to mention our unexpected arrival; all hands were needed. I couldn't ask someone to take time out to help me with what was clearly a personal issue. I studied the forest, trying to make up my mind.

I felt Agnarr's gaze on me and looked up at him. He'd been watching me unravel all the bits of string in my head. Time for some redirection.

"When do you think someone would be able to make the journey to the Snaerfírar tribe?" I asked, hoping I looked like I believed I was willing to wait.

Agnarr looked thoughtful. "Well, after the first snow, it will be more difficult, so it would require more men and more hestrs to carry supplies. I'd say it would be a couple of vikas before we are all settled into the season enough to spare the men who would be needed to make the trip."

Yeah, nope. I wasn't waiting a few weeks. By that time, I would be a wreck. If they couldn't spare anyone to take me sooner, I'd have to go on my own, but I wasn't telling Agnarr that. He was looking at me as if he could see the cogs in my brain working.

"A couple of weeks would be really difficult, but I think if I was able to speak to Emla daily, I could manage until then. But I would want to go with the men to the Snaerfírar tribe," I said, hoping to further throw him off.

If I insisted on traveling with them in a few weeks, Agnarr wouldn't suspect that I would venture out on my own.

"No. Absolutely not. You are new to Niflheim. There is no way you should travel to another tribe. What if the Snaerfírar tribe attacks you when you arrive? We know that they have had human women in the tribe in the past and have treated them as they would their own tribe's mate, but we don't know how they'd respond to a human woman traveling from another orkin tribe. We don't have the best relationship," he explained. "Also, you are tiny and fragile. Adding you to the journey would only add time to it."

Not only did Agnarr just tell me *not* to do something, but he called me tiny and fragile. Agnarr didn't know me well enough to know how contrary I could be. I wouldn't just go because I was impatient, I'd go to prove to him that I could. There was nothing more dangerous than telling me no. Maybe my body seemed tiny and fragile compared to his, but I had a will of iron; if it weren't for the need to make *some* preparations, I would have walked into the Niflfyiri then and there.

"I am not tiny and fragile," I said, putting my hands on my hips. "I am taller than most human women."

"Oh, really?" Agnarr grinned at me. "And how tall are most human women?"

"About this tall?" I said, holding my hand up to about my nose.

I wasn't really that tall, clocking in at five-foot-seven, but I was taller than most women I worked with—my best friend at work was five-one. I definitely looked small compared to Agnarr, but there was no way I identified as tiny and dainty. I wasn't one of those willowy girls that looked like they were born to do ballet or pilates; I was the epitome of pear-shaped. Not so perky C-cups up top with a dump-truck ass and thighs that looked like they could crush a skull. I was sure I could put them to good use on a trek through the forest.

"So, though you are the smallest of grown females I have ever seen, there are human females that are even smaller than you?" Agnarr asked, still grinning.

"Yes, a lot smaller!" I glared up at him.

"Well, personally, I find you to be just the right size," he said, assessing me with a heated gaze.

How did this become sexual? I clamped my legs together at the look he gave me. I knew he could smell it when I was turned on—talk about a violation of privacy. But the way he was looking at me, all that came back to my mind was a rushing jumble of images. Me on my knees with my lips wrapped around his heavy cock. Him using his teeth to nip and bite at my breasts…our lips and teeth gnashing together…

Shit. I drew a hand over my face and took a step back. I needed to get it together. Sex with Agnarr was not an option. Well, not an option right now.

"Well, I am glad you find my size so agreeable," I forced out, trying to control my voice and failing.

It came out as a sultry whisper. For fuck's sake, was I going to react to other orcs like this, or was it just something about Agnarr? I needed to put some distance between us before I jumped him. There were more pressing matters at hand. Agnarr took a step toward me. I could smell him. Thoughts of licking him from his neck down to the waist of his pants rammed into my mind. I had to physically shake my head like a wet dog. Nope, nope.

I had a plan and I needed to execute it. I put my hand up and gave him a stern look.

"Who should I talk to about planning a trip to the Snaer-fírar tribe?" I asked, attempting to get my voice back to neutral.

Agnarr looked so disappointed it was almost comical.

"Well, you would need to speak with the jarlin and the village elders. They would decide when it would be best to make the trip and ask for volunteers to make the journey," Agnarr explained.

"And where can I find the jarlin? And what is a *jarlin*? Tora mentioned it too and I didn't know what she meant," I asked.

Agnarr looked at me, assessing.

"You aren't going to give up on being included on the journey, are you?"

"Nope."

"Fine. A jarlin is the title for the leader of a tribe. Let's take you to ours. We can let her decide."

"You have a female chief?"

"Já, is that unusual on Earth?"

"More unusual than it should be. My country has never had a female leader," I said.

Now wasn't the time to explain the difference between president and jarlin. I was just pleased to find out their leader was female. Perhaps she'd be willing to listen to my case. I almost felt bad for my plan to sneak out in the night once if they didn't provide me with someone to take me. Almost.

Agnarr looked toward the village and then back at me.

"Do you want to meet the jarlin in my tunic, or would you rather change?" he asked.

Well, that was a loaded question. Meeting any of the leaders wearing Agnarr's clothes would be akin to allowing him to lay claim to me. I looked at him, arching an eyebrow.

"Do you want me to meet the jarlin in your tunic?" I asked.

Fair was fair. If he was going to ask me where we stood only hours after meeting each other, I was going to make him take the lead. This was his tribe.

"I don't want any other male even looking at you. Meeting tribe members and the jarlin in my clothing will assure that doesn't happen," Agnarr growled.

Oh, he had a possessive streak. Did I want to be his and his alone? Maybe. Probably. But I wasn't going to tell Agnarr that.

"And if I decide I'd like to pursue other options after meeting more of the tribe?" I asked.

Agnarr clenched and unclenched his fists, breathing through his nose. Oh, this was definitely going to be fun.

"Then I would have to respect your choice," he grated out.

"Okay then. For now, I will happily wear your tunic to meet the elders. But that doesn't mean we're boyfriend and girlfriend or anything as far as I am concerned," I said.

Agnarr looked confused. "It doesn't mean what?" he asked.

Rethinking my choice of words, I realized they probably didn't have the words boyfriend and girlfriend in Niflheim.

"It doesn't mean that we are committed," I said.

Agnarr narrowed his gaze at me and then abruptly said, "Fine."

"Yes, it *is* fine," I said, full of sass.

I had been there, done that. I knew what it was like to have a man lay claim to me without even discussing it with me. My first boyfriend at the tiny Christian college I'd attended had decided we were exclusive after one make-out session in the backseat of his car. I had no such intentions, but by the time I realized what he was telling people, word had spread through campus. Piper and Christopher were official. He was one of those Christophers that refused to be called Chris. It should have been a red flag. Christopher and I had dated for six months, long enough at our school for people to start throwing around "ring by spring." I'd never dumped someone, but after six months of sad hand jobs, I'd needed out. I'd let him down as gently as I could, but Christopher was pissed, saying he had already told his parents about me. I definitely hadn't told my parents about him.

Christopher had made me decide I was done with Christian boys all together. They had been one terrible experience after another. I was sixteen when I knew I was ready to explore my sexuality, but being raised in the church meant I was penned in. More often than not, it meant I was giving rather than receiving, then shamed for any of it happening in the first place.

After Christopher, I decided to study abroad in Europe. I lost what was left of my virginity in the first month and never looked back. I spent most of my twenties figuring out what I wanted out of sex and relationships, but I still had some lingering hang ups from my old life. It was definitely a work in progress, but I wasn't going to let Agnarr choose what I'd worked so hard to be able to choose for myself.

"All right, where to?" I asked brightly, ignoring the scowl on Agnarr's face.

"We need to go to the longhouse. Everyone will still be there taking their midday meal," Agnarr responded, still looking grumpy.

"Well then, let's go."

I started on the path that wrapped around the village.

AGNARR

I stared at Piper in disbelief as she started down the path—in the wrong direction. It appeared that once this female set her mind on something, there was no stopping her. She continued, not looking back to see if I was following her.

"Piper," I called, "you're headed in the wrong direction."

Piper turned around.."Oh...I hadn't realized. Why don't you lead the way?" she said, looking embarrassed.

"It's easiest to get to the longhouse if we take the path that cuts through the village," I said.

I didn't add that it would also ensure that anyone that was in the market was sure to see us, thus cementing my claim on Piper. Piper was welcome to make her own decision about whichever male she wanted to be with, but if the other males of my tribe knew I had taken interest in her, they would think twice before approaching. I was one of our trained guards, and it wasn't uncommon for us to defend our interest in females with physical violence. I didn't think that Piper would approve of me laying claim to her in that way, so I decided it would be best not to mention it.

We walked on the cobblestone path toward the center of town, Piper looking every which way as if trying to take in all the sights and sounds at once. We reached the market in the center of town that was lined with shops and booths. It was relatively quiet as most were probably still in the long-house finishing up their meal, but there were still a good two dozen orkin in the village center. A hush seemed to fall over the market as Piper marched through it, clearly on a mission. The orkin all stopped to look at her. Piper, clearly feeling several pairs of eyes on her, slowed her pace until I met her side.

"Are they all staring because I am human or because I am wearing your tunic?" she whispered to me.

"I don't know, what do you think?" I whispered back, giving her a mischievous grin.

She rolled her eyes at me and started walking again. She was not to be deterred. We headed through the town center and out the other side without stopping again. When the longhouse came into view, I pulled up short.

"Why are we stopping?" she asked.

"Because that is the longhouse right there," I said, indicating the building we were approaching. "I wanted to give you some tips on what to expect. Unless you'd rather just barge in there without a plan."

"Fine," she sighed. "Tell me what I need to know."

Piper was going to be approaching our jarlin and elders. Jarlin Astrid was a very fair leader; she didn't hold herself above the rest of the tribe like other jarls had in the past. When there was work to be done for the good of the tribe, she worked with us, side by side. She always aimed to say yes to reasonable requests and was known to be an excellent listener. I had no doubt she would listen to Piper's request to join a trip to Snaerfírarr and agree to her joining. This was exactly what I wanted. If Piper thought she would be heading out on a planned trip shortly, there would be no reason for her to recklessly charge off without guidance. This would buy me time to head off on my own ahead of the planned trip. I could obtain the herbs and the information I needed and be back before Piper ever left.

"Our jarlin, Astrid, is very reasonable. She will listen to your request. While I might not think it best for you to travel through Snaerfírar and up the Fjall Mountains during the cold season, if Astrid thinks you are capable, she will likely agree to you joining."

Piper looked at me shrewdly. "Why aren't you stopping me, then?" she asked.

She knew I didn't want her to go; I would have to come up with some rational reason why I was willing to help her that didn't involve me going before she ever got a chance to leave. She wouldn't accept that I was doing it because I wanted her to go.

"Because you are clearly a force to be reckoned with. Is there anything that is going to stop you from attempting to go?" I asked.

"No."

"Well then, I would like to stay on your good side all the same, and I will do what I can to assist you. Even if I think it is a bad idea," I responded.

Piper continued to assess me. I could almost see her trying to decide whether or not to believe me, her brows furrowed.

"Fine," she said. "Thank you for your help. Will you point out Astrid when we go inside?"

"Of course."

Piper still looked as if she didn't quite trust my intentions, but she must have decided it was worth it to continue on.

"Okay, let's go in."

"There will probably be a great deal more staring," I warned her.

"Do you think they will stare at me because I am human or because I am covered in hickeys that you clearly gave to me?" she asked, giving me her most devious smile.

I blanched.

"You aren't going to tell them I gave you hickeys due to inexperience, are you?" I asked.

"Maybe I am, maybe I'm not."

This female would be the death of me. She headed to the longhouse doors, leaving me to trail behind her yet again. I used my long strides to catch up with her before she reached the doors, opening them to let her through. I heard her breath catch as we both walked in.

CHAPTER 9

PIPER

I'd brushed past the orcs in the market without really giving them a second glance. There were only a handful of them going about their days. They'd stopped to stare at me, but I was on a mission. As I walked into the longhouse, I was greeted with a very different scenario. A hush fell as around eighty sets of orkin eyeballs fell on me. I looked at Agnarr, a blush creeping up my cheeks. He gave me a nod toward the back of the longhouse and started heading in that direction. I reached out to grab his hand, and he looked at me, puzzled. I'd just made it clear that I didn't want him taking ownership of me, yet I was now reaching for him in a very public setting. Gripping his hand more firmly in mine, I took a step toward him and gave him a quick smile. I needed the support in the face of the crowd; I could worry about my independence later.

We walked hand-in-hand to the far end of the longhouse,

stopping at a table full of orcs that looked to be at least thirty years older than Agnarr. All eyes were on us as we approached. I looked at the middle of the table to see an older female orc. Her long black hair was peppered with white and gray strands and woven in a simple long braid down her back. She was slim and willowy, but I could tell that she was definitely taller than me. I looked at her face, seeing the wrinkles of age and kind eyes the color of honey. I knew without having to ask that she was Astrid.

"Hi, I'm Piper, one of the human females that recently arrived?" I asked more than stated, a nervous habit I still held onto.

"Hello, Piper. I'm Astrid. I'm so glad to see you are awake. Are the other humans awake yet?"

"Not as of this morning. I haven't been back since Tora explained everything to me," I said.

"Where did you go after your conversation with Tora?" Astrid asked, her eyes glancing at Agnarr.

My brain was working in overdrive. I was going to have to explain Agnarr, whose hand was still in mine, in a way that didn't get him in trouble. But, other than knowing it would look bad on him to have dropped a tree on me, I wasn't sure if our encounter would lead to trouble with the jarlin. Damn my impatience. I should have asked Agnarr more questions about their tribe's culture. Well, I would do what I did with Emla and take all the blame on myself. I couldn't be expected to wake up on an entirely different planet and understand their society; I would be more quickly forgiven for any mistakes.

"I went on a walk to clear my head. A lot of the information was overwhelming."

"Understandably so. How is it you ran across one of our guards on your walk?" Astrid asked, assessing Agnarr.

"I was walking when I heard the sounds of a tree being chopped down. Without thinking, I walked toward the noise to see what was happening. Agnarr felled the tree. I was in the wrong place at the wrong time," I explained.

Astrid gave Agnarr a questioning look. "What were you doing felling trees?"

Agnarr shifted, looking uncomfortable. Silence hung in the air.

"Look, it doesn't really matter, does it?" I interjected. "Because Agnarr was there, though the tree falling on me wasn't the best, he was able to help me find the healer's cabin after. I really needed to speak with her, which is why we are here now. I need to speak with you urgently," I blurted, attempting to take Astrid's focus off Agnarr. Not just because I didn't think he deserved any punishment, but because I wanted to discuss traveling to the Snaerfírar tribe.

Astrid looked back at me, eyebrows raised.

"Okay, Piper. I will ask Agnarr for an explanation after we take care of your pressing issue. What did you need to discuss?"

"I need to travel to the Snaerfírar tribe as soon as possible," I said.

Astrid looked even more surprised.

"Why?" she questioned.

"I have seen your healer, Emla. I struggle with anxiety and take medication daily to assist me in managing it. Emla said you have an herb on Niflheim that you use to treat this but that this tribe doesn't have any currently. I am requesting to travel to the Snaerfírar tribe to get the baldrian herb," I said, trying to make it sound like an official request. What did I know about asking for a jarlin's permission? I just learned what jarlin meant.

At this, Agnarr stepped in front of me, surprising me.

"Jarlin, I have spoken with Piper, and she needs the baldrian herb as soon as possible. I would like to volunteer to travel to the Snaerfírar to trade with them."

Well, that was kind of him. There was no denying I wanted to spend more time with him. I would get to know him better if he went on the trip. But Agnarr continued.

"However, Jarlin, though I am sure Piper will have objections, I don't think she should join the trip. She is new to Niflheim and has been awake for less than a dagr. We will be able to travel faster if she remains behind."

Um, what? He told me that Astrid would probably let me go! He knew it was important to me! What a dick move. I was pissed. The sooner I got to the Snaerfirir tribe, the sooner I could start taking the medicine. I glared at his back and then stepped around him.

"Jarlin Astrid," I said, "if I go on the trip, I will be able to start taking the herbs as soon as we arrive rather than having to wait until their return." I crossed my arms over my chest and scowled at Agnarr. He seemed undeterred.

"Já, you will be able to take the baldrian as soon as you arrive, but it will probably take us twice as long to get there," Agnarr said coolly. "Do you know how to ride a hestr?"

I opened my mouth to retort, then shut it quickly. I had no response. I didn't even know what a *hestr* was, much less how to ride one. I looked at Astrid. She looked almost amused. With our sniping, Agnarr and I were making it very clear that something more than an unfortunate incident with a tree and a trip to the healer had happened between us. I blushed red and looked at Agnarr. Either he was unfazed or much better at playing it cool than I was.

"Jarlin Astrid—" I said only for her to hold her hand up. She looked at me.

"Piper, I understand your concerns and your need to visit

the Snaefirer. Yet, however insensitively he may have put it, Agnarr has a point. Sending three males on our hestrs would be much quicker than sending a group on foot," she said. I opened my mouth to argue, but she continued on. "Further, we are expecting the first snow of the season tonight. If the snow does come, we won't be able to travel for at least three to four dagrs."

My mouth dropped open. Emla made it sound like we might be able to leave right away. Now Astrid was saying she wasn't willing to let anyone even leave for three to four days? I would be a nervous wreck by then. There was no way I was waiting that long.

AGNARR

Though I felt Piper's gaze on me, I kept my eyes on the jarlin. She was as shrewd as she was kind, and she had already picked up on something between me and Piper.

I'd known Astrid for my whole life. She'd stepped in when my parents died, just as I came of age. As was custom in our tribe, Astrid could choose the next jarl and step down when they felt the time was right. Astrid and I had had many conversations about this, and I knew I was her first choice. Her eldest daughter, Inga, was in training to become a healer when Emla retired. Her son, Ottar, had no interest in leading the tribe, instead taking on the role of head cook. This had left Astrid to pick amongst any of the tribe she saw fit.

Astrid had started planting the seeds of her choice very early, just after my parents' death. I was newly in the guard, going through brutal physical training. Astrid would ask to meet with me regularly to see how my training was going and ensure that I knew I had someone looking out for me. I'd thought she was merely being kind, but it soon became apparent that she had goals for me. We went from discussing how my training was going to discussing how I fit within the guards and the wellbeing of the tribe as a whole. As I'd progressed with the guard, I was definitely one of the strongest, but I didn't have the ruthlessness required to make it into the top ranks. In hindsight, my lack of vicious tendencies was probably one of the reasons Astrid had sought me out. I was respected and well liked. As I continued with the guard, I gained more responsibility until I was eventually put in charge of the training of new members.

As my responsibilities grew, Astrid started talking to me more openly about taking on her role when she decided to step down. I knew I was doing well in the guard, but going from a mid-level leader to jarl seemed like a ridiculous jump. Astrid had brushed off my concerns, saying she was more concerned with how I would lead than with my current position.

Astrid had one condition she wanted me to fulfill before she stepped down. She wanted me to take a mate. She said it would settle me and help me see things from more than one perspective. I had a feeling that Astrid knew I was hoping to find my elska mate and that condition served multiple purposes. Not only would it give me time to get used to the idea of taking over, but it would also give the tribe time to adjust to the idea of a new leader.

Astrid studied me while Piper continued to glare. She must know what I was thinking. She'd likely seen straight through Piper's careful story about the tree falling on her—there was no reason for me to be out in the woods. Astrid had to know that I wanted to be the one to retrieve the herbs. She met my eyes and gave me the smallest of nods. It was all the permission I needed.

I needed Piper to stay put. I wanted her safe. Seeing the determination on her face made me realize the only way this was going to happen was to let her think she was going. Even if I had to look like an idiot in front of my tribe. I thought she might be willing to accept staying behind, but the look on her face said absolutely not. Piper took her gaze from me and looked back at Astrid.

"While I understand Agnarr's concerns," she said, voice cold, "I am sure I will be able to keep up. I am happy to ride to the best of my ability."

Now that Astrid understood my intentions, I was more than willing to eat my words.

"Apologies, Piper. If you would like to travel with some of the guards, I would happily escort you once the weather clears—"

Piper cut me off, "If it is all the same, I would rather have someone that believes in my abilities escort me, thank you."

I couldn't do anything but blink. She'd just rejected me in front of my entire tribe. Piper was unlike any female I'd ever experienced. She kept her eyes on Astrid, not even looking at me.

"Knowing it will be risky, are you willing to go on the journey?" Astrid asked, looking skeptical.

"Absolutely," Piper said, standing up a little taller.

"Very well. We will have to wait until the weather changes, but when it does, I will have our best guards escort you."

"Thank you, Jarlin. May I return to my room? Today has been very overwhelming, and I could use some time to myself."

"Of course."

I couldn't let her leave without trying to explain myself. "Will you permit me to show you the way back to your room?"

Piper assessed me. "Fine," was all she said before she turned and walked toward the longhouse entrance, all eyes still on us.

It left me no choice but to follow her, looking incredibly foolish. I had shown that I would do whatever Piper asked just to have her walk out of the longhouse without a backward glance. I could feel dozens of eyeballs burning into me as we headed toward the door. The tribe knew me for being level-headed and firm in my decisions. They respected me. Now I looked like a smitten youth. I couldn't bring myself to care. I was more focused on making things right with Piper. Using my long strides, I caught up to her in time to open the large furutré doors for her. She walked through them without even glancing in my direction. I had underestimated her. Piper was a force to be reckoned with.

She only slowed when we were out of view of the longhouse, whirling on me.

"You knew how important it was to me to go on the trip and you still tried to convince Astrid I shouldn't go. What the hell?"

"I still don't think you should go. It is dangerous. You don't know anything about the Snaefiyer or Niflfýri. How do you plan to survive the mist and the dangerous beings that lurk the woods?" I asked.

"Just because I am small in your eyes doesn't mean I'm not capable. I take care of myself on Earth and I can take care of myself here. And I wasn't asking to go alone. I was asking to be taken with someone. I would have happily had you escort me had you not just made a fool of me in front of Astrid and an entire tribe of orcs that have never met a human," she said, glaring at me.

I was at a loss. Piper had as much pride as I did. Our first time in front of the tribe together had been completely disastrous for both of us, and it was my fault. Yet, I couldn't help but notice how adorable she looked, glaring up at me, completely unafraid of my hulking frame. I was entranced.

"Well, are you going to hold my concern against me and

not let me be one of the guards to escort you?" I asked, hesitancy clear in my voice.

Piper was going to be mad as hell when I stole away in the night without her, but I could get there and return way faster than a team of guards escorting her could. At the very least, I could try to convince her that I still wanted to help her—even if it wasn't in the way she wanted.

"Maybe. I'd like to see my other options," she said, looking me up and down casually.

"I assure you, I am the best of options," I gritted out.

How was she so capable of getting under my skin?

"Well, how about we start with you escorting me back to my room? Today has been a nightmare, and I would like to rest. I assume I will be expected at the evening meal?"

"Has all of today been a nightmare?" I asked, thinking back to our time on the border of the wood.

A blush creeped up Piper's neck. Aha—she wasn't completely unaffected by me, just utterly pissed off.

"You ruined any part of today that wasn't a nightmare by publicly telling your tribe you didn't think I could journey to Snaerfírar myself. I am used to handling things on my own; I have for a long time. I hate the idea that I have to rely on others to get the support I need." She looked at me, no longer glaring.

A small part of me hesitated then. She was going to be a tornado of righteous indignation when she realized I'd left without her. But I had to. I could get there in a dagr and a half, easily, on my hestr. I might get there and back before Astrid even gave them permission to leave. Getting there before her would give me the time to get the baldrian *and* find out about humans' ability to have an elska mate. I felt it in my bones that Piper was my mate, but no marks had appeared. And Piper had made it clear that though she was attracted to me, she wasn't looking for a permanent mate right now. If she knew I wanted to ask the Snaerfírarr about being a elska mate, she might think I had lost my mind. No, even with my doubts, it would be best to steal away in the night without her. Even if I had to apologize on my knees when I returned.

CHAPTER 10

PIPER

There was no way I was waiting until Astrid deemed the weather appropriate to travel. I was going on my own. I wasn't going back to my room to rest; I was going to prepare. I was considering telling Tora of my plans, but I wasn't sure if I could fully trust her. Agnarr had made his thoughts about my abilities painfully clear; I definitely wasn't telling him. Even if his intentions were good, he'd just embarrassed me in front of the entire tribe. I would not give him the satisfaction of waiting around to be escorted by "more capable" men. Fuck the patriarchy.

Agnarr and I walked back to my room in relative silence. As we walked, I took in more of the tribe. Just past the longhouse, we walked by what had to be the kitchens, the smells of delicious food wafting through the air. I knew I would be expected to go to dinner with the tribe and actually meet my new tribe mates, but I hadn't decided if I was going to sneak off even before then. It would all depend on how quickly I could prepare to leave—and what sort of answers I could get out of Tora.

We approached the row of little log cabins and I recognized the one on the end as mine.

I turned to Agnarr. "Thank you for taking me back, I can handle it from here."

He looked at me; I could almost see the cogs working in his brain. I almost felt bad that I planned on disappearing right under his nose.

"You're sure you have everything you need?" he asked.

"Actually, do you know where Tora is? I would like to speak to her about getting some fresh clothes, given that my tunic is ruined. I will get yours back to you."

"I can find Tora and send her to your room," Agnarr grumbled, clearly displeased at what was an obvious dismissal.

"Thank you, I would appreciate it."

I turned on my heel and headed to my cabin, forcing myself not to look back. I walked, noting that it was quiet all around. I guessed the rest of the humans remained asleep. Opening the door, I found it much the same as I'd left it. Someone, probably Tora, had made my bed and shut my window. Even though I'd told everyone I wanted to return to my cabin to rest, I wasn't actually tired. My mind was buzzing with the need to prepare.

I was going to the Snaerfírar tribe alone, and I was going as soon as possible. I wasn't waiting until Astrid deemed it suitable, and I certainly wasn't letting anyone else to go on my behalf. I knew I was pushing the boundaries of what was logical and safe, but I'd always needed to do things for myself even when asking for help would have been much easier. I started looking around my small cabin for supplies. The dresser next to my bed had a surprising amount of clothes in it. All of them were clearly hand-me-downs, but they were clean and in good condition. I found multiple pairs of leggings, even some that were lined with something that looked a lot like wool. If it was actually going to snow soon, they would be my best option. There were multiple tunics and what appeared to be a cloak—like my Californian ass had ever worn a cloak before. I was busy rummaging through the dresser when a knock sounded at the door.

Shit. Every single dresser drawer was open and all the clothes were all over the bed. I was trying to determine what to pack and what to pack it in. Anyone who came in now would be very suspicious about what I was doing. I stared at the clothes, trying to make a hasty decision, when there was another knock, followed by a voice.

"Piper, it's Tora; Agnarr said you wanted to see me."

I was going to trust Tora. Even if she didn't agree with me heading off on my own, I didn't think she was going to stop me. I opened the door.

"Hi. Thanks for coming by. I need your help if you are willing," I said, somewhat flustered.

Tora surveyed the room. "Looking for something?" she asked, raising an eyebrow.

"Listen…can I trust you?" I asked.

She looked hesitant.

"I've just arrived on an alien planet and I am trying to figure out things the best I can. I need someone to trust."

"All right, you can trust me," she agreed.

"I am planning to leave for the Snaerfírar tribe on my own. As soon as possible."

"What?" she spluttered. "Piper, you don't even know the way there! The snows are coming! The Niflfýri is full of dangerous beasts, and it is easy to get turned around. Seasoned guards and hunters have been known to lose their way when the mists are especially thick."

"I know there are a lot of risks, but I can't wait until the weather changes. What if it snows for days? I need to get to the Snaerfírar tribe. Without treatment for anxiety, I know I will become overwhelmed by it, especially considering my current circumstances," I said, waving my arms to show I was clearly out of my depth.

"And what if your anxiety gets the best of you in the middle of the forest?" Tora asked.

"I know myself. I can use my anxiety to keep me going. It will fuel me forward. If I just sit here waiting, I will completely spiral. The best thing for me is to help myself," I explained.

I was resolute. I knew it was the truth as soon as I said it. Not only did I want to go do this on my own, it was the only way I would be able to keep myself sane. I needed to use my anxiety to get to the Snaerfírarr tribe. Sitting and wringing my hands would put me in such a dangerous place mentally, I'd be better off braving this strange planet. I was no wilderness expert, but I knew how to hike and I was physically fit—enough. If Tora was willing to provide me some help, I knew I could make it on my own. I might be a puny human in their eyes, but I had a will of iron, and my mind would not be unmade.

Tora looked at me.

"Okay, Piper. This is not a good idea, but I will help you. What do you need?"

I breathed a sigh of relief.

"Well, it looks like I have plenty of warm clothes, but I could use a pack to carry things. I also will need enough food for a few days and a way to carry water if you have something like that," I said, looking at her hopefully.

"You'll also need to know the way there," she said, crossing her arms.

"Tora, please, please tell me you understand that I have to do this on my own."

Tora sighed. "All right. I am all in. I will help you in every way I can."

I squealed and threw my arms around her. "Thank you. Thank you so much!"

Tora looked uncomfortable and patted me on the head.

"I didn't say I think it's a good idea. I am just going to do everything I can to make sure you don't end up dead."

"That's fair. Where do we start? How can I get ready and leave without drawing attention to myself?" I asked.

"Well, during that spectacular display in the longhouse, you said you were coming back to your room to rest," she said.

I could feel myself blushing again.

"You were there in the longhouse?"

"Yes. I've never seen someone be so assertive with Jarlin Astrid. And I've never seen Agnarr backpedal so quickly. What exactly happened between you two in the forest? I know what you told Astrid wasn't the whole truth." Tora looked at me knowingly.

I hesitated. Agnarr seemed all too willing to participate in our woodland romp, but I didn't know if I was ready to tell Tora about it. What if she looked down on me for giving the first male orc I ran into a blowjob? Did I have feelings for him already? What if he was already "mated" to someone else and lied to me? Oh shit, I was spiraling. I felt my cheeks growing hot. The only way to get answers to at least some of these questions was to ask Tora. I definitely wasn't asking Agnarr.

"Does Agnarr have a mate?" I asked, trying but failing to sound casual.

"No, he doesn't have a mate. Many females have expressed interest in him and he has"—Tora paused as if trying to choose her words carefully—"considered many of the options available. But none of the females he has been with have been more than a passing thing."

I am not sure if that made me feel better or worse. So he wasn't spoken for, but he had "entertained" many of the females of the tribe. I guess that made me feel better.

"Well, he was chopping down a tree. He said he had gone out into the woods to 'clear his head.' About what, he wouldn't say. He accidentally felled the tree in my direction. I was mostly unharmed, thankfully. The branches of the tree trapped me, but didn't cause any injuries. To free me, Agnarr and I had to get up close and personal. One thing led to another and, well..." I trailed off, not really wanting to give the specifics, especially considering Agnarr's reaction to the kissing and the blowjob. I looked at Tora and bit my lip.

Much to my surprise, Tora broke out in gleeful laughter. She clapped both her hands over her mouth.

"What?" I demanded.

Tora said nothing but continued to laugh, wiping tears from her eyes.

"What is so funny?"

Catching her breath, Tora said, "Agnarr is absolutely infatuated. It all makes sense. His weird behavior in front of the tribe, the backpedaling, the request to escort you to the Snaerfírar. That is all out of character for him. He's trans-fixed." She looked at me, smiling from ear to ear. "I can't wait to tell Brandr."

I opened my mouth to say something, but no words came out. I was the first female to grab Agnarr's attention. I couldn't help but be pleased by that. However, that didn't mean I wasn't still irritated as fuck at him for trying to stop me from going—in front of the entire tribe.

"Well, if he's as *infatuated* as you say, someone ought to teach him that embarrassing a woman you are interested in in front of a large group isn't going to earn him any points," I said, crossing my arms over my chest.

"Points? Do humans score their partners and select who they will mate with based on who earns the most points?" Tora asked, looking confused.

I dragged a hand down my face. Whatever translation device I had received definitely wasn't prepared for human slang. Then again, maybe a point system wasn't a terrible idea...

"No, it is a figure of speech. I just mean if he is interested in me, then his behavior in front of the tribe was a bad idea," I explained.

"Ah. Well, he is clearly concerned for your safety—if he cares for you, he doesn't want you getting lost or hurt on a dangerous trip, obviously."

"He may think he cares for me, but he barely knows me. Hell, I barely know him. He underestimated my desire to make my own decisions."

"Clearly."

"Listen, I know you think it is a bad idea. But I am used to doing things for myself, and I've never had anyone to rely on, so I've gotten used to relying on myself," I said, surprising myself with the dull ache the statement caused me.

I never had anyone to rely on, not as a child and definitely not as an adult. My parents were distant at best, neglectful at worst. They'd divorced when I was young and spent years fighting over child support and who got my sister and I on weekends and holidays. I don't think either of them particularly *wanted* us on weekends and holidays; they were just focused on not letting the other "win." We ended up with my mom most of the time. As a single mom, she'd worked all the time, barely making enough to provide for us. We were latchkey kids from a young age.

When we were at my dad's house, he pawned us off on

whatever relative would take us. We'd ended up spending most of our time with my great-grandma. I remembered her making homemade cornbread and feeding me buttered saltine crackers. She was the most parent-type figure I had, and I only saw her every other weekend. When I was twelve, my dad remarried, and we never saw Grandma Esther again. My dad's new wife hated my mom and wasn't shy about sharing her opinions. I stopped going to see him as soon as I was sixteen and the courts allowed me to decide for myself.

Neither of my parents had gone to college. I'd stopped expecting any sort of parental guidance or support before I was in middle school. Neither parent cared particularly about my grades, given that I was passing. I'd worked my butt off in high school to get into an out-of-state college. I got into the school of my dreams in the Pacific Northwest, took out a shit-ton of student loans, and set off on my own. No one had helped me with any of it. My dad was openly displeased that I was "wasting money" on a private school. My mom was indifferent.

Even though I excelled in college, I still had my walls up. I didn't want to rely on anyone that would disappoint me. I had too many experiences of my parents not showing up when I needed them. I would get through college on my own. It was in college that I was diagnosed with anxiety and started medicine. Seeing a therapist helped enormously. I had no shame in using store-bought serotonin. I'd graduated and gotten a teaching job about an hour from my mom's house. A bit close for comfort, but I was at a dream school. I had just started my eighth year. I lived alone and was close but not *too* close to my coworkers. My therapist was constantly asking me about expanding my small network of friends beyond my coworkers I ate lunch with, but I was happy. Well, I'd thought I was. I really did isolate myself in my attempt to keep myself safe from the disappointment of relying on others.

I had no reason to believe I could rely on Agnarr or any of the other orcs; this was something I was doing on my own —again.

I realized I had been silent for a few moments, reliving old memories. Tora had gotten to work, putting clothes into piles. She folded up each item neatly, placing it in one pile or another. I looked at her, questions in my eyes.

"This pile," she said, pointing to the pile on the left, "is what you will take with you. The other pile is clothing that you won't need."

Oh, thank the stars for Tora."Okay, what are we packing?" I asked.

"Well, you don't need any of the lighter clothing. I have picked out all the lined leggings and thicker tunics. I figure you can wear a pair and pack a pair so if you get wet one can have time to dry. I've packed you two extra tunics, considering you've managed to destroy one in less than a day," she said to me with a smirk.

"Hey!" I swatted her arm. "I didn't ask to have a tree dropped on me!"

"Well, I am sure Agnarr didn't mind your tunic being torn from top to bottom," she said.

She continued to organize the clothes, then walked to the corner, opening a door I had glanced over but hadn't inspected. It was a closet with more supplies. Tora pulled out a leather satchel about the size of a backpack. I spied other supplies—extra blankets, a second pair of boots, some bags hanging on hooks that looked like they might be waterskins. These rooms are oddly well equipped for a sleeping human.

"Tora, what are these rooms used for when you aren't hosting a bunch of unconscious humans?" I asked.

"They are usually for our unmated males who wish to

move out of their family homes but have yet to find a mate. When the humans arrived, we had the males move back into their family homes for the time being in order to make space," she explained.

I flushed. Not only had I arrived with no warning and in need of medical attention, but I had also apparently kicked a male orc out of his room. Wow. They must be really gracious —or really interested in human females.

"Weren't the males displeased at being kicked out of their rooms?" I asked.

"No. Your arrival was met with great enthusiasm by our unmated males. Our tribe currently has far more males of age than females. It seems Agnarr has already laid claim to the only female awake. Funny that she happens to be the one sleeping in his room," she said, her eyes sparkling.

I groaned inwardly. I was not ready to be claimed as anyone's mate. Yes, I was attracted to Agnarr, but I had always shied away from commitment. I didn't want the disappointment of falling for someone, then realizing I couldn't depend on them. Sure, I was down to maybe date, but lifelong commitment right away? Mmmm.. probably not. Yet, I couldn't ignore how my stomach flipped knowing I was staying in Agnarr's room. Either they had stripped it of belongings or he was into clean minimalism. I looked around the room with new eyes for signs of the previous owner. Other than the bed large enough to sleep three humans, there were no signs. Then I thought of the slippers tucked under the bed. Those had to be Agnarr's. I couldn't decide how I felt about wearing his slippers around. That felt oddly personal.

I looked at Tora. She was folding clothes and placing them in the bag from the closet. I was wasting time inside my head. I needed to go.

CHAPTER 11

PIPER

I checked my bag was secure one final time. It was stuffed full of extra things Tora had thought I might need. She'd insisted on a second cloak, in case the first one got too wet from the mist, packed me enough food for four days, and stuffed in an extra empty waterskin in case mine split.

It was time for their evening meal, and I was going to head out. Tora tried to convince me to leave the following morning, but I wasn't having any of it. Despite the spectacle Agnarr and I had made in the longhouse, none of the other orcs really knew me. They wouldn't be suspicious if I skipped the evening meal—they'd likely assume I was still tired from whatever the bad aliens had done to me. If I spent time with them now, they would realize I was missing if I didn't show up for breakfast. Best to leave before anyone missed me.

I was waiting for Tora to return with the last item I

needed before departure—a map. She'd said she would have to sneak one from one of the elders' cabins, but they likely wouldn't notice it missing. I was just starting to get antsy when Tora opened the door, scurried in, and shut it behind her quickly. She had a piece of very weathered rolled leather in her hand. She looked at me, eyes resolute.

"I took this from Jarlin Astrid's bookshelves," she said, handing me the leather.

"The jarlin?" I squeaked. "You couldn't have taken it from another elder?"

"Well, seeing as Jarlin Astrid is my aunt, going into her cabin would draw the least suspicion," she said.

My jaw dropped. "Jarlin Astrid is your aunt? Why didn't you tell me?" I exclaimed, a little too loud.

"It hadn't come up," she said, grinning at me.

I smacked her on the arm, chuckling. I already liked Tora, despite only knowing her for a day, but her sense of humor made me like her even more. I looked at the map. The words weren't in English, and thus no help to me. Whatever translator they had given me didn't extend to written language. But the markers and landmarks made sense, the language barrier aside. I knew where the Niflfýri started, and Tora had told me I needed to head due north. That information and the map were enough to get me to the Snaerfírar tribe. I took another minute to inspect the map, making sure I didn't have questions, before looking up at Tora.

It all made sense. She'd told me to expect a wide trail out of the village that narrowed down as it cut through the middle of the forest, and I saw the landmarks she'd told me to expect—the grove of young furutré, the Pjota River, and the caves roughly halfway through the forest. Tora had told me that the caves would be a suitable place to seek shelter if I didn't make it to the hunters' cabin, but to check for any animals using them. I had a flint tied to a cord around my neck in case I needed to make a fire. Then there was the last part, the most worrisome part for me—a light source.

Tora had explained to me that Niflfýri was filled with bioluminescent plants—that was a rough conversation to have, even with the translator implant I had received. But, based on what she'd explained, their ancestors had planted and encouraged bioluminescent mushrooms along the path and bioluminescent moss on the north side of the trees. She'd explained that because of the mist, without this, a hunter would be lost immediately upon entering the forest. She'd told me to follow the path and that it would be lit up on each side as if there were lamps. At the end of the path would be the hunters' cabin. The lack of light was the most worrisome part about the journey. It almost made me want to scrap my plans altogether and wait for first light, but I knew I had to leave before anyone found out about my intentions.

I adjusted my pack, ready to leave. Tora looked worried but determined as she handed me a dark metal bowl—made of the same metal as my water pitcher. It was full of a pale green moss.

"When you get to Niflfýri, use a stick to grind the moss. It will make the moss have a faint glow. Even though the forest path should be alight from the plants, having your own light will help you on your way," she explained.

"Are there bears in Niflfýri?" I asked, trying to keep the tremble out of my voice.

Tora cocked her head to the side, looking confused. It would have been comical if I wasn't so nervous.

"What is a bear?" she asked.

"It is a furred animal that is large enough to eat any human—or orc," I said.

"Hmmm…we don't have anything called *bears*, but quite a few predators call Niflfýri home. Most of them will not approach an orc because of our history of our size. Given that you carry the scent of orkin and walk upright as an orc would, I would hope they wouldn't dare approach you."

I blushed, thinking about why I smelled like an orc. It wasn't just the orkin clothing I wore; I was certain I still smelled of Agnarr. I wondered how he would react when he realized I'd snuck off in the night. Taking him with me would have been a better decision, but I dismissed it immediately. He wouldn't allow me to go. I was a weak human. One more time, I adjusted my pack and held the flint to my neck. I was ready. There was no more time to waste. I looked at Tora. Would she be in trouble for helping me go against the tribe's wishes? As if sensing my trepidation, she spoke.

"Don't worry about me. I will tell them there was no convincing you otherwise. Agnarr and Astrid will believe me. They won't need to know that I aided in your departure."

"Okay. If you're sure, I think I am ready," I said.

Tora took one last look at me and then rushed to me in a bone-crushing hug. I wasn't prepared, so my arms hung limply at my sides as she embraced me. I wasn't much of a hugger to begin with, but being hugged by an orc was definitely not something I expected. As she pulled away, I tried to pat her arm awkwardly. It surprised me to see her eyes wet with tears.

"I just worry. I think of how I would feel if Odin wanted to go through Niflfýri on his own." She sniffed, wiping her eyes.

"I know I am a 'puny human,' as Agnarr would say, but I would hope I am a little more capable than a child. You have prepared me with everything I need. I've got this," I assured her.

I gave her a last hug and headed toward the door. She stayed behind as I opened the door, looked both ways, then headed out into the night. Instead of taking the cobblestone road that would lead me to the longhouse and past the kitchens, I circled around the back of my cabin as Tora had instructed me. A narrow path behind the cabins would lead me to the larger road heading out of the village. I walked as quickly as I could without making much noise. The last thing I needed was to wake up one of the other girls. I needed to get out, and I needed to get out fast.

I got to the main road in almost no time. As Tora had assured me, it was deserted. Seeing no one on the cobblestone path, I headed quickly to the edge of the village, marked only by the cobblestones stopping and the path becoming hard-packed dirt. My heart was in my throat as I rushed out of the village. Any of the villagers could see me, stop me, insist on taking me to Astrid. I reached the end of the path and practically ran to the edge of the forest. Ducking behind a tree, I paused to catch my breath. I'd made it.

I looked around to assess my surroundings. I was still on the edge of Niflfýri, so the mist wasn't very heavy. It looked like a typical marine layer I experienced every May and June in Southern California. I could still easily see ahead of me. I looked for the bioluminescent plants Tora had told me would be along the path and, sure enough, they were there. They looked kind of like mushrooms—not the garden-variety mushrooms that grew in the lawns of suburban America, but the red-spotted kind that looked like something out of a fairy tale. They gave off a faint yellowish glow. I looked ahead and saw the path lit as far as my eye could see. Tora had told me not to eat the mushrooms under any circumstances. They were poisonous. Not only did their light deter predators, but all animals avoided them. This was going to be okay. I was going to make it just fine.

The sun was just sinking, so I didn't need the bowl of

moss Tora had given me quite yet. I decided I would reserve it until I truly needed it.

Well, I had made it to the forest. It was now or never. I stepped out onto the path and started. I was in charge of my own future. I was going to the Snaerfírar tribe. I had everything I needed to get there. The anxiety I felt served as a fire in my belly. I stepped out onto the trail, ready. I could do this.

AGNARR

I knew Piper didn't like decisions being made for her; every interaction with her had made that abundantly clear. But I didn't think she would be this reckless. I watched, crouched high in the branches of one of the massive furutrés at the edge of Niflfýri, as she stepped out onto the path. She had a large pack with her—I squinted and realized it was my backup pack, the one I had left in my room when they gave it to the humans. Someone had helped her prepare. She couldn't have walked into the kitchens and asked for travel rations without raising suspicions. Tora was behind this. I wanted to be mad, but knowing Piper's fierce nature, I knew she wouldn't take no for an answer. If Tora had refused to help her, she would have gone anyway, supplies be damned.

I sat in the tree as Piper marched resolutely down the path. This was everything I didn't want. I dragged my hand down my face in frustration. How had this tiny human literally crashed into my life and disrupted its entire trajectory?

I weighed my options. If I approached Piper now and tried to take her back, it would only work if I physically picked her up and took her back to the tribe. She would probably kick and scream the entire way. If I tried to join her, she might flee the moment she got a chance. She was still furious with me for the incident in the longhouse. She was bound and determined to do this on her own. I looked down, seeing her marching out of my line of vision, and knew I had to make a decision.

My hestr, Sindri, chuffed impatiently at the base of the tree. She was one of the fastest hestrs in our tribe. If Piper could be convinced to ride with me, we'd probably make it to the hunters' cabin before morning. I rolled my eyes. There was no way she'd ride with me. I had fucked that up completely in the longhouse. I was so certain that if I had insisted that hunters go without her and make a much quicker trip of it that she would agree. That exploded in my face spectacularly. Piper's will was far stronger than any female orkin I had encountered—no one could say no to her, not even Astrid. She was stubborn to the point of putting herself in danger. Sindri chuffed again as she munched on grass.

Sindri made up my mind. I would follow Piper at a safe distance to ensure her safety. I would only intervene if absolutely necessary. I didn't know how I would accomplish it, but I needed to get back into her good graces. Only when we reached Snaerfírar would I know for sure, but I felt the mating bond grow stronger every time I was in her presence. My marks hadn't appeared, but Piper was human. I needed to speak with the Snaerfírar to find out if mating marks even appeared with human elska mates, or if elska mating was even possible with humans. From our…encounter in the woods and the stories passed on from other tribes, I knew that *mating* was possible with humans, but I didn't know if they would feel the pull of being an elska mate the same way orkin did. Piper certainly wasn't acting like she wanted to be my mate for life.

I slowly climbed down the furutré, trying not to make any noise, though Piper was already long gone. I would be able to catch up with her on Sindri easily; following her undetected would be more difficult. I stood at the base of the tree, adjusting Sindri's saddle and packs. I'd packed enough for three days. I mounted Sindri and gently slapped her reins, setting her off at a slow trot. Sindri would travel much faster than Piper. It would take all of our considerable abilities to remain unseen. We stayed to the very edge of the path, traveling slowly. It didn't take long before I made out Piper's form in the distance.

The mist shrouded much of her figure. Only the bowl of light she carried made her visible. Tora was wise to rely on the bioluminescent moss to light Piper's way rather than a torch. I slowed Sindri to a walk, following at as much distance as I could allow without losing sight of Piper. From my limited interaction with her, I knew that orkin had more refined senses than humans. She couldn't hear or see me at such a great distance, though I could see her. I could follow her like this all the way to the hunters' cabin, given we didn't encounter any problems.

As I walked Sindri, I thought about Piper. I craved her. I thought of the smell of her neck and her hair. I lost myself remembering the look in her eyes as I had my fingers inside her. I longed to taste her and wondered about her fears about having a male's face between her knees. What had happened to her to make her doubt she would taste divine on my tongue? I shuddered and adjusted my leggings. My cock had grown painfully hard at the memory of her arousal. I would have to keep myself focused or risk losing her to the mist. Would there be a time she would let me have her in all ways? Would she be my elska mate despite being human?

I pushed my erection down, making my mind focus on the dangers ahead. Piper was just at the edge of my vision; I would lose sight of her if I didn't keep Sindri at a brisk walk. Sunset had come and gone, and darkness had fallen over Niflfýri. I could still make out the light from Piper's bowl, but she was farther away than I liked. Now that the sun had gone from the sky, I could risk getting a bit closer without her sensing me. I urged Sindri into a slow trot while steering her off the path. If I stayed at the edge of the path, Piper was less likely to see me, even if it made it harder for Sindri to navigate. As I skirted closer to Piper, I watched for any signs that she heard us, but there were none. She was on a mission and oblivious to the dangers around her. Any number of predators could be stalking both of us. Given my enhanced senses, I would notice any predators far before Piper.

It was too late in the season for the björn to still be about. With the snows upon us, they would have long hibernated into the tunnels under the furutrés. I didn't doubt that Piper would be able to dispatch smaller predators on her own, but that didn't make me any less worried. There was still the skogskatt, and I cursed Tora for not thinking of them. While smaller than the björn, the skogskatt hunted in packs and could be lethal to an untrained warrior. Given their dislike of bright light, it was unlikely they would venture toward the path, but if Piper strayed from it for any reason, she was putting herself at risk. I slapped the reins gently on Sindri's back, risking Piper hearing me in favor of being closer in the advent of danger.

CHAPTER 12

PIPER

I held the bowl of light in my left hand, peering down the path ahead of me. It continued as far as the eye could see. I hadn't factored in that I had no watch or way of telling how much time had passed. I felt like I had been walking for hours. I hadn't passed the caves yet, so I knew I hadn't even reached the halfway mark. I had never been any good with directions. The best I got was *headed toward the ocean or away from it?* I knew the caves were halfway and the Pjota River would butt up against the path before the caves. I didn't hear the sound of rushing water no matter how hard I strained, which told me I was nowhere near my destination. I sighed, but kept walking resolutely. I didn't want to make it to the caves before sunrise—I wanted to make it to the hunters' cabin. While Tora had assured me the caves would likely be safe, the idea of sleeping in a cabin before continuing on was much more appealing. I would feel much safer behind walls and doors.

I jumped at a noise. It sounded like an animal moving in the forest to the left of me. I looked into the darkness, afraid of what I would see, but I couldn't see much beyond the rows of mushrooms that lined the rough path. My eyes had adjusted to the dim lighting, but I still had a very limited view of anything off the path. I had kept any sort of panic from rising in my gut by walking resolutely with my goal in mind. Yet, with the sun completely down and the darkness starting to feel like a heavy blanket, I knew I was going to have to stay hyper-focused on getting to the hunters' cabin to prevent myself from descending into terror.

I walked and walked. I didn't tire; my anxiety was fueling, as I'd hoped it would be. Every once in a while, I heard what sounded like an animal in the distance behind me, but Tora had assured me it was unlikely any predator would pass the lit border of the path. I tried to hang on to those words. After what seemed like hours, I heard what sounded like rushing water to my left. It had to be the river! That meant I wasn't far from the caves. I didn't want to stay the rest of the evening in the caves, but they seemed like a safe space to rest and eat something, based on how Tora had described them. I picked up my pace, knowing I was near the caves. Tora had told me the mushrooms would line the entrance to the cave because the ground was especially damp.

I was so focused on reaching the caves that I forgot to pay attention to my surroundings. Before I heard anything, I saw the glint of eyes in the woods. Nearly a dozen pairs of glowing eyes were ahead of me on the path. They reflected the soft light the way a cat's eyes would. I shuddered to a halt, falling flat on my ass in my attempt not to run headfirst into what appeared to be giant bobcats. The light from the mushrooms was so dim, I couldn't see all the details of the cats I was facing. They looked to be larger than a bobcat, maybe the size of a coyote, with much longer hair. Being a suburban girl, I had little experience with wildlife. I didn't know what my chances were against a cat of that size, but I knew my chances against a dozen of them were very slim.

The cats had yet to approach me but were watching my every move. My heart hammered in my chest as I slowly scooted backward, still on my ass. Lifting myself slightly, I crab-walked backward, never taking my eyes off the cats. They gathered in formation, narrowing in on me as their prey. I scuttled back as fast as I could, not daring even to stand. The cat out in front was larger than the rest, clearly the leader. I kept my eyes on him as I tried to continue backwards. He lifted a paw to step toward me. That was all I needed. I couldn't stay scooting on my ass anymore. I spun around on my hands and knees and stood, ready to run as fast as I physically could.

I fled past the row of magic-looking mushrooms, putting one foot in front of the other as fast as I could. I made it just a few yards beyond the path when, instead of connecting with the ground, my boot made a splash. Immediately, I felt icy cold water seep into the leather sole. I stopped myself with just enough force to prevent myself from flying head-first into the river. The giant cats were still approaching when I spun around. I had to decide: face the cats or step into the river? I couldn't tell how deep the river was or how fast the current was, but cats of all kinds had to be afraid of the water, right? Right?

The largest cat in the front continued to approach me, teeth bared. His canines we three times the length of the rest of his teeth. They looked as if they could rip the flesh from my bones. I chose backing into the river. I stepped back, using my boot to feel for the ground underneath the rushing water. It didn't seem to get much deeper, so I took another step back, still facing the cats, arms out in front of me. I was ankles deep in freezing water, but the cats paused their approach. I stood, looking at them, feeling my toes go numb from the cold water. The lead cat growled, apparently frustrated his prey was just beyond reach. I took another step back into the river, still afraid that the water might not be enough to dissuade them from pouncing. As I stepped back, the shore dropped off. I stumbled, landing flat on my ass in the river. The cats, seeing my helpless position, resumed their approach toward me. I was done for.

AGNARR

I watched the scene unfold before me in horror. The skogskatt's fear of the water would only hold them off for so long. Piper had made the right decision to step into the river to get away from the pack, but now that she'd fallen, they'd risk stepping into the edge to get to her. I had to act. While skogskatts weren't a fan of water, they were terrified of fire. I had to hope that if I lit one of the torches in my pack I could scare them off without them attacking either of us. I was safer up on Sindri, but Piper was at the cats' mercy.

I was still several yards away from Piper, beyond her line of sight. My stronger orkin eyes were the only reason I could make her out in the low light. Hoping to keep the element of surprise, I quietly pulled the torch from my pack. I slid my hand into my pocket to pull out my flint. I knew there was no way Piper wouldn't be able to hear me, but I knew the skogskatts had excellent hearing. I was on borrowed time. As soon as I struck the flint, the cats would be alerted to my presence.

I struck my flint, lighting the torch, and the eyes of the dozen skogskatts swiveled to me. My torch just barely burned, the flame still low. The skogskatts hesitated, as if uncertain whether to flee or continue to advance on Piper. The head cat let out a growl of frustration low in his chest.

Piper, crouched in the rushing water, looked at me with giant eyes, as if she couldn't believe what she was seeing. The cats took advantage of Piper's distraction, and the head cat pounced. Before I could even get a shout out, she pulled herself deeper into the river. But the Pjota was deceptive; once you got past the first few feet, the bottom dropped off. The water was deeper than any orkin standing full height. I saw Piper's wide eyes one last time before it dragged her under.

I dug my heels into Sindri's sides, urging her forward. Sindri didn't want to go into the water much more than the cats did, but I had to get to Piper before it was too late. Sindri charged into the water, scattering the hissing cats. They would not take on a hestr carrying an orc with a torch. We charged along the river's edge, Sindri in the water up to her hindquarters, soaking my feet and ankles. I could make out Piper ahead of me, getting dragged into the middle of the river, arms flailing wildly as she attempted to grasp anything to hang on to. I had a rope tied to the outside of my pack. I grabbed it, unraveled it quickly, and tied a loop at the end.

"Piper! I am going to throw you a rope. Try to catch it, okay?" I shouted.

Piper's head was still above water even though she had to be in the deepest part of the river. I couldn't tell if she could hear me over the current, but she met my eyes, so at least she would see me throw the rope. I swung it over my head, throwing it as far as possible. It landed past her in the water. She tried to grasp it, but it slipped out of her fingers. I yanked it back and readied myself to try again. I looked at Piper just in time to see her head slip under the water. I started to panic. I had lost her. I strained my eyes, hoping to see her under the water, but it was too dark. I pushed Sindri forward, trying to get closer to where Piper had disappeared. There was a splash farther down the river. I saw Piper's head reappear, and without a second thought, I threw the rope again. I got the rope closer to her and almost cried out in relief as I saw Piper's small hands grab the rope.

"Take the loop and put it around your waist," I called over the noise of the rushing water.

Piper took the rope over her head and dragged it down to her waist. As soon as I saw it was around her, I pulled her toward me as quickly as possible. In almost no time, she was at the side of Sindri, and I leaned over, pulling her up to my lap. She was shaking and soaking wet; I needed to get her to warmth immediately. I used my free hand to pull Sindri's reins. We weren't far from the caves. If I pushed Sindri to a gallop, we could make it there in minutes. Piper said nothing, but clung to me, her face buried in my neck. We were both soaked. We would need a blazing fire immediately upon our arrival at the caves.

It felt like an agonizing amount of time, but we got to the caves quickly. I had to let go of Piper so I could climb off of Sindri and check the caves for occupants. I tried to place her on Sindri's saddle alone, but she clung to me tighter, a sob escaping her throat. I'd have to try to dismount while still holding her. Against my giant frame, she weighed barely anything, even though she was soaking wet. I shifted my weight and was able to swing a leg over and slide down Sindri while still holding her in my arms. I knew it would be safer to head into the caves with a torch, but I would be able to see any predators lurking, even in the relative darkness. I hoped the caves were stocked with the basic necessities. Anyone who used the cave was expected to restock supplies that were used.

I walked to the opening of the cave, leaving Sindri behind —I would return to tie her and feed her. She was a good hestr; she would stay for the time being. The cave opening was small, one of the benefits it boasted. Unless the traveler knew about the cave, they wouldn't know that it opened up into a cavern large enough to accommodate several orkin. I stooped through the opening, still holding Piper to my chest. After a few paces, the entrance got taller and opened up, allowing me to stand up straight. As my eyes adjusted to the darkness, I breathed a sigh of relief. There were sleeping furs rolled in the corner, a stack of firewood against one of the walls, and what I hoped were baskets of dried meat and other travel rations lining the other wall. We'd make it through the night.

CHAPTER 13

AGNARR

I walked to the furs. I needed to get Piper warm while I started the fire.

"Piper, I am going to have to put you down so I can get you warm. I'm afraid you are already going to experience shock from the cold," I said quietly.

Piper looked up at me with her big green eyes. "Please don't leave," she said.

"I won't. I want you to get out of your wet clothes while I start a fire. You can wrap yourself in some of the furs here while I get the fire going," I said.

Piper looked at the furs and nodded mutely. I noticed she still had her pack on her back.

"Here, let me take your pack. Maybe we can salvage some of the contents if we lay them out by the fire to dry," I said.

Wordlessly, she shrugged the pack off her back and started peeling off her clothes. I turned away quickly. I knew we had already shared stolen moments in the woods together, but I didn't want her to think my attempt to get her out of her clothes was about anything more than her survival. Though I had to admit that the thought of Piper naked in my arms was incredibly appealing, even under the current circumstances. I gathered as much wood as I could carry and took it to the fire pit. I stacked the wood strategically, then gathered the tinder stacked near the wood. I lit the tinder using my flint. It wasn't long before the flames were growing, providing warmth and light to the cave.

I headed back to the furs to find Piper wrapped in one of them, standing barefoot. She'd barely said anything since I pulled her from the river. I feared she was in shock.

"Do you want to come sit by the fire and try to get warm?" I asked.

She nodded and followed me back to the fire, taking a seat on a log designed for such a purpose. I looked down at her tiny feet poking out from the bottom of the fur. They were faintly blue. There were definitely more chips in the red paint than I had noticed the first time I saw her. I looked at her as she stared blankly into the fire.

"Piper, are your toes supposed to be blue?" I asked, somewhat confused.

"Wh-what?" she stammered as if I had pulled her out of a trance.

"Are your toes supposed to be blue?" I repeated.

She looked down at her toes as if noticing them for the first time. She wiggled them.

"Ha," she said softly, "they definitely shouldn't be blue. It's a sign that they are very cold. I can't feel them, which isn't a good sign."

Without thinking, I grabbed one of her feet with my hands. It felt like ice. I knew from the previous times I'd touched her that orkin ran warmer than humans', but her little foot felt frozen solid. Piper looked at me, startled.

"Hey! You can't just grab my foot, don't be a creeper!" she sassed at me.

I had no idea what a creeper was, but I was glad she was getting some of her fire back. The empty look she'd had in her eyes as we'd traveled to the cave had concerned me.

"I don't know what a creeper is, but I doubt it means someone trying to keep you from losing your toes," I said.

She sighed. "A creeper is the type of person who would touch someone's feet without asking."

"Listen, you are freezing. Not only are your feet ice cold, but I can also see you shaking. We need to get you warm. The Pjota is nearly frozen over this time of year. If we don't get you warm, there's a real chance you could get sick, then you'll never make it to the Snaerfírar," I said with a huff.

I stood and walked to gather more firewood. The fire was strong, but the cave was still too cold to warm her up from her frozen state. Not to mention that I was still soaking wet I added more wood to the fire, then looked at Piper. She was still shaking.

"I'm going to go out and tie Sindri to a tree and get my pack. Try to stay as close to the fire as you can." With that, I turned and stooped to exit the cave.

PIPER

Well, if that hadn't all gone to shit spectacularly. What made me think I could make it to the Snaerfírar tribe on my own, at night? It was absurd. But I knew I was driven by panic and the need to do things for myself. I couldn't believe Agnarr had followed me all the way through the forest. I'd clearly underestimated his commitment to keeping me safe. I shivered. Though I was as close to the fire as I could be without burning my toes, I was still cold. The fur I had wrapped around me was scratchy and roughly cut, clearly made to be left as a basic supply for anyone who found themselves stranded.

I knew I should be pissed at Agnarr for following me. And for embarrassing me in front of the tribe. But without him, I would be dead. He'd headed into the river on his hestr without regard for his safety. The weird giant cats could have attacked him. The current could have pulled him away into the darkness. I couldn't deny that I was insanely grateful. I blushed as I thought of the way I'd clung to him on the way to the cave. I'd been in shock. He felt so solid, warm, and comforting; I wanted to cling to him and never let go.

My mind screeched to a halt. That was definitely not a thought I usually had. I'd had many relationships since leaving college, but I kept them casual. I always kept my walls up. No vulnerability for me, thank you very much. They never lasted long; I considered six months a serious milestone. Even in my more serious relationships, there was a small secret part of me I kept to myself, locked away. I didn't want anyone to know me truly. I feared that type of exposure. I was afraid if someone truly knew me, they'd run, not walk, away. Now I was here, in a cave, with an alien orc, thinking I wanted to cling to him and never let go. What in the hell? Was I still in shock?

I stared into the fire, not really seeing it. My thoughts were a scrambled ball of string with no thread I could grab on to. I kept going back to the smell of Agnarr's neck as I'd warmed my nose on his skin. I returned to his hesitancy, then urgency, as he'd kissed me underneath the tree branches, to the way he'd respected my space as I spoke with Emla. Even the misguided way he'd tried to protect me in front of his tribe.

Fuck it. If I was anything, I was impetuous. Here I was, in the middle of the woods, on an alien planet, with an orc I clearly was developing feelings for. I was going for it. He had already seen me make ridiculous decisions and watched me careen off into the darkness against everyone's better judgment. If he was still interested, I would let him see all of me. I was in free fall with literally nothing to lose. If I let Agnarr see all of me and he remained, maybe he was the one for me. Maybe.

I was so lost in my thoughts that I didn't hear Agnarr come back into the cave. I jumped when he cleared his throat to get my attention, standing near the fire but far enough from me to be respectful. His clothes clung to him. I could see every muscle under his tunic. He must be just as cold as I was. My eyes traveled up to his face. He looked at me, concerned, probably worried I was still in shock. I stood and walked toward him, my feet still numb with cold. As I got close to him, I reached out and stroked his cheek with my icy fingers, shaking. He reached up and covered my hand with his. Though he was still in his wet clothes, his hand was much warmer than mine. His look of concern shifted to a look of confusion.

"Let's try to get you warm as well," I said, my voice sounding much smaller than I'd hoped.

I moved my hand to his tunic. I tried to pull it up over his head, but between trying to keep myself wrapped in the fur and him being so much taller than me, I made little headway with my one hand.

"Piper, you're still freezing. Your hand is ice cold and shaking. Getting me warm is the least of our concerns," he said.

I swallowed. It was now or never.

"How about we get each other warm?" I said, my voice stronger as I continued to pull up his tunic.

I couldn't get his tunic off, so I settled for stroking the planes of his stomach with my cold hand, hoping I'd made my meaning clear. He was right about orcs being warmer than humans. Even though he was cold, he was still warmer than I was. Agnarr looked down at me, the look on his face shifting from confused to heated. He stepped back, and for a moment, I was concerned. But then he pulled his tunic over his head and laid it next to the fire. He returned to me and took my face in his hands, stroking my cheeks with his thumbs.

"Are you sure? I don't want to do anything you'll regret. And I definitely don't want you to do anything because you feel you owe me for saving you. If I hadn't been so stupid in front of the tribe, you wouldn't have gone off alone."

"Agnarr, I went off alone because I was stupid and panicked. I was so worried about waiting that I didn't see that I was already making decisions out of anxiety. That's part of what having anxiety is like–sometimes you make decisions out of fear that make no sense. It wasn't your fault," I said, stepping closer to him.

I turned my face up to him, looking into his eyes. Seeing light gold sclera where humans had white was still startling, yet captivating. As he continued to stroke my cheeks with his warm hands, he bent down and brushed his lips against mine, gently. Oh, so gently.

"Piper—" he started to say, but I interrupted.

"Pip. Call me Pip. It's what everyone who really knows me calls me," I whispered.

His face still close to mine, I kissed him again, with more urgency.

"Pip," he said, voice low, "if we are going to do this, it isn't going to be some elegant thing where we slowly undress each other. I must get out of my wet clothes, and we need to get warm in the rest of the furs."

"I promise," I said, pausing to kiss his full lips again, "this is what I want."

Agnarr looked at me again, eyes searching. Then he

wrapped his arms around me, scooped me up, and carried me to the furs on the other side of the fire. I let out an undignified squeal at being unexpectedly lifted off the ground. Agnarr pressed a kiss to the top of my head, then set me down gently amongst the rest of the furs. I sat, looking up at him, curling my frozen feet under myself. He was shirtless but still had his soaking pants and boots on. I admired the bunch and pull of his muscles in his arms and shoulders as he unlaced and removed his boots. I bit my lip as he began to unlace his pants, remembering his impressive size from our tryst in the woods.

He removed his pants with difficulty. They were stuck to his skin, still wet from the river water. And then there he was, in front of me, utterly naked. My eyes zeroed in on his package. It was just as magnificent as I remembered. He was already hard, his thick cock pointing up to his stomach, already leaking from the tip. I admired the textures and patterns of it, wondering what those would feel like sliding inside me. I gnawed my lip further, looking from his cock to his eyes. As much as I wanted to admire him for a moment longer, he was cold too. And I wanted his skin on my skin.

"Well?" I breathed, unwrapping myself from the fur I was in, exposing my naked body.

Agnarr needed no further encouragement. His large body was over mine in an instant, wrapping his arms around me. He pulled the furs up over us. Even in his chilled state, I could already feel him warming me. His skin was deliciously hot compared to mine. I buried my cold nose in his neck once again. What was it about his smell that was so addicting? I pressed open-mouthed kisses from his neck to his ear, all the while trying to pull him closer to me, running my hands across every inch of his skin.

"Pip, your skin is so cold," he said, stroking his large calloused hands up and down my sides.

I smiled at his use of my nickname and paused kissing his neck to look up at him.

"Well, you will have to work extra hard to warm me up. Are you sure you're up for it?" I said, grinning at him.

Agnarr raised his eyebrows. "I'm always up for a challenge," he retorted before capturing my lips with his.

Agnarr slid his tongue along the seam of my lips, parting them. He brushed his tongue against mine. I moaned at how good it felt to kiss him again. I stroked my tongue against his, devouring the taste of him. The different texture of his tongue was addictive. We explored each other's mouths hungrily. It was his turn to moan as I dragged my nails up and down his muscled back and sucked his lower lip into my mouth. Agnarr shifted his large frame over me and I became very aware of his cock pressing into my thigh. My nipples hardened into taut peaks against the wall of his chest.

Agnarr took his kisses down the side of my neck and to my breast, taking my nipple into his warm mouth. He used his tongue to go back and forth across the stiff peak before sucking it deeper into his mouth. I groaned as I dug my fingers into his hair, pulling him closer to me still. He looked up at me, eyes smoldering while he continued to tongue my breast.

"Do you want me to stop?" he asked.

"Don't you dare," I murmured, pulling him by the hair from one breast to the other.

He gave it the same attention he had the first, alternating between licking and suckling, driving me insane with need. Each time he dragged his tongue across my stiff nipple, I could feel heat pooling in my core. I definitely wasn't cold anymore. Loosening my grip on his hair, I ran my hands down his chest, tracing the outline of his muscles with my fingers. He shivered as I stroked a finger down the line of muscle that pointed directly to his cock.

"You are distracting me from my work," he growled, nipping gently with his teeth at one of my puckered nipples.

"I was just thinking of all the ways I could warm my cold hands, and I thought of one I couldn't resist," I said as I wrapped my hand around his shaft and gave it a gentle tug.

Gods, it was thicker than I remembered. It made sense for him to be much larger than any man I'd slept with. He was taller than any human man I'd ever seen and built like a brick wall. I stroked him up and down, exploring the patterns and ridges on his cock. I stroked my thumb across his crown, feeling the wetness of pre-cum already leaking from the broad head. Touching him while he continued to lavish attention to my breasts had me dripping with need. Every time he sucked down on one of my nipples, my internal walls clenched, feeling the emptiness where I wanted his cock.

I grabbed his face and pulled him from my breasts to my mouth, kissing him urgently as I wrapped my legs around his waist. Agnarr devoured me, thrusting his tongue in and out of my mouth in a way that mimicked sex. I reached my hand down between us, grabbing his cock and notching it at my entrance. Agnarr paused and looked at me, eyes hooded with lust. He leaned forward and licked the shell of my ear before whispering, "Are you sure? We don't have to do this if you aren't sure."

"Mm. Sure. Very sure. Need you inside me. Right now," I panted, digging my heels into his ass to pull him in.

I was practically dizzy as I felt the fat head of his cock brush against my swollen clit. He pushed in slowly, inch by inch, stretching me almost painfully wide. I could feel every ridge and swirl of his cock as he pressed into me. When I thought he must be fully seated I looked down to see he was only halfway in. We hadn't even reached his knot. Agnarr continued slowly stretching me wider still. I gasped at the invasion, causing Agnarr pause.

He looked at me, concerned. Sweat beaded on his brow, showing what it was costing him to go slow for my comfort. He stroked my cheek, then pressed kisses to my neck while using his hands to palm my breasts and tease my nipples. Sliding one of his hands down between us, he used his thumb to circle my clit. Realizing he was taking his time to ensure I was wet enough to take more of him, I grinned into his shoulder. I was no quitter.

As he continued to stroke my clit and toy with my nipples, I was more and more aroused, getting wetter than I'd ever thought possible. I took my feet and dug them into his ass, silently letting him know I was ready for him to keep trying.

He chuckled quietly. "Impatient in all areas of life, are we?" he whispered huskily. He used his long tongue to lave the puckered tip of my nipple, sending zips of pleasure straight to my clit.

I groaned and used my heels to pull him further into me. I was so wet that even with his enormous size, I was ready for him to push further. Leaving the attention he was giving my chest, he looked me in the eyes.

"Do you think you can take my knot?" he asked.

I nodded frantically, ready. So ready. He shifted above me and pressed into me as I continued to pull him to me. I was stretched so wide I could feel every braided ridge and texture of him. His knot pushed past my entrance. I panted at the size of it. I had never felt stuffed so full. With one final push, he was fully seated. My breathing heavy, I looked at him. His pupils were blown out with lust, but he had a look of uncertainty on his face.

"Are we okay?" I asked breathlessly.

He dragged a hand across his face while using his other arm to support him.

"You're just so tight, Pip. Are you sure this doesn't hurt? I don't want to harm your perfect pink cunt. I'm not too much?" he asked.

I was a little shocked at the amount of times this man—I mean orc—checked in on me. How many times had I been rammed into by a clumsy guy in his twenties who didn't even bother to see if I was wet and ready? Agnarr was already surpassing all of my expectations. Not only was he stopping to ensure I was ready every step of the way, he was worshiping my body in a way I had never experienced. I was stuffed full and felt pinned to the floor by his monster cock, but I was more than ready.

I reached up and stroked his cheek before pulling him into a bruising kiss. I loved the flavor of him. I sucked on his tongue in a way that clearly provided an answer to his question. He kissed me back fervently, nibbling on my lower lip before sucking it into his mouth. I pulled away and looked up at him.

"Think we're ready to get this show on the road?" I asked.

"Show? What? Who is watching?" He looked around the empty cave.

I laughed. American slang clearly was going to be interesting with him.

"It's a human saying. It means fuck me like you mean it, Agnarr," I said.

Okay, maybe that wasn't quite what it meant, but it would do.

His face shifted from concern to a feral grin, pulling me into one more kiss before sliding all the way out of me and then plunging back in with one overwhelming stroke. After that, it was like I had finally broken the wall of his concern. He plunged in and out of me with slow, sure strokes. With every thrust, I could feel the braided, textured parts of his cock drag along my sensitive walls, making me see stars. As I adjusted to his size and got over the overwhelming sensations, I dug my fingers into his shoulders and thrust my hips up, meeting his. I kissed and licked his chest as he slid in and out of me before it became too much for me to do anything but focus on the mind-numbing fucking he was giving me.

He shifted his hands to grip my hips as his thrusts became faster. The sounds of our bodies slapping together echoed obscenely in the cave. I was so close. I could tell by the urgency of his thrusts, he was too. Just when I thought I was ready to go over the edge, he reached his hand down between us and circled my clit with the calloused pad of his thumb. Between that and each exquisite drag along my channel as he thrust in and out, I shattered. I pulsed around his cock, pulling it into me. My arms and legs jerked uncontrollably, and I came gasping his name.

I pulled him in for another kiss, running my fingers through his silky black hair and biting his lower lip. I shifted my legs, lifting them up higher to where I felt I was folded in half like some sort of erotic origami. Agnarr growled, *freaking growled,* at the shift of position. If I thought he was fucking me before, his thrusts went from measured and deep to frantic and overwhelming. I'd never been multiorgasmic before, but I felt another orgasm building as Agnarr continued to pick up the pace and thrust deeper. The muscles in his neck were corded with strain, and his eyes never left my face as he thrust in deeper than I thought possible, hitting the spot on the inside that had me coming again with a scream. With two more powerful thrusts, I felt Agnarr jerk and release inside of me, splashing my walls with hot cum. I felt his release pulse as my channel fluttered with the overwhelming sensations I had just experienced.

With one last jerk, he said, "Piper," in a low growl, taking my mouth with his again.

Agnarr dropped from his position over me, pulling me to him as we lay on our sides, facing each other. It didn't feel like he was going anywhere anytime soon. He was still throbbing inside of me. I wrapped one leg over his hip and pulled myself to his chest. I could feel his heart pounding under the wall of muscle.

"So it is probably a bit late for this, but how does this whole knot situation work again?" I asked breathlessly.

Agnarr stroked my hair, which was now nearly dry, and peppered kisses along my jaw and cheeks.

"We will be tied together until I release fully and my knot softens enough for me to pull out," he explained.

"And what is the point of this anatomically? Why have a knot?" I asked, trying to understand the differences in our anatomy.

Agnarr grinned. "It is to ensure I seed you well, making it more likely that our mating will lead to young."

Well, that thought would have walloped me, but hurray for birth control. I had an arm implant that lasted three years. I did not need to worry about carrying a giant orc baby anytime soon. Yet, being the anxious person I was, I hoped that wouldn't somehow offend Agnarr.

"Agnarr, do orcs have birth control?" I asked hesitantly.

"Já, not many use it because young are so rare, but there is a tea that females can drink if they do not want to get pregnant. Some of our females use it if they don't want to have another orkling quickly after their first. Do you not wish to be a mother? Because I am afraid I don't have any tea on hand," he asked, looking at me seriously.

As if I expected him to bring contraceptive tea on a rescue mission.

I laughed and kissed him, tightening my legs around him and scratching my nails up and down his broad back.

"Um, I don't know if I want to be a mother, but I definitely didn't expect you to bring contraceptive tea on your mission to save me from my foolishness. I am on human birth control. I can't get pregnant right now," I said, chuckling.

"Ah. I see. Well then, that is not a worry or a conversation for today," he said, pulling me into another kiss.

Well, that was much easier than I'd expected. In the past, I had never trusted my partners to take responsibility for contraceptives, so getting long-term birth control made the most sense to me. My foresight had saved me from getting pregnant with an orc baby, which I definitely wasn't ready for. Anxiety saves the day.

"Um, Agnarr, how long are we going to be stuck like this?" I asked. "Not that I am not enjoying you holding me, but is this like a few minutes or several hours situation?"

I felt him pulse inside me again. If the pulses I kept feeling were any sign of how well he'd "seeded" me, I was going to be overflowing with cum when we finally parted.

"Probably only a handful of moments more," Agnarr said quietly. "I'm in no rush, and more importantly, I am keeping you warm as we lay here wrapped together."

I hadn't even thought of how cold I had been since we'd torn at each other's clothes. Between Agnarr's much warmer body and the physical exertion, I was no longer chilled to the bone.

CHAPTER 14

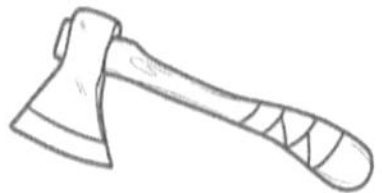

AGNARR

a s Piper and I lay in each other's arms, I stroked her tangled hair and pressed kisses to her temple and the top of her head. She stroked the fine hair of my chest and nuzzled into my neck. My heart was going to burst out of my chest; it didn't seem to be slowing down, even though we were no longer fucking. My mind was swirling.

Piper was mine. She was my mate, marks or not. The pull I felt to her was indescribable. In the short time I'd known her, she had become my everything. I loved every part of her, from her impetuousness, to her insane drive, to her need to care for herself and go her own way. How was I to convince her to let me provide for her and let me in? Sex was one thing, but was she going to agree to be my partner in all things, marks or no marks? I was still hoping that when I got to the Snaerfírar tribe, they would tell me that humans could take elska mates, whether marks appeared on them or not. If marks appeared on me, it would seal our mated status.

I continued to stroke Piper's hair and hold her to me. I noticed her breathing had evened out, slowing down. She'd fallen asleep. I studied her face. Her plump pink lips, swollen from the attention I'd given them earlier, were parted slightly as she slept. I had never experienced what humans called *kissing* before, but now I couldn't imagine going more than a few moments without taking her lips with mine. Piper's little nose was tiny and pert. Her cheeks were still flushed pink from our time together. I resisted the urge to stroke her face, not wanting to wake her, so I settled for admiring her, trying to burn every one of her features into my mind. As I studied her face and the tiny freckles she had down one cheek, I felt my eyelids droop. It wasn't long before sleep claimed me as well.

I awoke with a start, forgetting where I was. The fire had died down, but it was still dark outside. At some point, my knot had softened to where I could slip out of Piper. I was on my back, and she was lying with her arm across my chest and one of her legs over my waist, pinning my erection painfully into my stomach. She was still asleep, breathing softly. She would wake up chilled if I didn't get out from under her. I slowly shifted her and slid her off me, covering her with the fur. I stood and started to walk to the fire when I heard her call out to me.

"Agnarr?" she said in a muffled voice.

I looked, but though one of her hands was reaching toward where I had been, she was still dead asleep. That she was looking for me even as she slept sprung hope inside me. Maybe it wouldn't be so hard to convince her we were mates. I placed more wood on the fire and added more kindling until it was burning high and bright again. It would last until the morning with how much wood I had added. I could feel the cave getting warmer already. I was perfectly comfortable naked in front of the fire, but I knew Piper chilled more easily than I did.

I returned to the furs and was going to slip back into bed with Piper when I saw the mess we had created. Her cunt, thighs, the furs, and even her stomach were covered in my seed. I couldn't let her stay like that. I returned to my pack and grabbed one of the extra tunics I'd brought. After pouring water on it, I held it over the fire until it was warm. Walking back to her, I gently cleaned her stomach and her legs, wondering if she would find me cleaning her an invasion. I was considering my options when I felt her hand reach out and stroke my hair.

She looked at me dreamily, still half asleep. "Hi," she said softly.

"Hey, I need to get you cleaned up. I'm afraid I've made a mess of you. Is that okay?"

She looked surprised, waking up more fully.

"Agnarr, you are the most thoughtful. But, actually, I really need to pee. Is there someplace I can do that? I can clean the rest of myself up while I take care of that," she said.

I could tell she was trying to assure me it wasn't a dismissal. She was happy to have me touch her but needed to take care of her needs first.

"There's a hole behind the outcropping of rocks at the back of the cave that we've used in the past when we've been stuck in here during snow storms. I would rather you use that than go outside into the cold," I said.

I handed her the damp cloth, and she stood up, pressing a kiss to my cheek before heading to the back of the cave. I didn't even try to stop myself from admiring her lush back-side as she walked away from me. It was made to be grabbed by my large hands. She was absolute perfection. I briefly imagined watching her ass jiggle as I pounded into her from behind, but I wasn't even sure if that was a position humans partook in. It didn't stop my erection from becoming almost painfully hard thinking about it, though. I needed a distraction.

I didn't want her to assume I was staring at her as she did her business, so I returned and got another piece of wet cloth to clean the furs we were sleeping on. I was ripping the sleeves off my spare tunic, but I couldn't bring myself to care. When she came back, I had done my best.

"I left the cloth on the outcropping of rocks in case you need it," she said, looking at my swollen shaft with one eyebrow raised.

I looked down to see not only was I sporting a massive erection, but I was also covered in the dried combination of our juices.

"Ah, yes. I will be right back," I said, embarrassed that I hadn't noticed I was also a mess.

I walked to the back of the cave and used the now-cold cloth to clean myself. It didn't take long, and with the warmth from the fire, it wasn't uncomfortable. I headed back to Piper, expecting to find her asleep again. I was surprised to see her lying on her side, propped up on an elbow, waiting for me. Her eyes zeroed in on my erect cock.

"Ready to go again already?" She chuckled throatily.

"Mmm, around you, I always seem to be ready," I answered as I lowered myself to the furs.

Her eyes sparkled mischievously as she took me in, stroking the planes of my abs before stroking a finger along the full length of my cock.

"What did you have in mind?" she asked.

This woman would never cease to surprise me. With the last two dagrs she'd had, I would have assumed she'd need to rest for dagrs, especially given the taxing weight of carrying around anxiety in her head all the time. But as she continued to stroke my cock, now with her fist fully wrapped around it, she was making her desire very clear. I could smell the shift in her scent. I reached out and pulled her into a kiss. I had tried to be gentle with her our first time. Her perfect cunt looked so small, it amazed me when she could not only take all of me, but thrust me in deeper with each stroke. Knowing I hadn't hurt her, I didn't know if I could be as gentle this time.

I pulled back, and she looked at me quizzically as if to say, *well?*

"What?" I asked

"I said," she laughed, "what did you have in mind?"

Hmm, what did I have in mind? I wanted to rut her into the ground like a beast, but I was still learning the ways of human mating. Would she be interested in mating in the traditional position of orkin? Would she be offended if I asked? What if it was vulgar or unacceptable on her planet? I realized she was staring at me with concern. I was going to have to say what I was interested in.

"Would you be interested in mating in the traditional position of the orkin?" I asked hesitantly.

She looked at me, raising an eyebrow. "How could I possibly answer that? I don't know what the traditional mating position of the orkin is. How many orcs do you think I've slept with?" She was sassing me, and I loved it.

"Okay, fair, fair. The traditional position is you on all fours with me—"

"Fucking me from behind?"

Well, clearly, she was familiar with the position, so that was one concern off the table.

"Já, that is the position," I said, relieved she wasn't horrified. "You have this position on Earth?" I asked.

She laughed and went back to stroking my cock up and down with her small hand.

"Yes, we call it doggie style. It is one of my favorites," she said, grinning as she continued to tug on my cock.

I couldn't understand what *doggie* meant, but I was pleased. Yet if she didn't stop stroking my cock soon, we could not fuck in any position because I was going to come all over her hand. I took her hand and wrapped it around my waist.

"Well, if it is something that you are interested in, it is definitely something I had in mind. But you are going to have to stop stroking my cock if you want to get to any of this *doggie style*," I said, smirking down at her.

She grinned at me, moving her hand to my shoulder and pulling me into a kiss. Her kiss was hungry; she nipped at my lips and sucked on my tongue. She devoured me, leaving no doubt that she was in want. I kissed her fervently, ready to take her again. Piper dragged her fingers through my hair, loosening my top knot.

"I don't want you to hold back this time. I can take all of you," she said breathlessly.

I kissed her one last time before rolling her onto her stomach and hoisting her up on her knees. Her cunt was on display for me, pink and wet, glistening in the firelight. The sight of her full ass was almost more than I could handle. I kneaded her asscheeks with my hands, groaning at how soft they were. I lined my cock up with her entrance, kissing the soft skin of her cunt with the tip of my cock.

"Are you sure?" I said before going any further.

I was hesitant to claim her in this way. She wasn't an orc. Perhaps this position would be too much for her.

She wiggled her hips against me, trying to make my tip breach her entrance.

"Very, *very* sure, Agnarr," she said with a breathy moan.

I pushed my cock into her slowly, letting her adjust to my size. Hearing her pant and moan as I entered her was almost enough to be my undoing. As I pushed past my knot, she let out a garbled groan, leading me to pause.

"Do you want me to stop?" I asked, wishing to the gods that the answer was no.

"No, no, keep going. I want to take all of you," she whined.

I continued to push my way in until I was fully seated, admiring my flesh pushed against hers.

I leaned over her and kissed the shell of her ear.

"Do you hurt?" I asked, trying to mask the want in my voice.

"No. No, feels good. So full. Fuck me, Agnarr. Please," she said breathlessly.

That was all the permission I needed. I pulled back and thrust into her, savoring the tightness of her cunt. Her core gripped me like a vice. It was like nothing I'd ever experienced. I rutted into her again and again, driven wild by her moans of encouragement. When we'd first mated, I had no idea that I would be able to take her this way, her being human. Being able to see her ass jiggle and move as I plunged into her was almost more than I could handle.

"Harder, Agnarrr, more!" she exclaimed as I slammed into her.

I was losing all thought of her being a delicate human, given her response to me. I railed into her ferociously, holding nothing back. Her head lolled to the side as she gasped for air, caught in the pleasure of the moment. I pounded into her again and again, savoring her moans and gasps. With each thrust, I expected her to exclaim that it was too much, but she rocked back to meet me every time. Our bodies slapped together, my balls hitting her thighs with every thrust, filling the cave with the primal noises of our mating. I gripped her hips, pulling her toward me, wanting to feel all of her. Her core began to flutter and clench against me. I knew she was close to her climax.

Pleasure shot down my spine as I continued to buck into her. I was so close, but I wanted her to come first. I bent over her, snaking my hand down her stomach to circle her clit with the pad of my thumb. She jolted as I circled her clit, continuing to thrust into her.

"Is this too much?" I whispered into her ear.

"No. Don't stop...so good." Piper arched her back to meet each one of my thrusts.

I continued to piston my hips, stroking into her softness. I had *never* mated like this. My control was slipping but wasn't going to finish until I saw Piper come. As I used my thumb to circle her clit I leaned forward and kissed along the sensitive skin from her shoulder to her neck, stopping to suck on the skin just below her ear. I thrust into her as she rammed herself back onto me, causing me to lose my mind with lust. Piper gave as good as she got, and I was ill-prepared for her enthusiasm. None of the females I had mated with before had expressed such eagerness. I could barely contain myself. She swore breathlessly before saying *"oh gawd"* over and over again.

"Agnarr. Not *gawd*. Agnarr is the one fucking you," I growled into her ear before licking it from top to bottom.

"Oh fuck, Agnarrr, I am going to come."

She spasmed beneath me as I picked up the pace of my thrusts. I was an absolute beast, railing into her wildly. Piper was *mine*. With each thrust, I saw stars burst in front of my eyes. I never knew mating could be like this. My need to claim her was almost too much to bear. I pulled her up against me, her back against my front, delving into her with each upward thrust. I wrapped one arm underneath her breasts and used the other to pluck and tease her nipples as I continued to ram into her tight core. She cried out, and then

I felt her clench down on me as she came. I swore, feeling my sack tighten at my impending release.

"*Mine,*" I growled into her ear as I lost any semblance of control.

Piper's cunt clamped down on me as I jerked and tensed, shooting what felt like an endless amount of cum into her in burst after burst. I felt the rush of release as I emptied myself into her, feeling my knot lock us into place as I finished. I had never come with such force. I was completely spent.

I let out a ragged breath and held Piper against me as I slumped down on my knees. I could feel her heart beating rapidly under my arm as she continued to pant with the exertion of our furious mating. I nuzzled my face into the nape of her neck. She smelled musky and delicious, damp with sweat.

"Do you hurt?" I asked, knowing I had been much more forceful in this position.

She let out a small sigh and reached up to stroke my face even as she still had her back to my front.

"No, I feel boneless. Thoroughly fucked," she said, stroking my jaw with her fingers.

I grinned into her hair, running my hands along her stomach and thighs, loving the feeling of her soft skin.

"Should we attempt to lay down?" she asked, craning to look up at me from our current position.

Carefully, I leaned to the side so we could lie down while still joined. As we lay on the furs, I wrapped my arms around her, wanting to hold her as close as possible. Piper ran her hand along my arm, snuggling into me closer, letting out a contented sigh. I was enjoying lying with her, just relishing in our closeness, when I heard her let out a small snore. I smirked to myself. I had literally fucked her unconscious. I nestled into her, taking in the scent of her hair and her skin, and followed her into sleep in mere moments.

PIPER

I woke up to the light coming in through the mouth of the cave. From how dim it was, it still had to be early morning. Agnarr and I had shifted in the night. He was on his stomach with an arm draped over me. I was on my side, curled into him. I looked up to see our faces were mere inches apart. I studied him as he continued to sleep. His full lips and firm jaw wouldn't have been out of place on a male model—minus the tusks. Though, if I was being honest, I was a fan of the tusks.

Remembering the feel of them as he'd nipped at my nipples made my core clench, causing me to realize how much of a sticky mess I was. When Agnarr had slipped out of me, I'd leaked a literally inhuman amount of cum all down my legs—and him, by the looks of it. I needed to get up, clean up, and pee, but I wanted to lie and enjoy being with him like this for a moment more. I studied him more, noting the delicate points of his ears and the small silver hoop in the left one, the same ear that Odin had pierced. It must have something to do with their tribe. I filed it away to ask later.

I was admiring Agnarr's expressive black brows and his unfairly thick lashes when he shifted and opened one eye, looking down at me sleepily.

"How long have you been watching me sleep, Pip?" he asked huskily.

I grinned sheepishly.

"Um, not at all. I just woke up, I swear," I said, a little too quickly.

I was surprised at how raw my throat felt, then remembered the screams of pleasure from the night before.

"Not at all, hmm?" he asked, eyebrows raised.

His throat sounded just as raw as mine felt.

"Okay, well, maybe for a few minutes," I admitted. "I

didn't want to wake you. After last night, you needed your sleep."

Agnarr smirked down at me, then pulled me into a kiss.

"Last night was exquisite," he whispered as he stroked my side. "You're sure you don't hurt?"

While I didn't *hurt,* I was definitely sore. I'd been thoroughly fucked. Muscles I didn't know I had were stiff.

"I am a little sore, but I don't hurt. I won't be sore as much as I get used to your size," I said.

"Oh, so we'll be doing this more?" Agnarr grinned at me.

"Mmm, maybe we should focus on getting out of this cave before we think about next time," I replied, smiling back at him. "We both really need to clean up first."

Agnarr stroked my hair and brushed a kiss to the tip of my nose.

"That we do. Let me go get something for us to use," he said, getting up.

I couldn't help but admire his perfect, full ass as he walked to his bag. I heard a ripping noise and then pouring water. Agnarr came back a few moments later with what looked suspiciously like two ripped pieces of a tunic, wet with warm water.

"If you want to go clean up behind the alcove and take care of business, I know it is important for a female to do that," he said, handing me one of the cloths, "I will clean up here and then I need to check on Sindri."

I took the cloth and headed to the back of the cave. After I relieved myself, I set to cleaning up. Orc cum seemed to have the same viscosity as human cum, still creamy but with more of a sheen to it. It almost seemed to shimmer like that cheap eyeshadow I was into in middle school, ha. There was definitely much more of it. It was all over me. It took quite a thorough examination and cleaning to make me feel like I was no longer sticky.

When I walked back to the cave, Agnarr was gone, probably seeing to Sindri. I went to my clothes that had been drying by the fire all night. They had definitely seen better days but were still wearable. I got dressed and tried to run my fingers through my hair but found it was too tangled for even that. Agnarr had long hair. I wondered if he'd thought to bring a comb.

I was sitting down to pull my boots on when Agnarr returned. I tried not to stare, but he was shirtless. I had seen him naked but wasn't used to it yet. The thick planes of his pectoral muscles were lightly dusted with fine black hair. His abdominal muscles looked like something a Renaissance sculptor would have envisioned, with his V muscles pointing downward on either side of a happy trail of the same silky black hair. He bore many small scars that I'd have to ask him about, but they did nothing but make him even more appealing. I realized I had been looking for an extended period and snapped my eyes up to his.

"Do you still like what you see?" he asked, smirking.

I returned my attention to lacing up my boots, not looking him in the eye. "Well, aren't we confident?" I said.

He didn't say anything for a moment as I sat lacing my boots, and then I felt his breath on my ear as he whispered, "I guess I am pretty confident. After all, it was my name you were screaming as you came around my cock last night."

I turned and stared at him with open-mouthed shock. The audacity of this orc!

"Wha—I mean—what—" I sputtered, blushing to my roots.

"Oh, and now I've gone and left you speechless? I must be doing something right," he said, giving me a cocky grin before turning his attention to my pack.

My brain short-circuited as I tried to think of a clever comeback. I settled for lacing my boots up with determination and refusing to look in his direction. I looked around the cave for something to do to aid in readying us to leave and settled on straightening up the furs. There was definitely dried cum on them, but I decided that if Agnarr wasn't going to worry about it, I wouldn't either. I straightened them and then, having no other option, turned back to Agnarr.

Luckily, he was focused on my pack and didn't seem to feel the need to get in any other sly comments. It looked like the extra clothes I'd brought had dried overnight, but the food Tora had so carefully packed for me was definitely ruined. Great.

The endorphins of the night before were wearing off, and as I started to panic, realizing how far I still was from my goal of reaching Snaerfírar. I had now gone another day without any medication. I did a quick body scan. My heart rate was elevated and breathing shallow. I could tell I wasn't too far into a panic attack yet because I wasn't experiencing tunnel vision. Without saying anything to Agnarr, I walked to him and sat down on the log by the fire. I focused on my breathing.

In through your nose, out through your mouth. In through your nose, out through your mouth. In through your nose, out through your mouth.

I watched him as he carefully repacked my pack, not really seeing him but trying to break what felt like an insurmountable problem into pieces instead of catastrophizing.

Break it down, Piper. You got this.

I had been attacked by some sort cats and almost drowned in a river. That was bad. But I had made it to the cave, and now I had Agnarr. Definitely good. With him and his hestr, we could easily make it to the cabin at the end of the forest. From there, I knew I could rely on him to guide me up the mountains to the Snaerfírar. We would definitely get there faster than I would have on my own. All of these were good things. We could make it to the cabin. We could make it to the tribe.

My breathing was evening out. I was still watching Agnarr in a sort of unfocused way as I shifted to how he fit into all of this. I'd been so damned certain that I needed to leave as soon as possible that I didn't even think of the possibility that he might follow me. And now here he was. A beautiful, caring, alien orc, legitimately packing up my backpack like a high school boyfriend. I was going to have to let my walls come down with him. He deserved as much. He showed up for me even when I was unwilling to accept his help. If this hadn't shown him to be worthy of my trust, I didn't know what would. I worried at my lower lip, wondering what his thoughts were. Was he looking for a *mate,* as they called it? Was I ready to be a mate?

One step at a time.

AGNARR

I could tell Piper was trying not to panic as I packed things up around the cave. Her extra clothes had dried nicely. Though the food she'd brought was ruined, I had enough for both of us to reach the hunters' cabin. I wasn't sure what kind of mental support Piper needed at the moment, so I decided to press on, readying us to leave. When I left the cave earlier, I'd discovered that the first snow had fallen. It lay in a blanket across the forest floor. If I had let Piper make the journey on her own, the snow would have stopped her progress entirely. With Sindri, we'd have no issue reaching the cabin before the afternoon. Hestrs were built to travel through snow with their thick, curly coats.

I let my mind drift to the night before. Not only had Piper accepted the primal part of me, she demanded it. I felt completely unleashed as I took her from behind, and she loved every second of it, thrusting her perfect ass to meet each one of my punishing strokes. I knew there was no going back. Piper was mine. I felt even more urgency to get to Snaerfírar to find out what they knew of orkin-human matings. Could she be my elska mate as a human? I honestly wasn't sure if I cared anymore. She was my mate in my eyes, elska markings or not. But I needed to know everything I could about claiming her. The thought of another male in my tribe even approaching her filled me with rage. I finished packing all of our things and looked at Piper. She had calmed down. I wanted to ask what had suddenly troubled her, but it didn't seem like the time. We had a hard day of travel ahead of us. I was willing to see where the conversation went as we rode together on Sindri.

"Are you ready to go?" I asked.

Piper jumped."What?"

"I said, are you ready to go?"

"Yes, yes, I'm ready."

"It snowed overnight, so make sure you wear your cloak."

I watched as Piper gathered her cloak from the belongings I'd laid out to dry the night before. It might be stiff, but it would protect her from the wind and snow, which was all that mattered. As she fastened it, I finished packing her bag and handed it to her wordlessly. It was significantly lighter, considering all the ruined food. I gathered my remaining things, slipping on my extra tunic that was now missing a sleeve due to tearing it to use in the night to clean up. It wouldn't really affect me, and I still had my cloak. None of my things had been ruined in the river because they'd been packed on Sindri.

"Well then, I guess it is time to head out. We are still on a tight deadline, right?" I said, ushering her to the mouth of the cave.

"Yes; the sooner we get to the Snaerfírar tribe, the sooner

I can get the medication I need," she said, concern apparent in her voice.

"It's good I brought Sindri. She's the fastest hestr of our tribe," I said, grabbing her hand and leading her out into the light of early morning.

CHAPTER 15

PIPER

I gasped as I exited the cave. It hadn't just snowed; it had dumped piles of snow—mountains of snow. Was this normal? I was from LA, the only snow I saw was when we drove a few hours away to go sledding every few years. This seemed like an avalanche of snow. How were we ever going to continue traveling through this? The panic I had quieted in the cave returned in full force just when I heard an animal chuff near me. I jumped, startled, and looked at Agnarr's hestr.

"This is Sindri?" I said breathlessly.

"Já. " Agnarr approached her to adjust her saddle and his pack.

I hadn't looked at the animal when Agnarr pulled me from the river. She looked mostly like a horse but had a few differences. Most obviously, she had eight legs. Four in the front, four in the back. Honestly, it was a bit alarming, and I wondered how that would work, but she seemed to be doing just fine. Her fur was thick and curly as if designed to keep her warm during cold weather. Her muzzle was broader than that of a horse, almost like a combination of a horse and a cow. Looking down, I saw that her hooves were cloven, like a goat's. She seemed uninterested in me, eating grain that Agnarr must have laid down for her. The saddle she wore was enormous, definitely designed to fit Agnarr.

"We'll be riding Sindri the rest of the way?" I asked.

"Já. Is that a problem?"

"Well, where will I sit?"

"You'll sit in front of me. Not only will it keep you warm, but I will be able to protect you if we encounter any other predators," Agnarr explained.

I rolled that over in my head. I would be sitting in front of Agnarr on Sindri for the entire day. That shouldn't be a problem, not a problem at all. I looked from Agnarr to Sindri, one eyebrow cocked.

"You think you'll be able to keep your hands to yourself while I sit between your knees for the rest of the day?" I asked.

"I made no such promises," he said, smirking at me.

"Well, remember we have a goal here. I need to get to the Snaerfírar tribe as soon as we can."

"Oh, I promise not to detract from our goals," he purred. "Shall we get going?"

"Yes, yes, let's get going."

Without missing a beat, Agnarr picked me up as if I weighed nothing and sat me atop Sindri. He walked around the hestr once, looking her over to ensure everything was in its place before putting one foot in the stirrup and swinging up behind me in one effortless motion. Oh, wow, this was going to be a tight fight. My ass was pressed directly into Agnarr's groin, our thighs lining up tightly on each side. He wrapped an arm on either side of me to grab the reins.

"Is this too close for comfort?" He leaned forward, whispering into my ear, causing me to break out into goosebumps.

"N-no. No. Not too close at all," I stammered.

He straightened up and gently slapped the reins against Sindri's sides. The hestr started at a swift trot, causing me to bounce up and down on the saddle. Agnarr wrapped one hand around my waist, steadying me and pulling me closer to him.

"It looks like I am going to have to be careful to ensure you don't go flying off Sindri. She's not used to such light riders." He chuckled.

Agnarr navigated Sindri back to the path. It was barely visible due to the heavy snow. In the light of day, the mushrooms lining the path didn't glow at all. Only the tops of the largest of them were visible above the snow. I looked down to see that the snow was almost halfway up Sindri's legs, but she seemed to have no trouble continuing to trot through it.

"How long do you think it will take to get to the cabin now that we have Sindri?" I asked.

"Given the snow, I think we will probably make it by mid-afternoon," Agnarr replied.

"If we push on, could we make it to the Snaerfírar tribe tonight?" I asked hopefully.

"Sadly, no; it is rocky terrain, and I don't want to risk getting caught in the dark halfway up the mountain," he said.

I sighed. I was getting nervous that I would have a total meltdown at some point, but there was nothing to be done for it. I felt safer with Agnarr. His expertise improved my chances of getting to the Snaerfírar tribe dramatically. I settled into the saddle while trying not to lean back into him. It would have been very easy to lean into his broad chest and enjoy his warmth and the feeling of his solid body, but I still wasn't sure where we stood. We'd had amazing, mind-blowing sex twice now, but I didn't know what that meant for him. He'd said that he wanted more than sex with me, but maybe that was what he told all females. Maybe that kind of sex was a regular occurrence. With what I knew of Agnarr, I doubted that, but I worried at my lower lip as I thought about it. If I was going to let my walls down, this was conversation that needed to be had, and soon.

As we traveled, I took in all the sights around me. The giant furutré were covered in snow, and the ground was blanketed with it. It reminded me of Christmas. The path, while covered in snow, was easy to follow due to the lack of trees. We traveled in companionable silence, but after a while, I couldn't hold my spine straight anymore. Hesitantly, I leaned back into his broad chest, giving my screaming back muscles the break they needed.

I felt Agnarr shift behind me, but he didn't say a word. I settled into his body, allowing myself to get comfortable. As I leaned into Agnarr, I felt his cock grow hard and prod into my lower back.

So I wasn't the only one impacted by this proximity. I smirked to myself.

This ride had my anxiety rearing its head, and I knew the endorphin rush and the feel of his heated skin against mine would abate it. I shifted my ass against his hips, grinding into his hardened length and grabbing his thigh.

"Are we feeling hungry?" he whispered.

"Hmm, I believe it was you who made the first move," I said back.

"I can't help it; you pressing your body into me makes me react."

"How close are we to the cabin?" I asked, grinding my ass against him shamelessly.

"Not close enough," he hissed.

He pulled Sindri up to the base of a tree and swung

himself off before lifting me to join him. I didn't even have a moment to ask what his intentions were before he directed me.

"Hands on the lower branches of the tree. Hang on."

I grabbed the lower branches of the furutré, unsure of what to expect as Agnarr yanked down my leggings. It left my ass bare to the cold, and I shivered. His calloused hand stroked my ass, and I heard him growl in approval.

"Your ass is...divine. Watching the way it jiggles and bounces as I pound into you causes my undoing."

He really knew how to compliment a girl. He stroked my bare ass and then smacked it, hard, causing me to gush with want. He arched over me and whispered into my ear.

"Do you want it slow and drawn out or hard and fast?"

"Hard and fast," I choked out, barely able to contain my anticipation.

"Thank the gods," he growled.

He notched himself at my entrance, only giving me a second to prepare myself before he slammed into me. The feral noise that escaped me may have been a moan—it may have been a scream. All I knew was that Agnarr was seated to the hilt and I was stretched in a delicious mix of pleasure and pain. Agnarr pulled back and thrust in again. I felt every single one of the braids and ridges along his cock slide into me. He leaned over me and nuzzled the nape of my neck, giving the sensitive skin a nip before asking, "Is this all right? It's not too much?"

"Not too much. More. Need you. Now," I panted.

I had unleashed him. He pulled back and pounded into me again and again. Each thrust of his textured cock felt exquisite against my sensitive flesh. Just when I thought I was going to go over the edge, he grabbed my hair, pulling me upwards and exposing my neck."Whose cunt is this?" he asked as he continued to pound into me.

"Yours, only yours," I breathed, moments away from shattering.

He lowered his mouth and bit down on the throbbing pulse in my neck as I shattered around his cock. He thrust his hips twice more, then I felt him jerk and twitch, unloading jets of hot cum into me.

I had never experienced sex like this. Every single man I had encountered on earth had dealt with their own issues of repression and purity culture. A man—no, an orc—who was willing to claim what he wanted was enough to make me come on the spot.

Agnarr was still wrapped around me, breathing heavily as his knot slowly loosened.

"That was–" he said breathlessly

"Yes, yes it was," I said, cutting him off.

He slid out of me, and I felt cum gush down my thighs. If we were going to keep going at it like this, I was going to need more than some torn pieces of fabric to clean myself.

"I am afraid we are going to have to settle for snow for cleanup, Pip," he said, breathing still ragged. "As much as I'd like to take you to one of our hot springs and clean you from head to glorious toes, it will have to make do."

"I guess I can use your other sleeve and some melted snow," I said, grinning at him.

That we'd been using parts of his shirt to clean up after sex suddenly struck me as hysterical. I started laughing as he went to rip his sleeve. Agnarr looked affronted.

"Are you laughing at me?" he huffed.

"No, no," I said, still chuckling. "I'm just thinking we've now gone and made your tunic completely sleeveless. You look more like a lumbersnack than the day I first saw you."

This mollified Agnarr as he pulled his sleeve off and handed it to me. A sleeve and snow weren't the best way to clean up a ridiculous amount of orc cum. It was freezing and only moderately effective, but at least I wasn't sticky anymore. I pulled my leggings back up, and Agnarr lifted me back onto Sindri before swinging up behind me.

We rode in silence for a while, but my mind was whirling. He had, crudely, called my cunt his. He'd now laid claim to me in so many ways that it seemed time to have a conversation. I wanted to ask. I wanted to have this conversation before I put even more of my heart on the line.

AGNARR

Being back on Sindri with Piper between my legs was pure torture. I knew we didn't have the time to keep stopping, but all I could think of was the jiggle of her pale ass as I plowed into her. I squeezed my thighs against Sindri's sides, urging her into a trot. Piper leaned into me, turning her head to the side to lay her cheek on my chest.

"Not concerned about keeping the distance between us now that I've thoroughly sated you?" I asked.

"Mmm—maybe. Or maybe I think it's time we have a conversation," she said, drawing circles on my thigh with one of her fingers.

I tried to understand the meaning behind her words. A conversation was just that, two beings talking, but the seriousness with which Piper used the term sounded like there was a lot more meaning behind it.

"What kind of conversation, Pip?" I asked.

Piper remained silent for so long that I wondered if she had fallen asleep when she finally said, "We need to have a conversation about you and me."

"You and me? What do you mean?"

"Well, I don't know how relationships really work here outside of elska mates. Do you date? Do you have boyfriends and girlfriends? Have I fallen backward in time where you use the word courting? What is the normal situation when two orcs start sleeping together?" she asked, all very quickly. I rolled over Piper's questions in my head. She had voiced so many of the concerns that I was taking with me to the Snaerfírar tribe. If we were both carrying the same worries, I would have to be honest with her.

"Well, before you arrived, I had refused to take a chosen mate because I wanted to wait for my elska mate. Yet, none of the orcs in my tribe is my elska. I would have known by now. It is getting beyond the time when I should have chosen a mate and settled down."

I hesitated to continue. Piper didn't know that my choosing a mate was a condition of me taking on the role of jarl. I didn't want to deceive her, but I also didn't want my role in the tribe to impact her decision whether to be my mate.

"So you aren't interested in taking a mate that isn't your elska mate?" Piper's worried voice interrupted my train of thought.

The tension in her voice caused a new concern. What if she didn't want a mate, elska or not? I cleared my throat.

"Well, before you arrived, that was true. Circumstances have changed since then," I replied huskily.

Piper turned around as much as she could. I slowed Sindri to a walk. Piper's brow was knit with concern as she looked at me.

"How have circumstances changed?" she asked.

"Ever since I put you back in my bed the morning you woke up, I've felt a pull to you, Pip. Not like I've felt with any other female. I feel this all-encompassing need to be with you. I don't know what it feels like to have an elska mate, but it can't be more than how I feel for you."

Both of Pip's eyebrows shot up at this admission.

"Do you think we're elska mates? I thought they were supposed to have markings of some type?" she asked.

"Já, orkin elska mates have paired markings that appear down their spines. But I don't know if humans and orcs can be elska mates. We have never had humans in our tribe," I explained.

Piper scrunched up her face.

"But the Snaerfírar tribe has had human women, hasn't it?" she asked.

"That is what the rumor is from the trade routes."

I could almost see all the pieces clicking together for her.

"So you wanted to go to Snaerfírar to find out if we could be elska mates?" she asked, sounding shocked.

"That was my intention before I knew you also wanted to go to Snaerfírar to get baldrian. Once I knew you were on a mission, I wanted to get there before you. First, to get you the baldrian. Second, to find out if we could be mates. Things have not quite gone to plan."

At this, Piper went quiet. Trying to be respectful and give her time to process, I focused on the trail ahead. We were still a good way from the cabin. I pushed Sindri back to a trot. I did not want to be caught out in the forest at night again. We traveled in silence for a long stretch, Piper leaning into me but saying nothing. I regretted my admission to her. She clearly wasn't ready to take on a mate. It had only been two dagrs since she had woken up. Given her anxiety on top of everything, finding out that she had an orc that wanted to be her mate probably pushed her over the edge.

We continued in silence for the rest of the afternoon. I pushed Sindri as hard as I felt I could for Pip's comfort. Pip rode quietly, leaning against me with her hand on my thigh. If it weren't for her hand, I think I would have convinced myself that she wanted nothing to do with me. But that hand on my thigh gave me a small glimmer of hope that she was rolling things over in her head and considering me.

The mists weren't as bad as I remembered, probably due to the snow the night before. Yet, it was still hard to see a great distance ahead of me, even in the daylight. When the trail began to climb, I knew we were approaching the cabin.

I finally broke the silence and said softly, "We're nearly there, Pip."

She jumped, making an adorable squeaking noise.

"Sorry, I didn't mean to startle you," I said.

"No, it's fine, it's fine. I was just lost in thought. We're nearly there already?"

"It has been quite a while since we left the cave," I responded, looking down at her quizzically.

"Oh, sorry. I lose track of time when I'm lost in my own head," she explained.

"You have had a lot to think about," I said before I hesitantly reached down to stroke her cheek.

"I have."

She reached her hand up and placed it over mine before leaning in for a kiss. It was brief, but I knew it was Piper trying to reassure me even if she didn't have the words yet. She returned to leaning against me as we continued toward the cabin. As it started to appear out of the mist, Piper sat up straight as if trying to make it out.

"Can you see it?" I asked.

"Just its form. I know orc eyeballs are better than human eyeballs," she responded, sounding exasperated.

"Give it just a bit more—"

"I see it!" she exclaimed, interrupting me.

I couldn't help but laugh at her excitement. From my sketchy memories, the cabin wasn't much. I hadn't been in almost fifteen árs. I didn't even know what condition it would be in. As it appeared through the mist, it was larger than I remembered. It appeared to be in good condition, the glass solid in its two front windows and the door sturdy against the snow.

As we approached, I pulled Sindri up to a halt and dismounted before turning to help Piper. I lifted her off carefully and set her next to me. She shivered. Oh, I *had* been keeping her warm. I needed to get her to warmth.

"Let's get inside," I said.

CHAPTER 16

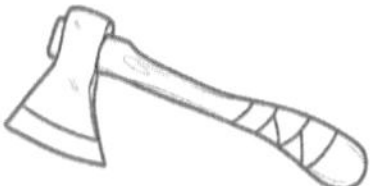

AGNARR

I approached the door, kicking the snow out of the way. The roof overhang had blocked most of it, but there was still some. Luckily, it was fresh snow and not ice, so there would be less danger of taking a spill. I reached the door and turned the knob, opening it with a creak. It wasn't locked. All in our tribe were free to use it. I pushed it wide open before turning to Piper.

"Let me just do a quick scan for safety?" I asked.

"Of course, of course," she said, teeth chattering.

I went in, quickly surveying the state of the place. It had been kept up well. While it wasn't much, it was clean and tidy. There was a solid wooden bed against one wall. On the opposite wall was a fireplace with two chairs and a low table. A small kitchen huddled in the back, and a door led to a small washroom. While not much, it was definitely better than a cave. I turned and widened the door for Piper to step in.

"This is nicer than I expected. I was thinking of a hut with barely enough room for one. This is a cute little cabin." She smiled up at me.

I grinned, glad to see she was pleased with the place. I was nervous and waiting on her response to our earlier "conversation," but I wanted to give her time. It was warmer in the cabin, but only barely. I needed to get a fire going immediately.

"Do you want to look in the kitchen and see if there are any travel rations we can use while I get some firewood?" I asked.

"Sure, I can do that."

I headed out the door, leaving her to get settled. I surveyed the surrounding area. The mist was still lighter than normal. I couldn't see the sun, but I could tell it was late afternoon. I went around the side of the cabin to find a decent stack of firewood piled up against the wall. Gathering several logs, I headed back to the cabin. When I returned, I found Piper rummaging through the baskets in the kitchen.

"Any supplies of note?" I asked as I placed the logs in the fireplace.

Still looking, she said, "There's a good amount of dried meat. What I think are dried vegetables and herbs and basic medical supplies. Plenty for us to stay the night."

She seemed happy, so I was happy. The anxious and absent Piper from our ride to the cabin seemed to be gone. I slowly built a fire, stacking it so that it would last for several hours. Piper sat down in a chair next to me as I worked.

"I have been thinking about what you said," she said, looking at me earnestly.

Piper

Agnarr looked up at me, face full of concern. I could tell that he'd been waiting for me to say something the entire afternoon—but my head had been a jumbled mess. Yes, I was falling for Agnarr. Yes, I was attracted to him. However, the idea of being mated for life through some fate I didn't understand scared the shit out of me. I'd decided I was going to be as honest with Agnarr as I could.

"Okay, so," I said quietly, Agnarr still looking at me.

"So?" His voice was full of questions.

"So, first things first. I'm an anxious person, and I know I have caused you a lot of anxiety by riding in silence. I'm sorry, but I needed time to figure things out. Finding out that someone thinks you are their fated mate is not even possible on Earth. It was a lot to grapple with," I said.

Some of the concern shifted from Agnarr's face, but I could tell he was still worried. He'd laid it all on the line and was waiting for my response. I took a deep breath.

"Agnarr, I don't understand how this whole fated mate thing works. If this were Earth? I would happily date you. Hell, I'd move in with you. But mates for life from day one? I can't wrap my head around it. It isn't the way I am used to things working for a couple." I looked at him, concerned he'd jump up in anger.

Instead, he shifted from where he was on his knees in front of the fireplace to being on his knees in front of me. We were eye-to-eye like this. He cupped my face in my hands, stroking my cheek with his thumb, looking deep into my eyes before gently kissing me. My breath hitched as I kissed him back, deepening it as I wrapped my arms around his neck. We kissed for a moment before Agnarr pulled back to look at me again.

"But you're willing to give me a chance? A chance to prove I am your mate?" he asked.

"I'm willing to take it one step at a time. I'm not committing to anything, but I am leaving the door open. I don't know what will happen when we get to the Snaerfírar tribe.

We don't know if humans and orcs can even be elska mates. But I am willing to see what happens."

Agnarr pulled me in for another kiss, this one hungry and devouring. I slid out of my chair and wrapped my arms around him, not only wanting to touch him everywhere but also grateful for the warmth he provided. He gently nipped along my lower lip until I opened for him, allowing him to snake his longer tongue against mine, licking the inside of my mouth everywhere. I moaned at the onslaught. Regretfully, I pulled back.

"As much as I appreciate where this is going, we should get the fire going first. After all, what kind of mate would let his delicate human freeze?" I asked playfully.

Agnarr huffed, but grinned. "Only a terrible mate would let his tiny, delicate, human…freeze." He punctuated each of his words with a kiss down my neck.

I pulled away and stood up, looking around the cabin. Despite being a bit bare, it was much cozier than I had expected. The bed did look very inviting, but there were other things to attend to. Telling Agnarr how I was feeling had relieved all the tension I had carried on the trip to the cabin, and I was anxious to get things done. I was an okay cook; I could get something going between the supplies Agnarr had in his pack and the supplies available in the cabin. But then I looked down at myself. I was filthy. What I really needed before food was a shower.

"Agnarr, is there running water here?" I asked.

"There is. Are you thirsty?" he replied.

"No, I desperately need a shower, as do you," I said, looking him over. We were both worse for wear. His tunic was torn and dirty and sleeveless.

"There are no baths here. There are hot springs a little ways away, but we would have to take Sindri."

I sighed. I didn't want to get back on the hestr. My

muscles were already sore from our journey—and our inability to keep our hands off each other. We had another long journey the next day if we were hoping to get to Snaerfírar.

"Hmm…we will have to think of another way to get clean," I said. "I think we should clean up before we try to make something to eat, no?"

Agnarr looked around the cabin thoughtfully. There was a large metal bucket on the floor near where I stood. His eyes zeroed in on it.

"We could use the kettle to heat water and clean using the bucket?"

"That doesn't sound very appealing, but I think we can make do."

Agnarr lit the fire while I went to figure out filling the kettle. Filling the bucket one kettle at a time was going to be slow going. I looked through the cupboards and found a large pot I could fill, at least hastening the speed at which we could get hot water. By the time I had both heating on the small stovetop, Agnarr had the fire roaring and I could feel myself thawing. The journey to the cabin hadn't been terrible, but it was only Agnarr's body heat that had kept me from being absolutely miserable. I hated the cold. Why hadn't the aliens dropped me in a tropical climate?

I looked around the cabin as Agnarr tended to the fire. One giant bed. Of course. Well, I guess there was no question about sleeping arrangements. It looked so comfortable and warm. Only my filth stopped me from crawling in and falling asleep. I had now had two days fueled almost entirely by my anxiety. I was long overdue for a solid nap. But Agnarr and I both needed to be clean, and I definitely needed food.

I opened the door next to the bed to find a basic toilet and sink setup. At least I wouldn't have to worry about going outside to go to the bathroom. I continued my meander throughout the cabin, but in one room, there wasn't much to see. It was warm and comfortable now that the fire was blazing. I was ready to strip off and get clean. I jumped when I heard the whistle of the kettle.

"You should go first, then we can bundle you up while I go," Agnarr said from where he was crouched next to the fire.

He had placed the bucket in front of the fire and filled it partially with cold water, leaving me to fill the rest with hot. Using the hand towels hanging by the stove, I grabbed the kettle and poured it in. I wordlessly handed the towel to Agnarr. He used it to lift the large pot of boiling water and poured it into the bucket at my feet. I knelt and tested the water with my hand. Hot, but not too hot. I eagerly started to pull my tunic over my head, then looked at Agnarr.

We'd already seen each other naked, but this was different. I would be standing, buck naked, in the middle of the cabin, washing in front of him. I looked at him uncertainly, but he wasn't looking at me. He stood up and strode to the bathroom, rummaging through the small cupboard. Seeming to have found what he was looking for, he returned. I looked down. He had a bar of what looked like dark green soap in one hand and a small washcloth in another.

He looked at me and then nodded as if making up his mind. "Will you let me help you wash?" His voice was so earnest, I couldn't say no.

"Yes, that would be—that would be very nice," I responded, trying to sound sure of myself.

I took a deep breath and lifted my tunic over my head. My bra was long gone, either taken by the bad aliens, or whoever had put me in pajamas on day one. So it was just me, standing there, topless, with my not-that-perky C-cups. I couldn't stop to think about it or I would lose my courage, so I toed my boots off and stripped my bottom half. I stepped into the large bucket and sighed at the feeling of hot water up to my calves before opening my eyes to see Agnarr, staring at me, slack-jawed.

"Mmm, sir, it is impolite to stare," I sassed.

Agnarr's cheeks turned a darker shade of green before he muttered, "Sorry, sorry."

He dipped the soap and cloth into the tub, lathering it before approaching me.

"May I?" he asked softly.

"Yes, I would love that."

Agnarr used the washcloth to wash me, starting at my shoulders. He scrubbed down each arm, leaving no skin unwashed, before returning to my chest. His eyes grew heated as he looked at my pebbled nibbles. I could almost hear his silent groan. He cleared his throat and then cleared it again before saying, "May I continue?"

Enjoying toying with him, I only stretched my arms out further, allowing him full access to continue. Agnarr, attempting to stay the course, swiped over one boob, cleaning the underside of it completely before shifting to the next and failing entirely. He started and then, as if abandoning all self-control, dropped the washcloth and the soap and pulled me to him. He grabbed one of my nipples gently with his teeth before sucking hard on it, causing me to gasp. It felt so good. I grabbed his head and held him to my chest, moaning into the sensation of him sucking on my nipple before coming to my senses. Clean. We needed to get clean. I leaned back and looked at him.

"Agnarr, I promise, once we are washed and fed, I am up for *whatever* you are imagining. Deal?" I said.

Agnarr's eyebrows went sky-high before he said, "Deal."

He grabbed the washcloth from the water and returned to washing me, carefully stroking down from each boob to clean my stomach.

"Who made these?" he growled, staring at the small scars on my midsection.

"Um, my doctor? I had my gallbladder removed years ago."

"Hmph. Was it causing you pain?" he asked, sounding skeptical.

"Yes, a great deal. I was very glad to be rid of it."

He seemed satisfied with that response, washing lower, washing each leg before staring at the apex of my thighs.

"Piper, I can smell your arousal. I don't think I can wash your beautiful cunt and keep myself restrained," he choked out.

Blushing, I grabbed the washcloth from him. It wasn't often I heard the words "beautiful" and "cunt" together, let alone used to describe *my* cunt.

"Why don't you get more water going on the stove while I work on the rest of myself? Maybe by the time you get more water going, you can help me with my hair."

Agnarr nodded vigorously and took the kettle and the pot to the stove. I washed the rest of myself except my hair. I wasn't sure about using bar soap on my hair, but I wasn't about to ask about shampoo.

"Agnarr, is there a pitcher or something I could use to wet my hair?" I called to him.

I heard rummaging, then Agnarr approached me with a metal pitcher and handed it to me.

"I am almost done. Think you could keep it together long enough to help me wash my hair?" I grinned at him.

"I shall try my best," Agnarr replied, bending down to fill the pitcher with water.

He stood behind me and poured it over my head as I tilted it back before lathering up the soap. He then proceeded to massage the soap into my scalp, starting at my forehead and working his way back. He did this slowly and methodically, kneading the soap into my hair. Goosebumps pricked all over my body, and I let out a small moan.

"Remember, Pip, we both need to get clean," Agnarr said, clearly mocking me for my previous statements.

"Well, I didn't know how good you were at hairwashing when I said that," I replied coolly.

"Still think you'll be able to hold off?"

"Oh yes. I can't wait until it's your turn."

Agnarr continued to lather my hair wordlessly before using the pitcher to rinse it.

"Are there towels here? Do orcs have towels?" I asked.

Agnarr looked slightly affronted. "Of course we have towels. Orcs love bathing. This is a sad attempt at a bath, but it has to do for now. Let me go find some in the bathroom," he said, walking in that direction.

I ran my fingers through my hair, pleased to find it feeling clean and soft, before I used the pitcher to rinse my body one last time. The water was tepid at this point. I was just getting cold when Agnarr returned with a pile of soft-looking brown towels in his hands.

"Wow, orcs must really take bathing seriously," I said, grabbing one towel, finding it not only to be as soft as it looked but large enough to wrap around me twice.

"We have very sensitive noses, as I think you've noticed," Agnarr said, his lips lifting into a feral smile.

"Ah, yes," I said, blushing again as I stepped out of the bucket.

I toweled myself off as Agnarr took the bucket outside to dump the water. He brought it back in and filled it partially with cold water before placing it in front of the fire again. As we waited for the next round of water to heat, I wondered if it would be weird to ask if Agnarr had thought to bring a comb. I walked to the entry of the cabin where Agnarr had placed both of our packs. Opening mine, I found Agnarr had thoughtfully folded my extra clothes after they had dried out in the cave. I slipped on a pair of lined leggings and a fresh tunic, already feeling a hundred percent better. I found a pair of thick, long socks in the pack's bottom and was thrilled. Pulling them on, I silently thanked Tora for thinking of socks. I heard the kettle whistle and turned to see Agnarr standing stark naked in front of the fire.

If I'd thought staying on task while he washed me was hard, washing him was going to be nearly impossible. My eyes scanned down his body, taking in every rippling muscle before my eyes fell on his fully erect cock. How had I fit that in my body? My heart rate increased just thinking about the way the braided texture had felt inside of me and clenched my thighs together just as I heard a low chuckle come from Agnarr. I looked up at his face to find him smirking at me.

"Are you sure we need to get me clean before...anything else?" he purred, still grinning.

"I'm—I'm definitely sure," I stammered. "Maybe I should let you wash while I start preparing something to eat?" I suggested.

"Oh no, I helped you bathe. I feel it's only fair if you help me," he murmured.

CHAPTER 17

PIPER

I readied myself and walked over to Agnarr, grabbing the bar of soap and a fresh washcloth from the low table. Agnarr turned and walked to the kitchen, leaving me with a view of his perfectly muscled ass. Holy hell. He walked back and emptied the kettle into the bucket before turning to get the large pot. Instead of ogling him, I focused on lathering up the soap and washcloth. I kept my eyes down as he emptied the pot and set it on the floor before stepping into the bucket. I stood up, washcloth and soap in hand, and blew a breath out my nose before looking Agnarr in the eye.

"How about I start with your back?" I breathed. I wasn't sure I could keep my composure standing in front of him.

"That sounds wonderful," he said, still smiling down at me. "Why don't you give me the bar of soap and I'll do my front while you do my back?"

Oh, thank fuck. I walked around behind him and started

to drag the washcloth over his muscled shoulders. It gave me the opportunity to ogle him further without having to look him in the eye. I admired his skin as I scrubbed down his back. I loved the dark shade of green he was. It no longer seemed weird and alien. Instead, it made me think of pine and warm comfort. As I washed him, I noticed small scars here and there. He had said he was in the guard for his tribe, but they made me curious.

"Where did you get all these scars?" I asked. He'd asked about mine, after all.

"Here and there. Some from training, some from a fight with a neighboring tribe árs ago. Nothing serious," he responded casually.

"Battle scars are nothing serious?" I asked, continuing to wash his back, biting my lip as I swiped over his muscled ass.

"Not when you are a guard. Plus, none of those scars are even significant. None of them required stitching."

"Well then, definitely not serious," I responded sarcastically. "Are you ready for me to wash your hair?"

It was still tied in the orc equivalent of a man-bun, but Agnarr managed to pull it off. He lifted his hands to his hair and untied it, letting it fall freely. I let out a gasp when I realized how long it was. It fell to the center of his back, a thick sheet of shiny black hair. I reached out to drag my fingers through it. It was much coarser than mine but still soft. I was only just tall enough to use the pitcher of water and pour it over his head. I poured the jug over several times as he tilted back so that I could get his hair thoroughly wet.

"Soap, please," I said, putting my hand out.

Agnarr wordlessly handed the soap back to me. I started lathering his hair, massaging the soap into his scalp. As I carefully cleaned his hair, I thought of everything I didn't know about Agnarr.

"Do you have any siblings?" I asked.

"I have two younger brothers," he said hoarsely.

My scalp massage was impacting him just as it had me. Ha.

"How much younger are they?" I asked, attempting to distract him while washing his hair.

"One is twenty-three árs and the other is twenty-five," he responded.

"Are you close?" I asked, now focusing on the hair that flowed down past his shoulders.

"Very close. I took care of them after our parents died." His voice hitched.

I continued lathering his hair, wondering how to proceed. I hadn't meant to stir up bad memories. I wasn't sure if Agnarr wanted to go through them with me. Then again, if he thought I was his fated mate, maybe he was?

"Do you want to tell me about it?" I asked softly.

"My parents died of an illness that gripped our tribe many árs ago. We lost many tribe members, including our jarl who ruled alongside Astrid. I was only sixteen," he said, voice barely above a whisper.

"Oh, Agnarr, I'm so sorry. Were you close to your parents?"

"Já. We were rowdy and gave our mamma a hard time, as three boys can, but we were very close," he said, clearing his throat. "They were elska mates, my parents. We haven't had any elska mates since the illness came. The tribe had all but given up on any new elska mates until Tora and Rune got their markings. I never did, though." He trailed off quietly.

Bath time just got very emotional. No wonder Agnarr wanted an elska mate. He wanted what his parents had. And he thought that was me. Oh boy. That was a lot to take in. I started rinsing out his hair, turning his words over in my head. We had no markings. We didn't know if humans were capable of having an elska mate. Agnarr pinned a lot of hope on me.

"Agnarr, what if we find out that humans can't be elska mates?" I asked.

"That doesn't change what I know," he said, his back still to me.

I scooped up another pitcherful of water and poured it down his back, finishing with his hair.

I set the pitcher down on the low table and walked around to face him. "And what is it that you know?" I breathed.

"I know that from the moment I saw you, time has stopped. Nothing has mattered other than being with you. I made a fool of myself before my tribe because I tried to protect you when you didn't want protection. When you left, I had no option but to follow. I don't want to be with anyone but you whether or not our markings appear." He held my gaze.

"Agnarr, I know that you think that the fates have aligned and that we are made for each other, but that isn't how it works on Earth." I dragged my hand down my face. "Some people on Earth believe in soul mates, but it isn't something I ever considered a possibility, especially not for me," I said, voice breaking.

Agnarr took my hand in his, bringing my fingers to his lips and kissing each of them before saying, "I am okay with one step at a time as long as you are willing to stay with me."

Holy hell. Agnarr was going to kill me with his never-ending patience. I couldn't say no to one step at a time.

"Yes," I breathed. "I will stay with you while we figure this out."

Agnarr pulled me into a bone-crushing embrace, pinning each of my arms at my sides. While I appreciated the sentiment, he was wet and naked and I was fully clothed. He pulled back and looked at my clothes.

"Sorry, sorry. I didn't mean to get you wet," he muttered.

"Oh, you didn't mean to get me wet? That would be a first," I said to him, grinning.

Agnarr laughed, a deep rumble, and I started laughing as well, breaking the tension of our weird, awkward half-naked hug.

"Let's get you dressed," I said, offering him one of the towels from the stack.

Agnarr wrapped the towel around his waist in a very human-like way before stepping out of the bucket.

"Do you happen to have a comb?" I asked, realizing my hair was still unbrushed.

"I do." He walked over and grabbed his pack, placing it on the bed and unpacking it.

He handed me a sturdy bone comb. I headed into the bathroom to find a small mirror above the sink and was able to comb out my hair. I looked at myself in the mirror for the first time since arriving on Nieflheim. It was almost odd to see that I looked exactly the same, no worse for wear. My wavy brown hair was starting to curl as it dried. I didn't have the dark circles under my eyes that I usually had at the end of each school day. Maybe I would get enough rest. I looked down to see the red toenail polish I'd had on while on Earth was even still there. It felt so odd to see me staring back at myself on an alien planet, in a rustic wooden cabin, with an orc I'd now fucked thrice.

I finished up with my hair and headed out to the living area. Agnarr was fully dressed when I returned. I handed him the comb, looking at his long locks. He combed through it quickly before putting it back into a bun at the crown of his head.

"Why do some orcs have braids while some wear their hair in a bun or a ponytail?" I asked, watching him.

He continued to tie up his hair, looking at me. "When a female accepts her mate, she does so by braiding his hair for him."

"I guess that works as well as wedding bands to let someone know you're off the market." I laughed.

Agnarr looked confused. "What are wedding bands? And what does it mean to be 'off the market?'"

"Wedding bands are rings you wear on your ring finger, the finger next to your pinkie, of your left hand. They signify that you are married—mated—or off the market, which means taken," I explained.

"Ahh," he said, looking thoughtful as he turned to place his comb back in his pack.

"Should we figure out something to eat?" I asked, suddenly very aware that I hadn't eaten since the day before.

"Já, let's," Agnarr said, looking through his pack. He pulled out what looked to be several pieces of fruit and some square packages that looked to be wrapped in wax paper. "I brought some basic travel rations, knowing the cabin would be stocked with some provisions."

"Do you know how to cook?" I asked.

I knew the basics, like making pasta, but I doubted I would get very far with alien ingredients.

"I do. Even though we tend to eat all together in the long-house, all orcs are taught the basics of cooking when they are young. I think with what we have here, I could make a basic stew," he replied.

"That sounds delicious. What can I do?"

"You could dice any of the dried vegetables that are available while I heat some water on the stove."

With that, we set to making a meal. It all felt very domestic, with Agnarr helping me with the ingredients I didn't recognize while chopping the dried meat. Once all the ingredients were in the pot, Agnarr poked around the kitchen more and found some earthenware jars of herbs, which he added to the stew. It bubbled away and started to smell delicious, causing my stomach to rumble loudly.

Agnarr looked at me, concerned. "When was the last time you ate?"

"Um, yesterday morning?" I confessed.

Agnarr looked chagrined. "What kind of mate am I if I can't keep you fed?"

"Well, we were a bit busy, first with you saving my life, then with you fucking my brains out."

At this, the green in Agnarr's cheeks deepened.

"Agnarr, I'm fine. What's important is that you are feeding me now. If you weren't here, I would have just gnawed on the dry meat that Tora gave me."

"All right, then, at least I am feeding you now," he assented. "Will you grab the square package on the bed? It has a loaf of bread in it, and the stew is nearly done."

I picked up the parcel as he ladled the stew into bowls, giving me easily three times what I would be capable of eating. He set the bowls on the low table before returning for spoons and a knife for the bread. I sat in one of the chairs, and he sat across from me. I scooped up a spoonful of stew, blowing on it before taking a mouthful.

I groaned at the taste of it. Agnarr could *cook*. Given the limited amount of supplies he had on hand, I was amazed. I took another bite and gasped as it scalded my tongue.

"Too bland?" Agnarr asked.

"No, no," I said, waving my hand in front of my mouth, trying to cool it down, "too hot!"

"Oh, I'm so sorry." He rushed to the kitchen and returned with two glasses of water.

"Thank you," I said, taking the glass from his hand.

He cut up the bread and we ate in companionable silence before I voiced a concern I'd had on my mind for a while.

"Do you think the Snaerfírar will be welcoming?"

"I can't really say. We trade with them, but bringing a human female to their tribe might cause violence."

"Violence? Why?"

"Because one of the males may want to lay claim to you. I will be forced to prevent that from happening," he replied blandly. "In our tribe, the fact that you smell of me would be enough to warn off any other potential suitors, but I don't know if the Snaerfírar tribe follows the same customs."

"And how would you prevent any other males from expressing interest?"

"By smashing them in the head."

Well, then. I returned to my stew, unsure of how to respond.

"Do you want to entertain any other advances?"

"No."

"Then we agree; I can smash anyone who approaches you."

"Um, that is not quite what I said, but sure."

I was very full and looked to see that I had eaten less than half of what Agnarr had given me.

"Agnarr, I know you aren't used to humans, but you gave me way more than I could ever eat." I hesitated, not wanting to offend him.

Without skipping a beat, Agnarr took my bowl and dumped the contents into his own.

He grinned at me. "Growing up with two brothers, food never went to waste."

"It must have been nice to have such a tight-knit family." I sighed.

"Were you not close with yours?"

"No, my parents separated when I was young. Neither of

them really wanted me or my sister, so we were just kind of ignored. After I went off to college, I only really talked to them on holidays."

Agnarr looked so sad I almost regretted telling him.

"I was used to it. My family was my family. There was nothing I could change about it. I didn't particularly want to be close to any of them."

"Who did you look to for support?"

"Uh, no one?"

Tears welled in his eyes. Jesus Christ, I was making Agnarr cry!

"Agnarr, it's fine! I'm fine. It was just how I was raised, honestly," I said hurriedly.

"It most certainly is not fine. You've already told me that your anxiety makes things harder for you and now you're telling me you had to deal with growing up and coming of age all on your own?" he said, almost angrily.

"When you put it like that, it is kind of depressing, but yeah," I admitted.

"You will never have to be alone again. I don't ever want you to face a problem on your own again. I don't want you ever to feel like you don't matter again," he growled.

Now it was my turn to well up. I'd never really thought about finding someone to rely on. It wasn't how I operated. If I didn't take care of myself, no one would. And now here was Agnarr, this orc I barely knew, telling me he would never let me feel that way again.

I wiped the tears from my eyes. "Agnarr, it might take me a long time to believe that. As my actions have shown, I try to do things on my own, even when it is a terrible idea," I said, giving him a weak smile.

He chuckled. "Yes, yes they have."

CHAPTER 18

PIPER

I sat quietly as Agnarr finished the last of his stew, pondering what it might be like to rely on someone. I didn't know if I would be capable of it. As Agnarr finished, he took my bowl and his and placed them on the counter near the stove. As he returned to me, I attempted to stifle an obvious yawn. It had been a long two days. Now that I had food in my stomach, exhaustion was kicking in. I was no longer in fight-or-flight mode, running on adrenaline.

I stood to go wash up the dishes when Agnarr grabbed my hand. "Let's go to bed."

"But the dishes…"

"The dishes can wait. You are clearly exhausted." He pulled me into a hug, and I melted into his arms.

I *was* really tired. "Okay, let's go to bed."

I looked at the bed and was suddenly self-conscious. All the physical interactions I'd had with Agnarr up to this point had been unplanned. Now we were going to get into bed together like a couple. I didn't even have pajamas.

"Um, I am guessing you didn't pack pajamas?"

"I usually sleep naked," Agnarr said awkwardly, rubbing the back of his neck.

As comforting as it was to know he also was aware of the shift between us that had taken place, I still wasn't sure how to proceed.

"Do you have a side of the bed you sleep on?"

"I've never shared a bed with someone long enough to establish that."

"Same."

We were both overthinking this. I approached him, placing my hands on his chest and looking up at him. "I think we are going to have to feel our way through this."

I pulled his shoulders down to me and kissed him softly.

"Give me your tunic. It will work just like a nightgown," I said, very aware that I wasn't wearing any underwear.

I changed into his tunic and put my clothes on a nearby chair before climbing into bed. It was surprisingly soft, considering it was meant to be a quick place to spend the night, with a thick, snuggly blanket. I sighed. Agnarr still looked uncertain. Lifting the blankets, I invited him in.

"I promise I won't bite. Unless you want me to." I laughed.

Agnarr climbed into bed with me in just his leggings. He propped his head up on his fist, leaning on his elbow, and looked at me.

"Hello."

"Hi."

"Ready for bed?"

"I think so," I said, looking out the window.

The sun wasn't fully set yet, but given the way the last few days had unfolded, I didn't really care. Agnarr looked at me.

"I don't think I've ever really slept with someone," he said, raising a hand to stroke my cheek. "Can I hold you?"

"We could, um, spoon?"

"Spoon? With...spoons? You want me to go get spoons?"

"Ha, no. No actual spoons. Here, let me show you."

I rolled over so my back was to him.

"Well, I don't like this," he grumbled. "I can't see you."

"Hang on a second." I scooted toward him until I felt his warm body. "Now you wrap your arm around me."

I curled myself into Agnarr, relaxing against his large frame. He wrapped an arm around my waist.

"Like this?"

"Yes, just like this. You can hold me as close as you want." I breathed in deeply, enjoying the warmth enveloping me and the feeling of a man—orc?—holding me close.

"Oh, okay. This is nice," Agnarr murmured. "Though I'd still like to see your face."

"You've seen my face plenty," I said, snuggling deeper into his arms.

"I want your face to be the only thing I see when I close my eyes," he whispered, stroking my hip lazily.

Agnarr was going to kill me with his devotion. He wrapped himself more fully around me. I had never spooned like this with a partner. It felt vulnerable in a new way. I evened out my breathing and tried to be present with Agnarr. I'd said I was willing to take this one step at a time, and right now, we were spooning. That was all I needed to think about. I stroked his arm and closed my eyes. I hadn't felt so at ease since I'd woken up on Niflheim. Agnarr nuzzled into my neck, breathing me in.

"You smell so damn good," he murmured.

I laughed. "I probably just smell clean. I've been a hot mess for the last couple days."

"No, it is your smell. Orcs have very sensitive noses. They also say you can smell your mate more acutely than others."

I rolled that over in my head. Thoughts of how much I loved Agnarr's smell and what that might mean were the last thing I thought of before I drifted off to sleep.

AGNARR

I woke up when it was still dark. I realized the fire had burnt to the embers and cursed myself for not building it up more before falling asleep. This would be the second time I'd let a fire go out with Piper. She'd distracted me with the lovely human custom of—what was it? Spoons? I'd have to have her explain again in the morning. Quietly, I slipped out of bed and headed to the fire. I was stoking it and adding another log when I heard a groggy voice call to me.

"Agnarr, where'd you go?"

I could make out her form sitting up in bed. Piper calling out to me from our shared bed made my heart clench. All I had ever wanted was calling out to me in the dark.

"I'm adding logs to the fire. I'll be right back."

I watched Piper lay back down and turned to finish tending the fire, stoking it up as high as possible to keep the cabin warm through the morning. Heading back to bed, I looked out the window. The mist was heavy. I couldn't see the moon, so I wasn't sure how late it was, but I guessed about midnight. I crawled back into bed, expecting to find Piper back asleep. Instead, I felt her reach out for me as soon as I slipped under the covers. She wrapped her arms around me and buried her nose in my chest.

"You're so warm," she said sleepily.

I stroked her hair, nuzzling the top of her head and inhaling her scent. My breathing hitched as I felt her press her lips along my collarbone, up my neck, to the sensitive skin underneath my ear.

"Pip, aren't you tired?"

"Not anymore," she said, planting kisses along my jaw. "If you're going to be with me, you're going to have to get used to waking up in the middle of the night. It's my favorite."

She stroked my chest and stomach while kissing down the other side of my neck.

"Are you tired?" she asked. She paused touching me, making her meaning clear.

"No, I'm definitely awake now. You can wake me up any time you like," I rasped.

"Excellent," she said, continuing to explore with her hands.

She slipped her hand down to my leggings, using the heel of her palm to stroke up my already hard cock. I let out a groan and bit down on my knuckle. If she wanted to explore, I was going to let her explore. She stroked me up and down a few more times.

"I don't think it's fair that you are wearing pants and I'm not. Can we do something about that?" she purred.

"Oh—definitely, yes," I breathed, moving my hands to untie the laces of my pants, pulling them off.

Piper's small hand wrapped around my knot, giving it a gentle tug. I could only see shadows of her face in the fire-light, but I stroked her cheek, nudging her chin up to look at me.

"You're sure you are awake enough to do this?" I questioned. Middle of the night sex was new to me.

Piper responded by grabbing either side of my head and pulling me into a kiss. She captured my lips with her own, flicking her tongue along the seam of my mouth before I opened it for her. She slipped her tongue in, dragging it along mine. I wrapped my arms around her to pull her closer, delighted to find myself gripping her bare ass. She was so soft. I kneaded her soft flesh as I kissed her fervently, plundering her mouth with my tongue. Piper returned a hand to my cock, tugging up and down and driving me wild. I wanted to be inside her.

"Piper," I hissed, "unless you stop, I can assure you, I won't last very long."

Piper released her grip on me, sliding her hand up my stomach and chest before swinging one leg over me and pushing me onto my back. She pulled my tunic over her head and tossed it aside. The fire had now grown large enough that I could see her in all her naked glory. I skimmed my hands up her hips and waist to cup her perfect breasts. I pinched each nipple gently, causing her to gasp.

"Ooh, harder," she panted.

I pulled her to me, taking one of her nipples into my mouth and flicking my tongue against it before nipping it with my teeth. She moaned. I filed the information away for further use. Piper's nipples were extremely sensitive. I sucked hard, earning a gasp from her before letting her breast release. I switched to the other, and she threaded her fingers through my hair as I feasted on her chest.

"Agnarr, I need more of you." Her breathing hitched as I sucked on her nipple.

She lifted herself up on her knees, reaching down to grab my cock. She dragged it up and down her slit, wetting herself with my leaking pre-cum. I groaned. If I wasn't inside her soon, I was going to die. I grabbed her hips just as she notched my cock at her entrance and pulled her down on me. We both moaned as I slid into her, down to my knot.

"Are you all the way in?" she breathed.

"No."

"Fuck, Agnarr, you're so big."

I continued to toy with her nipples, trying to loosen her

muscles so she could slide further down past my knot. She hissed in pleasure as she took all of me. She clenched her internal muscles as she adjusted to my size.

"Are you okay? Am I too much?" I asked.

She wiggled atop me and I clenched my teeth to stop myself from thrusting upward.

"No, not too much. I feel every ridge and braid of your magnificent cock. Fuck me like you mean it, Agnarr," she said.

I lifted her so only the tip of my cock remained inside her and slammed her back down, thrusting into her wet heat with everything I had. I would never tire of the feel of her. I thrust up into Piper again and she placed her hands on my chest to gain leverage. Fucking Piper was like nothing I'd ever experienced. I didn't know if it was her enthusiasm or that we were mates, but I could hardly contain myself. I pistoned my hips, repeatedly plunging into her as she bounced atop me. I grasped her breasts, enjoying the fullness in each hand, before I flicked my thumb over each nipple. Piper threw her head back and moaned as I hammered into her.

I reached down and used my thumb to slowly circle her clit. I circled it with the pad of my thumb, slowly increasing the pressure. She dug her tiny nails into my chest, panting each time she slammed herself down on me. I was so close, but she needed to finish first. I reached up with one hand and teased her nipple while still using my other hand to fondle her clit. She gasped and threw back her head as I felt her muscles contract around me as she arched her back.

"Oh fuck, Agnarr, don't stop," she hissed.

I continued to hammer into her, all the while stroking her clit. Her thighs stiffened on either side of me, and I felt her cunt clench around me as she reached her climax.

"I'm coming, I'm coming." She shuddered and twitched

atop me before I felt the final tense of her muscles, then the flood of her release.

She gasped and groaned above me as I plunged into her warmth. I continued to stroke into her, my own release building. My thrusts became erratic and wild as I held her atop me. It was mere moments before I followed her over the edge. I spasmed as I released into her welcoming body, shuddering at the feeling. Stars burst in my eyes as I climaxed into her. Even though I knew she was on human birth control, as I shot wave after wave of cum into her, I couldn't help but imagine her small frame, heavy with our child.

Thoroughly spent, I went limp as Piper leaned forward to pull me into an embrace. We were breathing heavily, both damp with sweat.

"That was—"

"Amazing?"

"Yes, amazing is a good word for it. I've never finished like that."

"Me neither," I breathed, stroking her hair as she melted into my chest.

I felt her rapid heartbeat slow as she settled on top of me.

"We should clean up," I said, hoping to catch her before she fell asleep.

"Ugh, I guess we should. Are there more washcloths in the bathroom?" she asked.

"Já, plenty."

As my knot softened, she lifted herself off of me, hobbling to the restroom as my seed leaked down her legs. I tried— and failed—not to feel pleased with how well I had filled her cunt. I heard the tap running in the bathroom and regretted not offering her warm water to cleanse herself. I cringed at the idea of her cleaning her delicate parts with cold water.

In almost no time, she returned to me. She placed her ice-cold hands on my chest.

"The water was freezing," she said as she pulled me toward her.

"I still need to clean up as well. I will be right back," I promised as I slipped out from under the blanket.

In the bathroom, I used a washcloth to give myself the quickest cleaning possible, eager to return to Piper. I used the restroom and washed my hands before returning to our warm bed. I stepped into the living area to see Piper propped up on an elbow, waiting for me.

"Hi," she said.

"Hey, ready to go back to sleep?"

"Now I am," she said with a grin as I climbed into bed with her.

She immediately plastered herself to me, pulling me tightly to her and sighing.

"You're so deliciously toasty," she murmured.

"Thank you?" I wasn't sure if it was a compliment or not.

As she nuzzled into my neck, I decided it was a compliment, letting myself melt into her, naked as we were.

"Do you need my tunic? Are you warm enough?" I asked.

"I'm plenty warm now," she purred as she wrapped herself around me.

Was this what it was going to be like with Piper? Falling asleep naked and content?

I slipped in around her, spooning her, as she'd called it. Spooning naked was so much better than spooning with clothes on. I felt Pip sigh and relax as I held her close to me, nuzzling into her neck.

"Is this what it is going to be like with us?" I asked.

"If you want it to be," she replied sleepily.

I drifted off, thinking it was all I had ever wanted.

CHAPTER 19

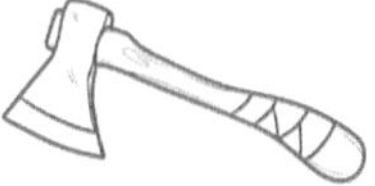

AGNARR

I woke to light streaming through the cabin windows. The mist was still heavy, but the sun had risen. Thankfully, Piper slept on as I slipped out of bed to rebuild the fire. I was well rested and alert, ready for the day's expedition to the Snaerfírar. I pulled on my leggings, regretful that Piper wore the extra tunic I'd packed. She snored softly, blissfully unaware of the preparations I was making. I repacked our packs before beginning a morning meal.

A quick look through the cupboards revealed grain and dried fruit that could be used to make grautr, which would sustain us for the rest of the morning. I slowly heated water to soften the grains and the fruit as Piper slept. It took all my willpower not to climb back into bed with her. Something had shifted during our uncomfortable bucket bathing. We'd both bared a private part of ourselves. It was no longer her soft skin and vahlnot hair that pulled me to her; I wanted to be the solid ground on which she landed, a place to lay her foundation.

I turned back to the grautr, pleased to see it thickened nicely. I searched the cupboards for cinnamon, cloves, and sugar, pleased to find each readily available. I would have to tell Astrid how helpful this cabin had been and ensure we kept it well stocked. As I added the cinnamon, it perfumed the air, and Piper stirred.

"Whass for breafast?" she mumbled in her sleep.

"Grautr with dried fruit," I responded, unsure if she'd hear me.

"Mmm…Odin loves grautr," she said before settling back into bed and snoring.

I quietly made tea, trying not to wake Pip. She'd had a hard enough time as it was. I didn't care if we left for Snaer-fírar at dawn or midday—she needed her rest. As I continued to stir the grautr, the smell of cinnamon and cloves grew stronger throughout the cabin. Piper sat up from our shared bed, looking disheveled and oh so inviting.

"Are you making breakfast?" she asked.

"I am. Are you hungry?"

"Starving."

She crawled out of bed and walked toward me before enveloping me in a warm hug. She kissed my rib cage, causing my cock to jump, but this seemed to be a good morning greeting for her.

"Thank you for making breakfast," she murmured into my skin before pulling away.

"Of course," I choked out, ignoring my growing erection.

She wandered toward the bathroom while I continued to stir the grautr and monitor the kettle.

I tried to focus on breakfast while she used the bathroom, adding more dried fruit from the cupboard. It smelled deli-cious, so I hoped it would be to Piper's liking. She returned from the restroom and crept up behind me, wrapping her small frame against mine. I relished the feeling of her warmth leaning into me.

"Are you ready for breakfast?" I breathed, trying to contain myself.

"Can I sit on your lap for breakfast?" she asked.

This female was going to kill me. "Of course," I choked out.

I placed two bowls of grautr and two cups of tea on the low table in front of the fire before taking a seat. Piper walked over to me and curled herself into my lap before pressing her lips to my temple.

"Thank you," she said before picking up one of the bowls.

Using the spoon I had laid for her, she took a large mouthful and moaned into it.

"This is way better than the grautr that Tora served me my first morning. What did you do differently?" she asked.

"It's cinnamon. They never add enough," I responded, grabbing my own bowl and spoon. I navigated around Piper so I could eat my breakfast while she enjoyed hers. Selfishly, I never wanted anyone else to provide for her.

"Is this what orcs eat every morning?" she asked.

"Mostly. Sometimes we have eggs, but grautr is the staple," I said.

"I like it. It's comforting. Like oatmeal," she said. I wasn't quite sure what oatmeal was, but her pleasure with our morning meal was enough for me.

I continued eating, watching to ensure Piper had gotten her fill. I was still getting used to what a human could digest in one sitting. She placed her bowl back on the table when it was two-thirds empty and leaned her head against my bare chest, sighing.

"Are you full?" I queried, just to be sure.

"Yes, very full. Ready to head to Snaerfírar," she responded as she stroked my thigh, leaning into my chest.

The sun was barely rising, as far as I could tell through the mist. We would easily make it to before sunset.

I washed up the dishes and placed them back in the cupboard before attending to my own belongings. I grabbed my leggings from the night before and put them on, pulling on my boots before looking to Piper for my shirt. She lifted her arms and pulled my tunic off, revealing her glorious chest. I groaned but tried to keep myself in check as I put my tunic on and fasted my belt. Piper grabbed her tunic from the previous evening and pulled it over her breasts. I mourned the lack of accessibility but reminded myself that Piper was committed to me whether or not her chest was on display. I hesitated to meet the Snaerfírar tribe, but Piper was mine, so I tried to quiet the anxiety rising in me. What did it matter if another male expressed interest? Piper was mine and mine alone.

Once we were both fully dressed, I used the excess water from our bathing to extinguish the fire, leaving the cabin as we found it. Piper had even made the bed and placed the pillows atop the blankets.

"Are you ready?" I asked.

"Yes, very ready," she responded, taking my hand in hers.

I led her outside to Sindri, who was chuffing impatiently. I laid some grain from my pack down for her as I readied Piper for the ride.

"The trail to the Snaerfírar is narrow and sometimes treacherous, but Sindri knows the way, okay?" I said, lifting Piper and placing her on Sindri's saddle.

"I'll be okay as long as you're with me." She shifted in the saddle to get comfortable.

I swung myself up behind her. "Don't worry, Sindri won't go anywhere other than where I direct her. I promise." Sindri had been my hestr since I came of age, and I did not doubt her willingness to trust me. I grabbed the reins and gave Sindri the lightest of taps, causing her to move forward in the snow.

Sindri led us out of the forest and to the mountain's base. The trees started to grow sparse as we ascended, but Sindri continued to climb. Looking out, the valley was shrouded in mist as far as the eye could see. As we climbed, we started traveling on a series of narrow switchbacks, leading us higher and higher up the mountain. The wind was picking up, and it was desperately cold. I was grateful that my large frame shielded Piper from most of it. We traveled in easy silence all morning. As the sun reached its peak in the sky, I pulled Sindri up to a stop. There was a flat rock jutting out from the side of the mountain; it was a good place to stop for a midday meal.

I swung myself off Sindri, then lifted Piper off. "Are you hungry?"

"Yes. I guess it is about lunchtime."

I assumed lunchtime meant the midday meal.

I found the supplies I had packed for our meal. We had dried meat, the rest of the loaf of bread from the night before, and two pieces of fruit I had packed before leaving the tribe. I removed my cloak and laid it down for us to sit on.

"Agnarr, you don't need to do that. It's freezing," Piper said, shivering even in her borrowed cloak.

"I run warmer than you. And I am not having you eat sitting on a cold rock."

She huffed, but sat down. I handed her some of the dried meat.

She took a bite and chewed thoughtfully. "Hmm, it's like spicy beef jerky."

"Is that a good thing?"

She laughed. "Yes, it's a good thing."

I sat down with her and laid out the rest of the food before grabbing myself some dried meat and bread.

Piper picked up the fruit, inspecting it. "What is this?"

"It's an epli," I said. "It is a bit late in the season for fruit, but epli are the last to harvest."

She took a bite and chewed, looking thoughtful. "It's like a combination of an apple and a pear."

"Do you like apples and pears?"

"Yes, I do." She continued munching on the epli. "How far are we from Snaerfírar?"

"We should be there by late afternoon if we can keep up this pace."

Instead of looking comforted, she looked concerned. "Is there a certain way I should act?"

"I know your nose isn't as sensitive as an orc's, but you smell of me. That should ward off any unwanted advances," I said.

She smacked my shoulder playfully. "I'm not worried about whether or not I am spoken for. I am worried about whether or not they'll attack us."

"They won't attack us unless we give them a reason to. We clearly aren't coming to start a war, it is just the two of us. If we intended to bring violence to Snaerfírar, we would have brought several more guards."

"True," she said, looking thoughtful.

We finished up our meal and cleaned up the remaining food. I placed what was left of the bread and dried meat back in my pack while Piper shook out my cloak. She handed it back to me, looking around.

"Are you okay?" I asked.

"I need to pee," she said, blushing.

"Pip, that's nothing to be embarrassed by. We've been

riding all morning," I said, looking around. There was an outcropping of rocks ahead that would provide her privacy.

"If you go behind those rocks ahead, I will take care of my own business further down the path," I said.

Piper headed toward the rocks while I traveled down the path a few paces, so I was out of eyesight. I took care of my own business. As I was lacing up my pants, I heard a shrill scream come from Piper. My heart dropped to my stomach as I turned and ran to her.

PIPER

I walked around the outcropping of rocks to find a little ledge to use. I had never been good at peeing in the wilderness; I always ended up peeing on my shoes. I was finishing my business when something white and feathered flew directly at me, painfully latching talons into my hair. I let out a high-pitched shriek as I tried to figure out what the fuck was happening. I couldn't see the creature because it was literally on my head, but it seemed to be a bird of some sort. I fell backward, landing hard on my ass on the rocky terrain, pants still around my ankles. I winced as I felt the rocks cut into my flesh.

I tried to pull whatever it was out of my hair, but it continued to root around, claws holding my hair. Whatever it wanted from me, it wasn't letting go. As I started to panic, Agnarr rounded the corner.

"What the fuck is this thing? And why does it want my hair?!" I gasped.

Agnarr rushed to me and yanked whatever it was out of my hair, taking several of my hairs with it. Without hesitation, he threw it directly off the side of the mountain before turning to me. "It was just an örn. It probably wanted your hair for its nest."

"An örn? What the fuck is an örn?"

"It's a type of bird. They are common this high up in the mountains."

"So it wasn't trying to eat me?"

At this, Agnarr started to laugh, a full belly laugh, mouth open, tusks on display. I would have been annoyed if I weren't so distracted by how handsome he looked when he was happy.

"What is so funny? I thought it was going to kill me!"

"From how you shrieked, I thought you were being attacked by a björn," he said, still laughing.

"Okay, I don't know what a björn is, but I was definitely afraid for my life. Thank you very much," I said, crossing my arms and scowling at him.

He continued to laugh, wiping his eyes, and after a while, I couldn't help but laugh with him. I wasn't injured and had clearly scared him; it felt good to enjoy some humor in relief. After he composed himself, he pulled me into a quick embrace and smoothed down my tangled hair.

"A björn is a furred beast with teeth and claws that could rip you to shreds," he said.

"Ah. Nope, no björn here. Just a scary ass bird."

Agnarr offered me his hand, and I stood, suddenly painfully aware that my pants were still around my ankles. I attempted to pull them up hastily, but Agnarr stopped me. He turned me around and bent so he was eye level with my backside.

"Um, what are you doing?" I demanded.

"I'm checking you for injuries. You have scrapes all over your lovely bottom," he said.

I dragged my hand across my face. I had a handsome orc checking my ass for cuts. I didn't know if it was possible to be more embarrassed. "It's fine, honestly. Let me just pull my leggings back on."

"No," Agnarr said firmly, "I packed some of Emla's healing salve. We should put some on first."

Agnarr strode back to Sindri and started rummaging through his pack. He returned with a small pot of white cream.

"Let me apply this to your cuts," he said.

I could feel my face burning as I bent over a rock, and Agnarr applied salve to my cuts. It felt cool and tingly as he swiped it across each cut and scrape. He meticulously checked every cut, even lifting and parting my ass cheeks to ensure he'd caught everything.

"Agnarr, I'm fine, I promise," I said, exasperated.

"As long as you are mine, I will take care of every injury, no matter how small," he responded seriously. "When I heard you scream, I feared the worst. If something happened to you, I wouldn't be able to forgive myself."

I yanked up my pants and turned to him. He still held the salve in his hands. I grabbed him by the shoulders and pulled him into a kiss.

"I know you want to protect me in all ways, but I am okay, I promise. I've never had an alien bird attack my hair, so screaming was a reasonable response. I am fine."

Agnarr ran his hand through my thoroughly disheveled hair. "Are you sure?"

"I'm sure. At first, I thought I was being attacked by a pterodactyl, which would have been much scarier, but I can handle a bird looking for materials for its nest."

Agnarr looked confused. "What is a pterodactyl?"

"It's—you know what—it's too hard to explain. We've both had a scare, but I'm fine. Let's get going."

Agnarr, seemingly satisfied that my injuries were minor, scooped me up and walked me back to Sindri.

"Um, hey, I can walk, you know!" I exclaimed.

"I know, but I prefer this much more," he purred as he kissed my temple.

He placed me on Sindri before seating himself behind me.

"Are you ready?" he asked.

Ignoring that my ass was tingly from the salve, I responded, "Yes, let's get to Snaerfírar."

Agnarr gently slapped the reins, and Sindri started at a trot. I leaned into him, grateful to be back in his arms. As we climbed higher and higher up the mountain, it got colder. We continued in silence for a length of time before I finally mustered up the courage to ask Agnarr something.

"Agnarr, what if your mating marks appear for one of their females?"

I knew being someone's mate was too much right now, but I definitely didn't want Agnarr to mate with anyone else. I'd let my walls down with him. Seeing him happy with another female would crush me.

Agnarr was silent for a long time—so long that I started to freak out internally. Maybe he would mate with someone else if they were his elska mate.

Finally, he spoke. "I don't know how elska mates work with humans, but I know I have never felt this way about anyone else. You are my mate, marks or not," he said.

The finality in his voice comforted me. He wasn't going to bail on me for an orc chick. I breathed a sigh of relief. Reflecting on the last few days together, I wondered if I could believe in fated mates. For one, Agnarr had mentioned how elska mates were in tune with each other's scent. I'd never been as attracted to a man's scent as I was to Agnarr's. For two, my desire for him was insatiable. I was a sexual person, sure, but I had never experienced the type of lust I had for Agnarr. We'd been with each other for three days and had sex more times than I'd had in the prior three months. I was also weirdly calmer when he was near, as if he was the orc equivalent of a security blanket. I might have to drop my disbelief and acknowledge that mates *did* exist here. It seemed a whole lot easier than Tinder.

We continued to ride, the calm silence enveloping me as we climbed the mountain. The sun continued to arc over us as we journeyed higher and higher.

The sun was close to the horizon when Agnarr said, "We're nearly there."

I started to get nervous again. What if they refused to let us in? What if they refused to share their supply of baldrian? What if they attacked me for being human? I gripped Agnarr's thigh tightly. We reached the crest of the mountain and started to descend. From where we were, I could see a small settlement nestled in between the mountains. Rather than the houses being made of wood, as they were at Fýrifírar, they were made of stone. We continued down and down. As we approached the tribe, the path widened and became more distinct. As we passed a set of rough stone pillars, and I could hear the change in Sindri's steps as the path shifted from packed dirt and rock to smooth cobblestone.

"We should dismount and lead Sindri now that we are approaching," Agnarr said, swinging himself off the hestr.

He turned and lifted me off. I smoothed my hair and clothing. I looked travel-worn, but at least I was relatively clean. We continued to approach the village center, and I noticed that there weren't any orcs milling about.

"Where do you think everyone is?" I whispered.

"Given the time of day, I'd guess they are all sharing their evening meal. Most orkin eat communally."

In the center of the village, there was a long, low stone building.

Agnarr tied Sindri to a post before grabbing my hand. "Are you ready?"

"Nope. But we need to do it anyway," I said weakly.

He took a step forward and pushed open the large double doors. We stepped in together, hand in hand. I scanned the room. The first thing I noticed was that the Snaerfírar tribe was much smaller than Fýrifírar. From what I'd seen in the longhouse, Fýrifírar had over sixty members. Here, there seemed to be maybe forty orcs eating their evening meal. There was a raised table at the far side of the building, which must be where the jarl was sitting. Agnarr and I walked toward it.

I tried to take everything in, wishing I had more eyes. The orcs looked very similar to those in Fýrifírar. Maybe because I was human, I couldn't detect any distinguishable difference between them. As the orcs realized we were walking through the center of their dining hall, a hush fell over the large room. Pair after pair of eyeballs swiveled toward us. I felt my heart rate rise and my breath become shallow. I stumbled. Agnarr grabbed me around the waist, pulling me into him as we continued to approach the high table.

Finally, after what seemed like an eternity, we reached the jarl's table. There were several older orkin sitting there, but the male that was unmistakably the jarl sat at the center of the table, currently eating what looked to be meat pie. He looked at Agnarr and me, eyebrows raised.

"We rarely get visitors from Fýrifírar outside of our normal trading routines, let alone a visitor with a human female. What brings you to Snaerfírar?" He didn't seem harsh or upset, just surprised. I chose to take that as a good sign.

Agnarr spoke. "About five dagrs ago, a group of twelve human females were abandoned just outside our tribe. All have remained in a deep sleep. This is Piper. She was the first to wake up. Based on what we know of Snaerfírar, you have experience with human women?"

"Já, that we do. Unfortunately, we no longer have any living here. We only had one abandoned several turns ago, and she has long passed. But we may be able to help you with your questions," he responded, pressing his fingers together while resting on his elbows. "We have a personal interest in ensuring that any humans that stumble across our path are cared for."

"Oh?"

"Yes. We should probably introduce you to Steve," he said blandly. "Steve, would you join us up here?" he called.

At this, an orc with very light green skin stood and ambled up to us, clearly at ease. As he approached, I noticed that he was much shorter than the rest of the orcs I'd met. He was also leaner. When he was finally within speaking range, I noticed other subtle differences. His ears weren't pointed like other orcs, but rounded like a human's, and his tusks were much smaller.

"Hi. I'm Steve," he said, grinning at us. "I'm a half-orc."

My jaw dropped. "A what?"

"Yep. My mom was the most recent human to be abandoned here. That was about forty years ago now. She passed away a few years back, but she lived a long, happy life here."

"Holy cow," I whispered.

Agnarr looked confused, but Steve laughed. "You'll get used to the human sayings eventually. I grew up with them." He looked at Agnarr. "You must be her elska mate?"

At this, Agnarr's eyes grew wide. "That's one of the reasons we're here. Fýrifírar has never had humans abandoned near our village before. We wanted to find out if it was even possible for orcs and humans to be elska mates."

It was Steve's turn to look confused. "My dude, have you

looked at your back lately? Your marks are popping out of the neck of your tunic."

Steve turned to me. "Mom was from San Diego. I grew up on surfer slang," he said deprecatingly.

I laughed but was quickly distracted by Agnarr pulling his tunic over his head. Sure enough, there was an outline of what looked like planets, moons, and stars all down his spine. I whirled around so my back was to Agnarr.

"Do I have marks?" I asked, breathless.

Agnarr pulled up my tunic, only halfway so as not to expose me in front of the entire Snaerfírar tribe. I felt his warm finger stroke down my spine. "Yes," he said softly.

Holy shit. Agnarr was my elska mate. I had an elska mate. I felt my heart rate spike and my breathing go shallow. Black circles closed in around my vision. I was going down.

AGNARR

As I told Piper she had marks, too, I felt her pitch forward. I grabbed her just in time, finding her limp in my arms. Steve looked unfazed.

"When my mom found out she was my dad's elska mate, she threw up, so fainting seems pretty standard," he mused. "Humans don't have fated mates. It is a lot for them to take in at first."

"As comforting as that is, Steve, can we get her to your healer?" I asked, trying to keep the panic out of my voice. I knew Piper had fainted before, but I still couldn't handle how she lay lifeless in my arms.

"For sure. They aren't far," Steve responded, heading to the exit.

I followed him without a backward glance at the rest of the tribe. The sun had set while we were inside, and it was much colder. I wrapped my cloak around Piper and me, following Steve along a cobblestone path. Mere moments passed before Steve veered off to approach a low stone building. Light came from the windows, which I took as a good sign. Steve walked up to the wooden door and opened it for me, ushering us inside.

The room we entered was very similar to Emla's. There was a workbench along the back wall with various healing aids and equipment. On one side, there were multiple padded cots, and on the other, chairs. I laid Piper in the closest cot as an older female orc came in from an adjoining room.

"A human female found out that this guy was her elska mate. Fainted on the spot," Steve said with a grin.

"It isn't just that she found out she had an elska mate," I said, outraged. "She has anxiety! One of the reasons we are here is we don't have any supply of baldrian at Fýrifírar."

"Okay, okay," the elderly female said, attempting to placate me. "We will get her taken care of in no time. We have plenty of baldrian on hand."

She turned to her workbench and started a kettle while rummaging through her supplies. She pulled out two different earthenware pots and showed them to me.

She held up the first. "This contains aromatic herbs that will rouse her," she said before holding up the second. "This has baldrian root that will calm her nerves. I will make the baldrian tea before waking her so I can give it to her as soon as she wakes. Does that work for you?" she asked.

I felt instantly relieved. They had the herbs we'd traveled all this way for, and they were willing to share them.

"Já, já. That works wonderfully. What's your name?" I asked, still looking down at Piper.

"I'm Revna. I am the healer for Snaerfírar. Your mate is in good hands," she said, turning to attend to the kettle and the tea.

"Thank you."

Out of the corner of my eye, I saw Steve grab two of the chairs from the other side of the room and place them next to Piper's bed. He took a seat and then turned to me expectantly. I hesitated, then sat down next to him.

"Are you sure you want to stay with me?" I asked.

"Of course. While Revna patches up Piper, I can tell you a little bit more about human females being raised by one."

"Oh, I hadn't thought of that. Is there anything in particular I should know?"

"Well, for one, there are no fated mates on Earth. I'm sure that Piper has told you about that already, but it really freaked my mom out initially. If a couple doesn't work out on Earth, they just split up."

"Yes, she expressed a lot of concern about being with someone for life without having a say in it. She hasn't even agreed to be my mate. She said she would take it 'one step at a time,' whatever that means," I said mournfully.

"Yeah, Mom said she went through that too. They take a lot longer to settle on a partner on Earth. She said that she'd dated around a lot before she was abducted and that she didn't even want to get married, as they call it on Earth."

"Hmm," I said as I thought about his words.

I'd never even considered whether or not Piper had planned to take a mate. "Did it help your mom when she discovered she could reject the elska bond?" I asked.

"Yeah, it made her feel much more comfortable with the whole thing. She still ended up choosing my dad, but to her, having a choice was really important."

I would have to tell Piper that she could reject the bond when she awoke. That was something I had neglected to mention.

"Is there anything else I should know right away?" I asked Steve, grateful for his expertise.

"Some human women don't want children. My mom didn't at first, but after being with my dad for several years, she decided she did."

"Ah, yes. Piper and I have already talked about that. As much as I would love to have orklings with her, if it isn't something she wants, I will be happy to be with her for the rest of my days," I said solemnly.

"Well, if you've already talked about those things, you are off to a good start. My mom always valued open communication. She constantly told me, 'we don't keep secrets in this family.' She and my dad talked about everything."

I rolled that around in my head. Piper and I had already had important conversations. That made me feel better. I heard the kettle whistle and looked toward Revna.

"The tea needs to steep for a couple of minutes, then we can wake her," she said calmly, attending to the supplies on her workbench.

CHAPTER 20

AGNARR

$\mathcal{I}$ looked back at Piper. She looked so pale and fragile in the cot made for an orc. I grasped her hand in mine. We settled into silence as Revna finished up her work. She brought over the aromatic herbs in a small dish and held them up to Piper's nose. I saw Piper's nose twitch as she took in the strong scent before she reached her hand up to push it away, her eyes fluttering open.

She propped herself on her elbows, taking in the healer's quarters before looking at me. She looked almost fearful.

"Agnarr, I didn't pass out because I don't want to be your mate, I swear. I was just overwhelmed that it had happened. It isn't that I don't want to be with you," she said, voice full of concern.

I reached down and stroked her cheek. "Pip, I was never worried. I know it is a lot to take in," I said gently.

Piper looked relieved and continued to assess the space. "Where are we?" she asked, looking around Revna's cottage.

"We took you to the healer when you passed out. This is Revna," I said, nodding toward her. She held a cup of tea in her hands.

"Your mate tells me you require some baldrian," she said, handing the cup to Piper. "It takes a few minutes for you to feel the effects, but it should last for a good while."

Piper sat up properly to take the cup of tea, swinging her legs over the side of the cot. She blew on it before taking a hesitant sip. "It tastes kind of like licorice," she declared.

"Is that a good thing?"

"If it is something I am going to need to drink daily, there are worse things it could taste like," she said, grinning at me.

I leaned in and placed a gentle kiss on her forehead. "Are you sure you are okay?"

"Definitely," she said, taking another sip of the tea. She turned to Revna. "Is there a mirror in here?"

Revna looked startled at the question but replied, "Já, there is a full-length mirror in the washroom." She indicated a door in the corner.

Piper got up, tea in hand, and walked to the washroom. Wondering what her intentions were, I followed. She entered and then looked at me.

"You can come with," she said.

I walked in before she closed the door behind us. She set her tea down on the sink before removing her tunic. She looked in the mirror, then turned completely so her back was to it while attempting to look over her shoulder. It appeared as if her markings matched mine completely but were smaller, given her smaller build. She looked at me expectantly. "Well, come on, let's see yours," she said.

I pulled off my tunic to reveal my markings. Piper leaned closer to inspect them, drawing a finger down some of the patterns. "Why are they only outlines?" she asked quietly.

"While you were asleep, Steve told me there are a few

more things I should tell you about elska mates that might make you feel more comfortable."

She walked around to face me. "Such as?"

"Well, the markings only fill in when the bond is accepted. You can choose not to accept the bond, and the outlines will fade over time. Steve said that, for humans, choice is really important. I didn't even think to tell you that you could reject the bond because I don't know anyone in our history who has. Then again, I don't know other humans."

Piper's eyes went wide. "What happens if you reject the bond? Is there a possibility of another elska mate?"

"Eventually, the marks fade, but you only have one elska mate. So you can take another mate, but they won't be your fated mate, as you call it," I explained.

"Hmm..." Piper thrummed her fingers against her lips. "If we choose to accept the mate, how do we go about that?"

"A mated pair takes the journey to the hot springs near the cabin and spends the night at the springs. They bathe together and spend the night together. In the morning, the female braids the male's hair so that when they return to the tribe, all will know the mating bond has been accepted. The tribe will have readied one of the empty family cabins as a homecoming. This shows the tribe officially accepts the newly mated pair."

Piper looked thoughtful for a moment before speaking. "What do you think made the marks appear?"

"That's something I was wondering, and as odd as it sounds, I think it might be when the örd attacked you."

"Me being attacked by a bird caused our marks to appear?" She looked skeptical.

"If you think about it, for a moment, both of us thought your life was in danger," I said, trying to suppress a chuckle.

Piper's eyes widened. Then she clapped her hand over her

mouth, but not before a delicate snort escaped her. She erupted in giggles, her whole body shaking. I joined in with her until we were both belly laughing in the tiny washroom of the healer's cottage. We laughed until tears streamed down our eyes. It felt good to let go of some of the stress and anxiety that had built up over the past few days.

Piper finally took a deep breath and pulled me into a tight embrace. "You don't know what it means to me to have a choice in this," she said before nestling her face into my chest.

"I don't think I fully understood in the beginning, but I am starting to now," I said, stroking her hair. "With your contrary nature, I can see that being forced into any relationship would make you want to run in the opposite direction."

Piper looked up at me, face in a mock scowl. "I do not have a contrary nature!"

"Oh, really?" I raised my eyebrows.

She just laughed and nuzzled into my chest again. We held each other tight for a moment before a knock came at the door. "Um, not to interrupt," Steve said, "but Revna says no mating in her washroom."

Both Piper and I laughed again before I pulled the door open. Steve gave me a quizzical look before I said, "We were just looking at each other's marks."

"Ah," he said, letting the matter drop.

I escorted Piper back to the cot and she took another sip of tea. After a few minutes, Revna approached us.

"I've packed up enough baldrian to last six mánuthurs for someone with moderate anxiety," she said, handing me a large parcel wrapped tightly with string. "If more of your humans wake up with anxiety, you'll need to return sooner."

I took the parcel, stunned. "You are going to give us this at no cost?" I asked, skeptical.

Revna sighed. "I would, but you'll have to go through Jarl

Skarde. He has a soft spot for Steve, so maybe you can get him to help you out," she said, nodding in Steve's direction.

As if summoned by the mention of him, Jarl Skarde entered the cottage.

Revna gave him a searching look before they nodded to each other. Revna turned back to her workstation. I looked at Skarde. He looked serious, but not angry.

"As you know, I can't hand over our entire stock of baldrian without some sort of trade, especially considering the strained relationship our tribes have had in the past," he said.

I nodded but did not speak. I wanted him to make the first offer.

"Knowing that you have had several human women abandoned at your tribe, I would like to send some of our eligible males back with you to see if they can find their elska mates."

Piper made an indignant noise, and I shook my head vehemently.

"There's no way. They weren't even awake when we left. They are going to need time to get accustomed to our planet and our tribe before we introduce them to another set of males looking for mates. We don't even know if they will want mates. Piper hasn't even accepted our bond," I said.

Skarde swiveled his eyes to Piper, looking shocked. She didn't hold back.

"On our planet, there are no fated mates. People enter a relationship out of choice, not out of some fate that I don't even understand," she said flatly, eyes steely.

Her claws were out, and she was ready for a fight. "None of the women who have had their lives turned upside-down are going to be handed off to be brides."

"Well then, Piper," Skarde's voice was deceptively calm, "what would you suggest is a fair trade for the baldrian you desperately need?" He sneered.

"I'm not trading their freedom for my comfort," Piper retorted, standing and crossing her arms. "All the women that were left here will have a say in choosing a mate, if they choose one at all."

Skarde crossed his arms as well. "What are your terms?"

Piper's voice was clear and firm. "First, you may not send any of your males until after the snows, giving our women some time to acclimate to their new home. Second, when your males do arrive, they are not to pressure any of the women into any relationship, regardless of markings. The women must know that they can reject any offer of mate-hood, elska or not."

Skarde looked murderous, but nodded. "Fine, I agree to your terms. You and your mate may stay the night in one of our unused cottages. I will have a meal delivered to you. Steve, show them to the cottage at the end of the path when they are ready." With that, Skarde left in a huff, leaving us sitting in silence.

Finally, Revna cleared her throat. "He's not as terrible as he seems. Our numbers are dwindling, and we need more females. He is in a desperate position," she said apologetically.

"That doesn't excuse him for withholding medication that would help my mate's mental health," I said harshly. "She's been here a mere handful of dagrs and has already experienced enough trauma to last her a lifetime."

Revna nodded glumly. "I understand, but I wanted you to know it is out of the needs of our tribe, not spite or anger, that his demeanor comes."

"I understand, but I have to put Piper first," I said before turning to Steve. "Can you lead us to where we can rest for the night?" I asked.

"For sure," he said, completely unfazed by the seriousness of the situation.

He picked up my pack and headed to the door. I helped Piper stand, and we walked out into the night air.

PIPER

I was emotionally spent. Standing up to Skarde had taken all of my energy. There was no way I was leaving without the baldrian, but I was unwilling to trade away my fellow humans' freedom. Agnarr wrapped his arm around my waist, sheltering me from the cold as we followed Steve along the cobblestone path. Steve was a conundrum. It was like I was talking to someone from home who had insider information about life here.

We walked for a few moments before we approached a small stone cottage with darkened windows.

"You'll have to light the fire, but all the basic supplies should be there. I will send someone over from the kitchen with food and I will have your hestr taken to our stables," Steve said.

"Thank you so much. We really appreciate your generosity," I said sincerely.

"No worries, it's nice to see another human. I haven't seen a human since we lost my mom. I wasn't sure if I ever would again," he said sadly.

Steve turned and headed back down the path before I had a chance to respond.

Agnarr pulled me in close. "Well, should we go inside?"

I nodded and headed up the steps.It was too dark inside for me to make much out, but with Agnarr's superior eyesight, he was able to find his way to the fireplace. I could only see his form squatting down and working with something, then there was the noise of metal on metal and a flash of light. A small fire started almost immediately. I saw that the fireplace had been filled with logs and tinder, ready for any unexpected guest. It made me think a tiny bit better of Skarde, but only a tiny bit.

Agnarr continued to feed tinder to the fire and it grew, enveloping the whole room in a soft orange glow. I looked around. We were in a small living space with a kitchen on one wall and a fireplace on another. There were two doors on the far wall, which I guessed would lead to a bedroom and a washroom. As the fire continued to grow, the room got warmer.

I headed to one door and opened it, finding a small but well-equipped bedroom. There was a large bed and another fireplace with a small seating area in front of it. There were hooks along one wall to hang clothing. I stepped out and peered into the other room to find a *very* well-equipped bathroom. Not only was there a toilet and sink, but there was a bathtub large enough to accommodate at least four orcs. The tub had two taps, which really could only mean one thing: hot water. I nearly jumped in glee before turning back to the living area.

Agnarr had lit some oil lamps, and there was a tray of steaming food sitting on the table in the kitchen space. It smelled delicious. I walked to the tray to find hand pies, what looked like part of a roasted chicken, and a bowl of steamed vegetables that I didn't recognize. I felt saliva pool in my mouth. I looked over at Agnarr, who was lighting the last of the lamps.

"Hungry?" I asked.

"Starving," he replied, walking to join me by the table.

He pulled a chair out for me and indicated I should take a seat. He then went to the cupboard and grabbed two plates. He started loading one up with pies and veggies. Before he could continue, I said, "Remember, I can't eat nearly as much as you think I can."

Agnarr looked somewhat perturbed but put back two

hand pies and a small pile of vegetables before handing me the plate. He proceeded to pile himself a plate with three times the amount I could eat and then took a seat. I picked up one of the pies and took a bite of it. The flavor burst in my mouth. It was full of minced meat, something similar to a potato, and a savory gravy. It was delicious. I looked up to see if Agnarr was enjoying his meal to see he was already on his third pie.

"I guess you like them?" I asked.

"These are delicious. They definitely have different herbs up here," he said, wolfing down another pie before turning to the vegetables and meat. I looked at the tray as I finished off my first hand-pie and noticed that there was an earthenware pitcher and another covered dish still sitting on it. I picked up the pitcher and poured some of the liquid into each cup, looking to see what it was. It was a light amber color. I lifted one of the cups to my nose and took a sniff. It smelled kind of like apple juice. I took a small sip and nearly choked. It was hard cider. *Really* hard cider.

I handed a cup to Agnarr.

He took a large swig. "Mm, excellent."

"What is it?" I asked before taking another small sip. It was sweet but burned a bit going down.

"It tastes like locally brewed cider. They must have a different variety of epli up here in the mountains," he said before taking another swallow.

We sat in silence, eating. I surprised myself by completely clearing my plate. I was hungrier than I'd thought. I felt loose and relaxed. I didn't know if it was the effects of the baldrian or if I was just coming down from the heightened level of anxiety I had been experiencing since I'd left for Snaerfírar. As we finished up our meal, I took the tray and plates to the kitchen area. Agnarr grabbed the pitcher and cups and headed into the sleeping area.

"What are you doing?"

"I figured we could finish the cider in bed if you'd like," he said, grinning at me.

"Actually, have you looked in the washroom?" I responded.

Agnarr's brows shot up. Instead of heading into the bedroom, he went to the washroom. I busied myself with cleaning up the dishes. I thought back on the events of the afternoon. I was definitely feeling the effects of the baldrian. My brain felt clearer than it had all day.

For how Agnarr had described relations with the other tribes, I'd expected a much more hostile reception. Things had gone much smoother than I'd dared to hope. And then there was the small fact that Agnarr and I had discovered we *were* elska mates in front of the entire Snaerfírar tribe. I wasn't sure if it was the knowledge that I had a choice in the matter or that I was ready to come to terms with being someone's mate, but I was able to think about it without getting panicky for the first time.

Mates for life. It was still a lot to take in, but it didn't scare me anymore. Just the knowledge that I could say no made me want to say yes all the more. Agnarr had proved himself to me time and again. He'd chipped away at my walls in an astonishingly short amount of time. He wanted to take care of me and demonstrated his ability to do so through his words and actions. I had shown that I was willing to accept that care. Maybe Agnarr could be the family I never thought I would have. I was so lost in thought that I shrieked and jumped when I felt warm arms wrap around my waist.

I whirled around to see a concerned Agnarr.

"Are you okay, Pip?"

"Sorry, I was just lost in thought. I didn't hear you walk up behind me," I explained before pulling him into a hug.

"I'm fine, just finished cleaning up from the meal. What did you think of the bathroom?"

Agnarr gave me a wicked grin. "That's a very nice bathtub."

"It is, isn't it? I am surprised they've given us such a comfortable place to stay given the way you've explained relations between Snaerfírar and Fýrifírar."

"That probably has a lot to do with you and the knowledge that there are other human females at Fýrifírar," Agnarr said ruefully. "You did a masterful job negotiating with Skarde."

"No matter how much I needed the baldrian, I wasn't willing to trade away the other women," I said simply.

"I know you don't think of it this way, but that was a high level of self-sacrifice for others you don't even know," he said before pulling me into a kiss.

I melted into him, taking the kiss from a gentle brush of his lips to a hungry capture of his mouth.

"Why don't you get the fire going in the bedroom while I figure out how to work the bathtub?" I asked, making my meaning clear.

"That sounds perfect," Agnarr said, eyes hungry.

I headed to the bathroom while Agnarr headed to the bedroom. There was a long cupboard across from the tub. I opened it to find a stack of towels, several bars of soap, washcloths, and what appeared to be some type of bath oil. I pulled out towels, washcloths, a bar of soap, and the bottle of bath oil and set them on the sink before turning to the tub.

The tub had two taps but no indicator of which was hot or cold. I hesitantly tried the first one and let it run for a second before putting my hand under the water. Ice cold. Plugging the tub, I turned on both taps and adjusted until the bath was hot but not too hot. Grabbing the bath oil off the counter, I poured a bit of it into the tub. It smelled heavenly.

I turned my attention to getting the soap and washcloths ready when Agnarr's voice came from behind me.

"Um, what did you do to the bath Pip?" he said, sounding amused.

I looked at the bathtub to see it was now piled high with light pink bubbles.

I laughed. "Well, that wasn't what I was expecting. I added some of what I thought was bath oil to the water, but I guess it's bubble bath."

Agnarr smirked. "Well, I hope you are ready to be covered in bubbles," he said, grabbing the hem of my tunic. "Arms up."

I lifted my arms to let him remove my tunic before kicking off my boots and pulling off my leggings. The tub was now nearly overflowing with bubbles, so I turned off the water before dipping a toe in the water. Hot but not too hot —perfect.

I climbed in and turned to find Agnarr completely naked already. "That was quick," I teased.

"Can you blame me?" he asked, climbing in behind me.

He leaned into the back of the tub and pulled me to him. I nestled myself between his thighs, laying my head on his chest and letting out a comfortable sigh. Agnarr started kneading my shoulders with his warm hands, causing me to break out in goosebumps. It felt entirely too good.

Agnarr's voice rumbled behind me. "Do you feel like the baldrian is working?"

"It's hard to tell. I feel relaxed and at ease right now, but that could be simply because we've finally reached Snaer-fírar, come to an agreement with Skarde, and I am in a warm bath with my lumbersnack," I said.

I felt Agnarr shake with laughter behind me. "Okay, fair enough," he said before beginning to plant kisses down my neck. I stroked his muscular thighs, leaning into his kisses.

"Lean back," he said, starting to scoop water up with his

hands and pour it over my hair. He started lathering up the soap and massaging it into my scalp. I groaned. In the past few days, I had gone from never having had a partner wash my hair to having Agnarr wash my hair twice. I could get used to this treatment. Agnarr washed and rinsed my hair thoroughly, massaging my scalp the entire time, leaving me a limp puddle of goo.

"Why don't you go get ready for bed while I finish up here? I can tell you are thoroughly relaxed. I am more than capable of washing my own hair," he said.

"Are you sure?" I asked.

"Definitely. Rinse yourself off and get one of the towels. The bedroom should be nice and warm by now," he said.

I stood and stepped out of the tub, grabbing one of the giant towels and wrapping myself in it.

As I went to leave the bathroom, Agnarr said, "You might want to look in the closet in the bedroom. I found some items you might find interesting."

"I'll definitely take a peek," I said, giving him a broad smile before leaving the bathroom.

I blew out all the oil lamps in the living area before heading into the bedroom. With the fire and two lamps lit on either side of the bed, the room was filled with a warm glow. I opened the closet door to find two fluffy robes and two pairs of slippers. Next to the closet was a small vanity. I opened the top drawer to find a comb and hand mirror. I took out the comb and started combing through my hair as I continued to explore. The other drawers had different oils and creams that I was hesitant to use, given my experience with the bubble bath.

I turned to the dresser next to the fireplace and opened the top drawer. Inside were cream-colored lacy things, folded neatly. I picked one up to find it was a sheer lace nightgown. This must have been what Agnarr was referring to. Holding it against me, it was almost small enough to fit me. I bet Revna and Steve were behind the accommodations in the cottage. I laid the nightgown on the bed and continued to comb out my hair. I dried myself thoroughly before hanging my towel on the hook on the back of the door. I slipped on the sheer nightgown. It was a little loose in the body, but I filled out the bust. Agnarr had said my boobs were bigger than most orc females. I tried to look at myself in the vanity mirror, but it wasn't big enough for me to see my whole body.

I heard the tub start to drain and nervously grabbed one of the robes from the closet. My lacy nightie underneath would be a surprise. I took a seat in one of the chairs by the fire and waited for Agnarr to arrive. I adjusted my robe nervously as I stared into the fire. Though we'd slept together several times now, this was the first time it felt like a special occasion. It didn't take long for Agnarr to walk in, towel slung low around his waist, hair hanging loosely. Now that I knew what it meant for his hair to be braided, I was itching to do it for him, but I loved the look of it loose and flowing free.

"Hi," I breathed.

Agnarr's face turned downcast. "I must admit, that is not what I was hoping you'd be wearing."

"Oh really? Was there something else you wanted to see me in?" I teased.

Agnarr mumbled something about the top drawer but moved to the closet to pull out the other robe. While his back was to me, I quickly removed the robe and climbed onto the bed.

AGNARR

I turned from the closet to see Piper lying on the bed, legs spread, in a completely see-through nightgown. I nearly choked on my own saliva. She was a vision.

It took all my restraint not to climb on top of her and rut her into the bed like a beast.

"Um," I said hoarsely, "ready for bed?"

"I don't know that I'm *that* tired," she said, hiking up her nightgown to give me a view of her perfect pink cunt.

I breathed in and out through my nostrils, trying to contain myself. I could smell her arousal, perfuming the air.

"Piper, remember how you said I could do *anything* I wanted after we bathed at the cabin at the edge of the wood?"

"Yes?" she said, looking at me skeptically.

"I want to lick your delicious cunt until you come screaming my name," I said, voice ragged.

Piper didn't slam her thighs shut as she had the last time, but she did look nervous.

"Every time I have done that before, the man treated it as a chore—something he had to do to get what he wanted. It made me *very* self-conscious. I haven't done it more than a few times and it was years ago. I don't want you to do this if it isn't something you want to do."

"Piper, do you like the way you see me come undone when you lick my cock?" I asked.

Piper blushed but said, "Absolutely."

"Well then, you see how with some open communication, it could go both ways? I assure you, I want to feast upon you until you shatter under me. You smell delicious."

Piper bit her lower lip and looked up at me. "I believe you —that this is something you want. I am willing to try, given you help me warm up to it a bit."

Ah, I knew what she needed. I lay on the bed with her, taking her face in my hands. I pressed a gentle but intentional kiss to her lips before kissing down her neck and using my long tongue to lick across her delicate collarbone. She grabbed my loose hair, yanking me to one of her breasts. I licked and sucked it through the thin material. Piper groaned, her breathing growing rapid as I sucked one of her nipples.

"Fuck, Agnarr, don't stop," she moaned.

I continued to suck on her nipples before gently nipping at one with my teeth. I was rewarded with a delighted gasp. I nipped along her chest before gently biting down on her other nipple, causing her to buck underneath me.

"Agnarr, I need you now," she breathed.

"I need you to take this off unless you want me to ruin it," I growled.

Piper propped herself up on her elbows, looking at me. She slowly maneuvered the nightgown over her head, never taking her eyes off me. She removed it and tossed it aside, laying bare before me.

I kissed my way from her breasts down her stomach, positioning my shoulders between her thighs and making my intentions clear. Reaching her hip, I kissed along it before kissing her from her knee to the apex of her thighs.

"Are you okay with this?" I asked, trying to keep the want out of my voice.

"As long as it is something you really want to do," she said, unable to hide the hesitancy in her voice.

"It is something I *really* want to do," I replied, unable to keep the eagerness out of my voice.

"Okay," Piper said, leaning back on her elbows.

I continued to kiss along her thighs while admiring her cunt. I wanted her to be comfortable. I kissed and nuzzled her soft skin until I felt her relax beneath me. I shifted my attention to her cunt with the thatch of brown curls covering it. Using my fingers, I spread her open so I could see her clit. I drew a breath, inhaling her delicious scent before licking her slit from top to bottom, pausing to circle my tongue around her clit. Piper shuddered beneath me and slammed her legs into my shoulders.

"Is it too much?" I breathed.

"No, no, not too much. Just more than I'm used to," she replied quickly, words almost jumbled together.

I licked her from bottom to top, again and again, using more pressure with my tongue as I circled her clit. A flood of her juices released as I continued to lick her, devouring her taste. I looked up at her to see her head thrown back in ecstasy, clearly no longer self-conscious about having my head between her knees. I flattened my tongue and dragged it across her clit slowly as I reached up and inserted two fingers into her warm channel.

She was so wet and ready for me, but I needed her to come before I flipped her over and rutted her like the beast that I was. Reaching up my hand, I slid two fingers into her core. I pumped my fingers in and out of her while I sucked her clit. She squirmed and panted at the overwhelming sensations.

"Oh fuck, Agnarr, I'm so close," she said, gripping my hair harder.

I continued to pump my fingers, adding a third to stretch her to accommodate my cock. All while still licking and sucking her clit. I could feel her thighs begin to jerk and shake. She was close. She was gripping my hair almost painfully hard.

"Fu—Agnarr, yes, don't stop," Piper keened as her muscles locked up around my shoulders.

I continued licking her clit and thrusting in and out of her with three fingers, then curled my fingers to reach the sensitive spot along her inner wall. Piper shrieked and clamped down on me as a flood of delicious release hit my face. I lapped it up without hesitation, loving her taste and smell. I continued to lick up her juices until she released my hair, legs flopping to either side of my shoulders.

"Agnarr, stop. It's too much. I need a break," she said breathlessly.

I lifted my face from her cunt and licked my lips, giving her a feral smile. I climbed up her body before letting my weight settle atop her, nuzzling her neck.

"How was that?" I asked.

"Well, that was the first time I've come from someone… licking me, so I would call it a success," she breathed, still coming down from the high.

"It would be a privilege to make you come like that every single day," I said, grinning.

"That might take me a while to get used to, but I am definitely open to it," she said, returning my grin.

I kissed and sucked on her neck before returning to her lips, giving her an open-mouthed kiss where our tongues could slide across each other.

"You taste of me. It feels dirty. And delicious," she said before capturing me in another kiss.

I settled myself between her hips as I continued to kiss her. Piper groaned at the feeling of my hard cock against her. She reached down and spread her lips for me, encouraging me.

"Are you sure?" I breathed.

"Agnarr, I have never been so wet and ready," she said, reaching down to grab my cock and notch it at her entrance.

I slid into her slowly. I knew she was ready, but my cock was much larger than my fingers and I didn't want to hurt her. As I continued to push into her, she gripped me like a glove. My eyes rolled back into my head at the sensation as I slowly slid into her. Piper panted through it, encouraging me.

"I can take you, don't hold back," she said breathlessly.

I continued to thrust slowly, knowing she had to stretch to accommodate my knot. I felt her breathing hitch and stopped.

"No, keep going," she breathed. "I want to take all of you."

Hesitantly, I pushed further until my knot was fully inside her. I felt her flutter at the invasion and saw her take deep breaths.

"Are you good?" I asked skeptically.

"So good," she breathed, clearly enjoying the girth of my knot.

I thrust into her, unable to contain myself any longer. She gripped my shoulders and curled around me before whispering, "more" in my ear.

I didn't know what I'd done to deserve Piper, but I was going to give her everything I had. Hesitantly, I gave her a shallow thrust. She groaned, her eyes closing. I took this as all the permission I needed. I let myself loose. I thrust into her wet heat repeatedly, pistoning my hips. She gripped me tightly with every thrust. She lifted her hips to meet every thrust, as insatiable as I was.

"Let's flip," Piper gasped mid-thrust.

Before I could even register what she meant, she'd rolled me onto my back with her on top. I grabbed her hips, lifting her up so only my tip was inside before slamming her back down. Piper groaned and dug her nails into my chest as I continued to lift her up and down off my cock. She slammed into me, taking me close to the brink. With each slam of her hips, stars burst into my vision. I wouldn't be able to hold off much longer. I slipped a finger down and circled her clit. I wanted her to come again before I did. Using one hand to circle her clit, I used the other to coax both her nipples into stiff peaks.

She shuddered above me, clenching her thighs around me. I circled her clit slowly before pressing down on the small nub of flesh. She climaxed above me, her legs jerking before going completely limp. She fell forward, wrapping her arms around me as I continued to thrust up into her. I bucked into her several more times before I came, shooting jets of cum into her with each thrust. Stars appeared before my eyes with my release. I felt as if I would pass out from the pleasure.

Piper lay limp on top of me, her breathing ragged, as I slowly came back down. I never wanted to have sex with anyone else. I closed my eyes and hoped that Piper felt the same. She stroked up and down my arms.

"That was—" she started.

"Incredible?" I finished.

"Well, I was going to say earth-shattering, but I guess that doesn't really apply here," she said, giving a soft laugh.

She grabbed my face in her hands and pressed a gentle kiss to my lips. "Agnarr, I want you to know, sex with you has been the best sex I have ever had, no question. I had always been afraid to let a man use his tongue on me because of negative experiences I've had, but that was...mind-blowing."

I kissed her back fervently. "I would lick your cunt until you screamed my name every day if you let me. There's no place I'd rather be than in between your knees," I said earnestly.

At this, Piper's cheeks grew even pinker, and she pulled me into an embrace while we were still locked together.

"I love you," she whispered so quietly I barely heard it.

"I love you too," I said, stroking her back up and down.

We lay like that for a long while while our breathing evened out. Finally, Piper said, "I think we should clean up."

She slipped off me and hobbled to the restroom to take care of herself, trying to keep her knees together so my cum wouldn't drip down her legs. I grinned to myself, knowing that I had seeded her well. I knew she was on human birth control, but that didn't stop the satisfaction I felt at the thought of my cum dripping down her thighs. I heard the water running and then the toilet flush as she took care of her needs. She returned moments later, naked but no longer pressing her knees together.

"You're welcome to go clean up if you would like. There are clean washcloths and warm water."

Looking down and seeing I was a mess of fluids as well, I stood and headed to the washroom. There was a damp washcloth on the counter. I ran the hot tap and got more water to rinse myself off. Using the bar of soap, I cleaned myself thoroughly. I assumed we were done for the night, but you never knew with Piper. Once clean, I used one of the towels to dry myself before heading back to the bedroom.

I found Piper curled under the blankets, looking serene and satisfied.

"Hi," was all she said.

"Hi. I know there were nice pajamas set aside for you, but is there anything for me to wear to bed?" I asked.

"Open the second drawer of the dresser," she instructed.

I did as she directed, finding a drawer full of soft pajama shorts in varying colors. I picked the top pair, a shade of light gray, and slipped them on before climbing into bed with her. She was wearing a midnight blue nightgown with less lace but still soft to the touch.

"Steve and Revna really did think of everything, didn't they?" I asked.

"I think Steve was so pleased to see another human that

he pulled out all the stops," she said before pulling me into a hug. "I hope he comes with the other eligible males in the spring. I think he'll be a hot commodity. I bet many of the human females will find his understanding of Earth comforting."

"Mm," was all I said before wrapping her into a tight embrace. We settled into an easy silence, enjoying being with each other, and I let my mind wander. Piper hadn't said she was going to accept our bond, though all signs pointed in that direction. I didn't want to push her, and we were so warm and comfortable together that now was not the time to bring it up. I stroked her still-damp hair and inhaled her scent. She was mine whether or not she was ready to admit it, No orc, either at Snaerfírar or Fýrifírar would lay claim to her. She was covered in my scent, and I would defend my claim on her to the death. As I stroked her hair, I felt her breathing slow and even out until she was emitting soft snores. At the very least, Piper was comfortable around me.

I pulled her loose form to me in an embrace before letting sleep overtake me as well.

CHAPTER 21

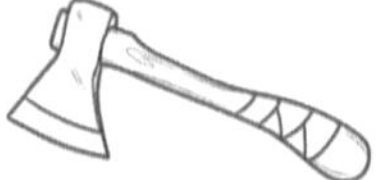

AGNARR

It was barely light outside when I woke up. We'd neglected to close the curtains the night before. Up above the mist, I could actually see the sun starting to climb. I slipped out of bed, closing the curtains quietly before heading into the living area. It was chilly, and I stoked the fire as I heard a quiet rap at the door. I was only in my sleep shorts but answered anyway. It was Steve, holding a tray of food and grinning at me.

"I know it is early, but I figured you and the missus might be hungry after last night," he said knowingly.

I thankfully accepted the full tray, and Steve headed off without comment. As I headed inside our cottage, I looked at the provisions they'd given us. There were pastries and fruit and what looked like their version of grautr. It smelled delicious. I set the tray down on the table while heating the kettle and getting the tea ready. I smelled the different earthenware pots of herbs and settled on a reviving morning brew for me and baldrian for Piper. I knew all the basics of cooking and tea making; Astrid had taught me well.

It wasn't long before Piper appeared in the doorway of the bedroom, still wearing her barely there midnight blue nightgown.

"Something smells delicious," she mumbled.

"Steve delivered breakfast. Why don't you take a seat?" I said as I finished the tea.

Piper wobbled to the table, clearly unsteady on her legs, before surveying the tray.

"This all looks amazing," she breathed before grabbing a pastry.

"Again, I think Revna and Steve are to thank for the hospitality we've received. We must stop by to thank them before we leave."

Piper nodded vigorously before taking a large bite of a flaky pastry. She moaned.

"It's like an apple fritter," she said.

"I'm guessing that is a good thing?" I asked as I finished up the tea.

"It's the best thing," she said, grinning at me and taking another large bite.

I finished the tea and poured it into two earthenware teacups before joining her at the table. I grabbed one of the pastries she was enjoying and took a bite. They were filled with seasoned epli and they were completely delicious. I demolished it in no time. Regretfully, I realized I hadn't even offered Piper the tea I had carefully brewed and handed her a cup.

She took it and held it to her nose. "You made me the baldrian? That was so thoughtful." At that, she took a sip and sighed. I was learning the ways of keeping my human fed and comfortable. It was hard to keep my pleasure contained.

"Are you ready to leave today?" I asked.

"I think we've gotten everything we came for," she said.

"So you're ready to go?" I asked hesitantly.

"I am if you are. I want to get back to the other women and help them settle into Fýrifírar," she said.

"Well, we have everything we need from Skarde, including his agreement that he won't send eligible males until after the snow. I have a feeling that if Steve is on the mission, he will be snatched up quickly," I said, laughing.

"Yes, Steve provides a comfort from home that other orcs don't have—he will be a hot commodity at Fýrifírar if he chooses to come," Piper said with a laugh.

"All right, let's head out," I said.

Piper returned to the bedroom and put on her traveling clothes, much to my chagrin. I preferred her in the lacy transparent nightgown but acknowledged it was probably not the best for travel. She had donned lined leggings, boots, and a fresh tunic before pulling on her cloak.

"Should we pack up the extra food to take with us?" she asked.

"Steve already provided us with a parcel of travel rations," I said, nodding toward the bundle at the door.

"That was so thoughtful!" she exclaimed.

"I think you remind him of his mamma. He wants to make sure you are taken care of."

"He is going to make one female very happy, my money is on it," she said, tying the bundle tighter. "What else do we need to do?"

"Skarde knows we are leaving, Revna has supplied us with plenty of baldrian, and Steve has given us provisions for the journey. I think we are safe to head out," I responded. "Is Sindri tethered outside?"

Piper stepped to the window, drawing back the thick curtains. "She is. She's tethered to a post outside and looks to be happily munching grain that Snaerfírar has provided."

"Well then, if you are packed and ready, we can start our journey home."

PIPER

I was ready to head "home," whatever that meant. I gathered the few belongings we had, including the provisions for our midday meal, and stuffed them into my pack.

"I'm ready," I breathed.

Agnarr couldn't possibly know, but I meant I was ready to journey back to Fýrifírar and start a new life as his mate. I hadn't told him yet, but I was ready to accept the elska bond. I'd let that be a surprise for when we reached the hot springs near the cabin. He ushered me out the door and lifted me atop Sindri before ensuring all the packs were tightly closed, especially the one containing the baldrian. After his inspection, he swung up behind me, his warmth providing a calm comfort.

He slapped Sindri's sides gently, causing her to start a trot out of the village. While they hadn't treated us poorly, I wasn't sorry to leave, even if we did decide to sneak out without thanking Steve or Revna. Though all of our interactions had gone smoothly, neither Agnarr or I were in a place to meet more of the tribe.

We headed down the cobblestone path and out of the Snaerfírar tribe with little fanfare. It was still early. I assumed everyone in the tribe was sleeping or getting ready to go to their great hall for breakfast. I liked that communal eating was part of life for orcs. It reminded me of college, where I got to sit with different friend groups every day. I would enjoy getting to know my new orc community during meal times.

"Will we be able to get to the cabin more quickly now that we are headed down the mountain?" I asked.

"It may be a little less effort on Sindri, but we'll have to keep the same pace. The risk of tumbling off a ledge is too great," Agnarr said gravely.

I looked over the side of the path. It was a long way down. I sighed. Not that I didn't enjoy riding Sindri while leaning into Agnarr, I just wanted to get to the hot springs and let him know my decision. I was a terrible secret keeper.

"What did you think of Skarde and the Snaerfírar?" I asked.

"I think that we could have a much better relationship with them if we didn't keep ourselves so isolated," Agnarr responded thoughtfully. "Skarde treated us well. Though he wanted something in return for the baldrian, I don't think it was an unfair deal. I would hesitate to say it might even be good for both tribes that they are sending some of their single males in the spring. Maybe it can lead to a stronger connection between the two of us."

I considered his words and realized that Agnarr was wise to look at this as an opportunity to bridge the two tribes rather than seeing it as Snaerfírar males coming to take our females.

"Agnarr, does Astrid have, like, a team of elders or something that helps her run the tribe?"

"She has a person from each varying position that provides feedback and helps in decision making. I am the representative for the guards," he said. "Emla is the representative for the healers and midwives. There are others."

"Wow. Why didn't you tell me you were on Astrid's council?"

I could feel Agnarr shrug from behind me. "It never really came up. I was too busy trying to get you to see that you were my mate and stop you from, you know, dying tragically on a mission to Snaerfírar to stop and talk tribal politics."

I let out a small laugh. "Okay, okay, that's valid. Who

becomes jarl when Astrid dies? Is she in the position for life?"

"No, no. We used to do it that way, but in recent times, leaders have stepped down and picked their replacement with the approval of the sitting council."

"Is Astrid ready to step down?" I asked.

"That she is."

"Why do I get the feeling I know who she is going to select?"

"Já," Agnarr admitted. "Astrid and I have been in talks for a long time about me transitioning to being the jarl. She's getting quite impatient, actually."

"What were you waiting for?" I asked.

"You. I was waiting for you. I didn't want to rule alone as an unmated male."

Oh, holy hell, Agnarr was going to melt my heart. He didn't want to take on his new position without someone by his side, and that someone was *me.*

"Agnarr, does that mean I will be jarl as well?" I asked anxiously.

"It does if you want it to be. Astrid and Ulf ruled together. I think of the new human females we have, and I would love for them to have a champion," Agnarr responded.

I didn't respond, instead rolling over this revelation in my head. Agnarr didn't know I had decided to accept him as my elska mate. If I agreed to be jarl—or jarlin?—with him, it would reveal my intentions, and I wanted to keep my acceptance of the bond secret until we got to the hot springs.

I traced my finger over his thigh. "Well, that is definitely a lot to think about." A good noncommittal response.

"You don't have to decide today or tomorrow—or even next vika. You have time," he reassured me.

"I appreciate it," I murmured, comfortably cradled in his arms.

It was about midday when we reached the base of the mountain. Agnarr pulled up Sindri's reins, halting her before swinging himself off her saddle. He turned and lifted me off, placing me on the ground and planting a kiss on the top of my head. He took off his cloak and spread it out on the ground before turning to one of our packs. I didn't know when I'd shifted from thinking about them as his pack and my pack, but the shift felt significant.

I took a seat on his cloak, and he joined me, hands laden with food. He arranged all the food in front of me. There were cold meat pies that looked similar to those from the night before as well as fruit, a loaf of bread, and what looked to be a pot of jam. I grabbed one of the pies instantly. They were almost as good cold as they were hot. I wondered if Fýrifírar had anything similar. I took several large bites before stopping myself. I was sure I looked like a chipmunk, mouth full of pie. I looked at Agnarr. He was completely unaware. He looked to be on his third meat pie. I laughed to myself. This was going to be our life together, me figuring out how much he needed to eat while he continued to over-feed me. It made me undeniably happy.

I finished up my first pie before grabbing a second, looking up at Agnarr.

"How far are we from the cabin?" I asked.

"A few more hours, we'll reach it mid-afternoon," he said, demolishing another pie.

I reminded myself I needed to keep an eye out for any other paths as we headed toward the cabin. I grabbed a piece of fruit as Agnarr continued to demolish meat pies at a light-ning rate. Taking a bite and munching quietly, I thought of how Agnarr would react to my want to commit fully at the hot springs. I couldn't help but grin, knowing he'd be thrilled. I packed up the food, but not before Agnarr finished yet another pie.

He shook out his cloak while I put the remaining food in the pack attached to Sindri, before I looked to him to help me up. He lifted me as if I weighed nothing, as he always did, and placed me on Sindri. Agnarr put his cloak back on before swinging up to join me on Sindri.

I would need to remain alert for the rest of the journey so I didn't miss the turnoff to the hot springs. I sat up straight, alert and ready to redirect Agnarr when ready. We were no longer beyond the treeline, so we entered the forest with a hush. All was quiet as we traveled. Eventually, I leaned into Agnarr, not wanting him to think anything was amiss. We traveled in silence for a long while. I noticed the bioluminescent mushrooms as we started along the path back to Fýrifírar. They were dull, but the sun was still high in the sky. It was a sign that we were headed home.

After a few hours,we reached a fork in the path, and I grabbed Agnarr's thigh. "Where does the path to the right go?" I asked.

"The path to the right takes you to the hot springs. The path to the left takes you to the cabin," he said.

"Let's take the path to the right." I breathed, finally letting Agnarr in on my secret. I turned to look at him.

"Are you sure?" He looked at me, both eyebrows high.

"Very sure. How long does it take to get to the hot springs?" I asked.

"A few hours at most," he responded. He was failing to keep the hope out of his voice.

"Let's head to the hot springs," I said confidently.

I felt Agnarr loosen behind me as he navigated Sindri to the path on the right.

"What does heading to the hot springs mean for you, Piper?" Agnarr asked, voice husky.

"I think you need to wait to find out," I responded, unwilling to let him off the hook just yet.

"Hmph," was all Agnarr said before leading Sindri down the path to the hot springs.

We continued to travel, though the silence felt a bit strained. I knew what was coming, but Agnarr did not. I was committed to keeping it a surprise for him, even if he was annoyed. We traveled further in silence while I tried to organize my thoughts. I was committing to Agnarr for life. Unexpectedly, I felt no anxiety or fear. I was ready.

After what felt like an eternity, Agnarr pulled Sindri up to a halt. There was nothing on the path to indicate we were near hot springs, so I was unsure of Agnarr's intentions. He swung off Sindri before lifting me off and taking my hand. We walked through a small grove of trees before reaching what looked to be a narrow cave entrance. I would have dismissed it entirely if it weren't for the bioluminescent mushrooms growing on either side of the entrance. Agnarr stooped to enter the cavern, my hand still in his. We walked along a dark tunnel before it opened out into a cavern. There were a multitude of bathing pools, steam rising from each of them.

"What do we do now?" I whispered, feeling as if I were on holy ground.

"We commit to each other," he said simply.

He stalked forward to one of the hollows on either side of the bathing pools. I followed. In it, I found a bed, a dresser with basic clothing necessities, and a small room with the orkin equivalent of a toilet.

"Are you sure this is what you want?" Agnarr asked, looking skeptical.

"One hundred percent sure," I said.

"Okay, then we need to strip and join together in one of the pools," he said.

I immediately pulled my tunic over my head and tossed it

onto the bed. I toed off my boots and removed my leggings, leaving myself completely bare to Agnarr.

He groaned as he did the same, then we were both naked. He grabbed my hand, looking at me. "Are you sure?" he asked.

"Very sure," I breathed as we headed toward the springs.

Hand-in-hand, both ready for the commitment we were about to make. As we reached the hot springs, my skin broke out in goosebumps, acknowledging what was likely to come. I stepped into the water, finding it hot but not too hot as Agnarr followed me. The pool was deep. I had to pump my legs to keep myself above water. Agnarr seemed to have no such issues.

Agnarr grabbed me around the waist. I took it as an opportunity to stick to him like a barnacle. He said nothing but held me tight as I clung to him.

"Is this what you want, Pip?" he breathed.

"You are everything I want," I responded without hesitation.

He waded deeper into the pool until he was up to his chest. I had no way to reach the bottom. He disentangled me from him so we were only holding each other's arms. He looked me in the eye seriously before saying.

"Piper, do you accept me as your mate for life, willingly and without reservation?" he asked.

I treaded water as I looked at him. Agnarr was a solid wall of beautiful muscle, but there was still some insecurity in his eyes.

"Agnarr, I accept you as my mate for life, willingly and without reservation. Do you accept me as well?" I said, attempting not to stumble over the formal language.

"I do," Agnarr said before pulling me into a tight embrace. I wrapped my legs around him, snaking my arms around his neck and pulling him into a deep kiss. A warm tingle shot up my spine as I wrapped around Agnarr. I pulled away from him, turning so he could see my back.

"Have the marks filled in?"

"Já, they have," he said, turning his back to me. "Mine as well?"

"Yes, yours as well. Does this mean we're bonded for life?" I breathed.

"It does. Are you ready for that, Pip?"

"More than ready," I said without hesitation.

At that, Agnarr grabbed a bar of soap from the edge of the spring and began lathering it in his hands. He set the bar aside and lifted his fingers to my scalp, massaging in the soap. I whimpered at his touch. Agnarr kneading my scalp was something I would never tire of. He massaged my scalp and then down the length of my hair, all while I shuddered beneath his touch. Using his hands, he cupped the water to pour over me, rinsing my hair of soap repeatedly.

It was then my turn to wash his hair, and my anxiety and excitement built. I stepped around behind him, seating myself on the ledge of the pool. I grabbed the bar of soap and lathered it in my hands before kneading my fingers into his scalp. He groaned at my touch, and I redoubled my efforts, massaging his hairline and his neck. I loved washing his hair. Though we were just at the beginning of our relationship, I wanted to ask him never to cut it. The beautiful black strands slipped through my fingers as I massaged his scalp.

Having fully lathered his hair, I rinsed it using water I'd cupped in my hands. Now was the moment of no return. I hesitated, but only for a moment. Using my fingers to divide his hair into three even parts, I started a French braid, beginning at his crown. Agnarr shuddered beneath me.

"What are you doing, Pip?" he asked.

"I'm braiding your hair," I said, voice confident as I gathered his hair in bunches.

"You know what that means in my tribe, right?" he said hesitantly.

"Oh, I am well aware. A male with braided hair is a man that is spoken for, one that has met his mate."

"So everyone will know we are mates when we return to the tribe," he said.

"Well, unless they are really dim, that is kind of the point. I don't want anyone else attempting to lay claim to you."

"Mmm," was all he said as he reached back and squeezed my bottom.

Glad to see we were on the same page. I braided his hair all the way to the tips before asking him for the strip of leather he kept on his wrist to tie it off with. I used my legs to propel myself around him and admire my handiwork.

"You look very respectable," I said.

"Respectable?" He laughed.

"Well, you said the braids were a sign of a committed male. You definitely look committed," I said in response before pulling me to him and nuzzling him into an embrace.

"Does this mean you will rule beside me as Astrid asked?"

"I will, to the best of my ability," I breathed, confident in my capacity to represent the needs of the females of Fýrifírar, human or not.

Agnarr wrapped his arms around me tightly, kissing the top of my head before leading me to the edge of the pool. He set me on the edge of the pool, mist swirling around us. Just as I wondered what his intentions were, he pushed my legs apart, making space for his broad shoulders. Having just experienced his skilled tongue, I wasn't sure if I was ready for it again, but I attempted to lie back and relax. I felt his lips and tusks kiss up each thigh, readying me for him. I was quivering with anticipation and nerves when he used his fingers to spread my lips wide, exposing myself wholly to him.

Agnarr didn't hesitate in licking me from bottom to top, swirling his tongue around my clit. I shuddered underneath him but fought the urge to clamp my legs shut. He ate me like a starving man, erasing any doubt about his willingness to continue. Agnarr reached my clit and suckled it with single-minded determination, adding his fingers into the mix. He slid two fingers inside me, slowly pumping in and out as he continued to lick my clit with unprecedented enthusiasm. I was so close to the edge that my grip on his locks had to be painful as he pumped in and out of me.

"Agnarr, I want all of you," I said breathlessly.

"You're sure, Pip? This is a commitment we can't go back from," he said.

"Very sure." I'd been sure since he'd fed me grautr the first morning at Snaerfírar.

With that, I felt Agnarr shift over me. I could feel his hard length between my thighs. I reached down, guiding him to my entrance.

As he notched himself at my core, I could see him breathing through his nostrils, his attempt at restraint.

"This is what you want?" he asked.

"More than anything," was all the response he needed before he thrust into me. My vision blacked out as he pinned me to the ground, unable to comprehend his length and girth.

He thrust into me again, tentatively, looking for confirmation in my eyes. I opened them and nodded just in time, giving him the permission he needed.

He unleashed himself, pounding into me with grunts and groans that spurred me on. Before Agnarr, I had never experienced a cock that dragged along every sensitive part of my core rather than leaving me feeling vaguely full. I was in unknown territory and experiencing ecstasy I didn't know was possible. He slipped a hand to my clit, rolling it between his thumb and forefinger. I shattered at the intensity, my muscles locking up before loosening entirely. As I loosened under him, his knot locked us together as he continued to thrust shallowly into me, causing my breathing to hitch with each one of his movements. I didn't know if I was already coming again or if it was the first orgasm still rolling through me.

Agnarr pistoned his hips up and into me, causing me to gasp for air. I still wasn't used to how his knot felt. He was so big, rubbing against my inner walls. I breathed through my nostrils, thrusting my hips up to meet his. Agnarr growled "Mine," as he shot wave after wave of cum into me. He shuddered and then dropped to his elbows above me, peppering my face with kisses.

"My Piper, my mate," he said huskily, pulling back to look at me.

I reached up and stroked his cheek. "Yours, forever," I said before pulling him in for another kiss.

Agnarr shifted us so we were side-by-side on the edge of the pool. He stroked my face and my arms, dragging a hand up and down my side.

"What's next?" I breathed.

"Well, we return to the tribe. I am sure the other human women have awoken. Astrid will be eager to start the transition to me as jarl. She's been waiting for me to take a mate for quite some time. She wants to relax with her garden and her grand-orklings," Agnarr explained.

"Will there be a ceremony?" I asked.

"Já, both you and I will be officially recognized as the new jarls of Fýrifírar, and there will be a feast in our honor."

"Oh wow, that is a lot," I mused.

Large parties weren't my strong suit. Good thing the baldrian seemed to be working almost exactly the same as Lexapro.

"It is, but my tribe knows all of this is new for you. They won't expect you to get it all right the first time," Agnarr assured me. "Plus we need a ruler that will keep the human women's best interests in mind."

I nodded as I stroked Agnarr's arm. I gave him another quick kiss before sliding back into the pool. I rinsed myself off and then looked up to Agnarr, still on the ledge. "I don't suppose you have towels here in this magical elska mate hot spring?" I said teasingly.

"That we do," he said, grinning.

He stood and walked to the alcove where we'd undressed, opening a small closet I hadn't seen before. He pulled out a set of towels and robes before heading back to me.

"Why is it that every orkin space, no matter how rustic, has all the supplies needed for bathing and fucking?" I asked.

"We like to bathe and we like to fuck," Agnarr said, shrugging.

I couldn't help but laugh. "I guess that makes sense."

Agnarr slipped into the pool with me, leaving the towels and robes on the edge of the water. After all the hestr riding and fucking I'd done in the last few days, the hot water felt amazing on my sore muscles. I rinsed my hair once more before stepping out of the pool and wrapping myself in one of the towels. Orcs were so much larger than me. I could get used to always having a giant towel to dry off with. I grabbed my robe and headed to the alcove.

I had dried myself thoroughly and was wearing my robe when I heard Agnarr approach the alcove. He grabbed me in a rough embrace from behind, kissing me from ear to collarbone.

"Hey," I said, "we both need some sleep, none of that."

"Hrmph," he grumbled.

"Agnarr, I just committed myself to you for the rest of my

life. You can fuck me every day from here on out. Sound good?" I said sweetly.

"Mm," he murmured into my shoulder, "yes, very good."

"Also, I was *very* into our middle-of-the-night sleepy sex in the cabin. If you ever want to wake me up by making your needs clear, I am consenting to that from this point forward," I said.

"Well then," Agnarr breathed, "you have my consent to wake me up in any way you see fit should you find yourself in need in the middle of the night."

"Challenge accepted." I grinned, thinking of all the ways I could drive Agnarr out of his mind.

Agnarr toweled himself off and then opened the drawers of the small dresser. There was a plain and too large nightgown for me and sleep shorts for him.

"Usually, couples come with their own supplies to the hot springs; we'll have to replace what we use," he said ruefully.

"That's fine," I said, grinning. "It will give us an excuse to come back here and spend more time together."

Agnarr handed me the nightgown while he donned some sleep shorts.

"How long will it take for us to get home tomorrow?" I asked as I crawled into bed.

Agnarr climbed in with me, wrapping himself around me to spoon.

"If we leave when the sun rises, we should be home by mid-afternoon," he said.

I didn't know when I'd started to think of Fýrifírar as home, but I was ready to get there. I wanted to be there for the other human women. I wanted to immerse myself in Fýrifírar and understand their culture. I was ready to go. Agnarr had blown out the oil lamps. It was completely dark in our little alcove. If it weren't for Agnarr's warm body around me, I would have been afraid to be in the pitch-black.

"Agnarr?"

"Já, my mate?" he said sweetly.

"You'll help me, right? You'll make sure I don't make any serious mistakes or offend the tribal leaders?" I said, voicing a concern I had been carrying with me.

"I will help you every step of the way," he said. "We can even set aside time to discuss the norms and culture of Fýrifírar on a regular basis so you don't make any missteps."

"I would like that," I said drowsily.

"I will do everything I can to make sure you succeed," he said, pressing a kiss to my temple.

I shuddered a long sigh of relief, letting go of the fear I had been holding. Agnarr was going to be an amazing jarl. He would be with me always. I pictured us ruling together, helping ensure the tribe flourished. It was the last image in my head before I drifted off to sleep, Agnarr's arms around me. I was truly unafraid of my future, ready to start a new life with him.

EPILOGUE

Three months later...

PIPER

It was barely light when I woke up. Agnarr snored peacefully, arms and legs wrapped around me in a tight embrace. Over the last few months, I had grown accustomed to waking up with him gripping me while still snoring. Gone were the days of me sleeping in my bed like a starfish. Agnarr was a snuggler which I found equally surprising and adorable. It was a big day for us, probably why I woke up so early. We were to be ushered in as the new jarl and jarlin of Fýrifírar. It was going to be full of celebration and feasting. The whole tribe had been preparing for weeks. My stomach flipped, thinking of being front and center all day. I was nervous about the spotlight on me but knew that Agnarr would be by my side.

Looking over at my handsome mate as he slept, an idea sprouted, something I'd wanted to do since we got back from

Snaerfírar. Just because it was an important day didn't mean we couldn't have a bit of fun before it officially started. I slowly shifted myself out of Agnarr's grip, trying to keep him asleep for as long as possible. I only had one thought on my mind: his magnificent green cock. Over the last few months, the "mating frenzy" as they called it, had worn off, but we both were still pretty insatiable. Scooting down the bed, nestling myself between his thighs as he snored on.

I took a moment to admire his package, in all its green glory, before licking it from root to tip. Agnarr twitched but didn't wake. I licked him again, watching his cock bob, fascinated by it. I wrapped my lips around the head of it and sucked deeply. It was his day too, after all. I wanted to make it memorable. I suckled the head of his cock with all my might, causing his eyes to fly open and jolt up onto his elbows.

"Piper!" He gasped.

"Yes?" I responded in a sultry tone.

"What are you doing?" he said breathlessly.

"Just something I've been wanting to do for a while," I said casually before taking him into my mouth again.

I hollowed my cheeks, sucking him down until felt the tip of him bump the back of my throat, and I let out a moan. Only able to reach halfway down his cock with my mouth, I used my hand to fist the base of him, stroking up and squeezing his knot. I could see his hands clutching his thighs, large fingers digging into his skin. I slid my mouth off of him and looked at him from under my lashes.

"Agnarr, how many times do I have to remind you you can grab my hair? How many times have I pulled yours?" I said.

He sighed, "I know, I know. It just feels like such a treat to begin with. Grabbing your hair seems like too much."

"It is not too much. I want you to take what you want. After all, not every girl gets to give the jarl a blow job." I said, grinning before I took him into my mouth again.

Agnarr ran his hands through my hair before gently gripping each side of my head. He raised and lowered me off his cock tenderly, still hesitant. I hummed in approval as he gained confidence in maneuvering my head. Each time he pulled me up and down, I sucked and nibbled him, using the flat of my tongue to tease the sensitive underside of his cock. He thrust me up and down more earnestly, bucking his hips up and fucking my face.

Ah, yes, this is the unleashed Agnarr I wanted. He surged into my mouth again and again, allowing me to take him as deep as I could down my throat. I hummed, knowing it would add to the intensity he was feeling. I felt his grip on my hair tighten and readied myself for him to cum, but to my surprise, he pulled me off him, using my hair to tilt my head up and look me in the eye.

Agnarr's eyes were blown out with lust, "I don't want to finish without you coming first," he growled.

He was tugging on my hair to maneuver me, and I couldn't help myself from finding it inexplicably hot. We were still figuring out each other's turn-ons, and I *loved* when Agnarr was like this. He knew exactly how to manhandle me without actually hurting me.

Still grasping my hair, Agnarr lifted himself to his knees and swung around behind me. Pressing down on the center of my back, he pushed me down so I was on my elbows and knees in front of him. Agnarr wrapped his warm body around mine, letting my hair go and putting an arm on either side of mine. He kissed from my shoulder to my neck before sucking and lightly nipping at my earlobe. I panted and pushed my ass against his cock.

Agnarr reached behind me and slipped one, then two figures inside me.

"Fuck, Pip, you're so wet already," he said while pumping his fingers in and out of me.

"What can I say," I breathed, "just thinking of your cock makes me wet and ready."

Agnarr, groaned and slipped another finger in, still pumping in and out of me. He continued to do so for a moment longer before adding the pad of his thumb and circling it around my clit. I breathed through my nose as I braced myself on the bed. I couldn't take it anymore. I slammed back on his hand, riding it in earnest.

"Are you ready?" Agnarr asked, voice gravelly.

"More than ready," I panted while still riding his fingers.

He pulled his fingers out and I almost wept at the emptiness I felt. Agnarr didn't make me wait long though. I felt him notch the broad head of his cock at my entrance and slowly begin to push into me. I wiggled my hips in impatience.

I heard Agnarr chuckle behind me, "Am I not meeting my mate's needs?" He said, unable to keep the grin out of his voice.

"I need you *now*," I whined, attempting to slide his cock deeper into me but unable to pass Agnarr's knot without his help.

"Well, lucky for you, little Pip, the feeling is mutual," he said as he slammed himself to the hilt.

I let out an inhuman noise that might have been a groan or might have been a garbled scream. Agnarr gave me only a moment to adjust before pulling himself all the way out again and impaling me once more. We'd fucked more times than I could count since I'd landed on Nilfheim, but each time was just as intense. While I enjoyed the slow, languid love-making we did in the early evenings, I couldn't resist when Agnarr let his primal dominant side out and fucked me like he owned me. At first, he was hesitant that he would hurt me, and I could tell he was holding back. After much coaxing, we'd finally reached a place where he was comfortable manhandling me.

Agnarr pulled himself out all the way, pausing to knead the globes of my ass. I let out a grumble of impatience, earning me a swift smack to one cheek.

I gasped in delight as Agnarr chuckled, "Always impatient, aren't we, Pip?"

Agnarr grasped my hips again and plunged into me again, wrapping his body around mine. He kissed and nipped down the side of my neck. I tilted my head to give him better access, but couldn't help but tease.

"Remember, we're being presented as the new leaders of the tribe today—no hickeys."

"Oh, you don't think it would impress the tribe that their new jarl can keep their jarlin sated?" He growled in my ear, continuing to stroke deep into me.

"I think they are already well aware. Everyone has noticed your habit of leaving hickeys down my neck," I said.

"What can I say, Pip? You're delicious," he murmured as he continued to kiss down my neck before leaning back on his knees.

Hands still on my hips, he pulled me to him, impaling me once again. I groaned as I felt him slide into me. He set a punishing pace, gripping my hips so hard it would leave marks. Stars burst behind my eyes as I felt his knot drag in and out of me.

"Pip, I can't hold back. You smell too good," he said through gritted teeth.

"Agnarr, I never want you to hold back," I breathed as I reared back to meet him thrust for thrust.

I dug my fingers into the covers as Agnarr thrust into me.

My sensitive nipples dragged across the blankets with each punishing thrust, causing goosebumps to rise on my flesh.

"Agnarr, I need more," I cried desperately.

He took one hand from my hip and snaked it around to my front, sliding his fingers between my folds until found my clit, rolling it between his thumb and forefinger. I gasped, and my muscles locked up around him as he continued to rut into me while stroking my clit.

"Oh fuck, don't stop. Don't fucking stop," I panted.

"Come for me, little Pip," Agnarr snarled, pressing down on my clit.

I opened my mouth in a silent scream as I clamped down on him, feeling myself pulse around his cock as I went over the edge. Agnarr's thrusts became even more erratic as he chased his own climax. He pulled my limp body up against his chest as he pistoned into me. He snapped his hips up one last time and came with a bellow before biting down on my neck. I felt pulses of Agnarr's hot cum coat my inner walls.

Agnarr slumped back on his knees, pulling me tightly against his warm chest. He nuzzled my neck and stroked my skin all over as I leaned into him.

"Good morning," I murmured. "I've been wanting to wake you up like that for a while."

"You can wake me up like that any time you'd like, as long as I can do the same," he replied huskily, still stroking my skin.

"Deal," I said, grinning and turning to capture his mouth in a kiss. "We have a big day ahead of us."

"Já, we do. Are you ready, Pip?"

"As ready as I'll ever be. Are you ready?"

"Knowing I have you with me, I'm ready for anything," he said, kissing down my neck again.

Agnarr knew just what to say to bolster my confidence. I was ready for the day, but that didn't mean I wasn't nervous.

"I wouldn't be able to do this without you," I said, my voice coming out smaller than I'd hoped.

"I wouldn't do it without you," he responded, wrapping his arms more tightly around me. "I love you, Pip."

"I love you too."

* * *

THE END

LEXICON

Old Norse is a parent language to many of the Northern Germanic Languages. It is a "dead language" and there is controversy between scholars and historians about the pronunciation and use of many words.

The language used by the orkin is a combination of Old Norse, present day Icelandic, and some proto-Germanic terms. It is not meant to reflect any specific language, history, or people.

While some Old Norse mythology has inspired some aspects of the universe *Abandoned on Niflheim* takes place on, there is little correlation between what I have depicted and any original texts, myths, histories or oral traditions of Old Norse and present day Northern Germanic cultures.

Planets

Niflheim /niv-uh l-heym/ – planet where Piper and other females have been left.

Midgard /mid'gard/ – orkin term for earth.

Tribes

Fýrifírar /fy:ri-fi:rar/ – orkin living in the forest of Niflheim.
Vátrfírar /va:tr-fi:rar/ – orkin living on the coast of Niflheim.
Snaerfírar /stnai:r-fi:rar/ – orkin living in the snowy region in the highest settlements of the Fjall Mountains.

People and Sayings
Já /ya:/ – yes.
Jarl /yärl/ – chief or earl (masculine).
Jarlin /yärl-in/ – chief or earl (feminine).
Kveoja /kʰvɛðja/ – language spoken on Niflheim.
Elska mate /ˈɛlska/ – fated mate.

Flora and Fauna
Hestr /hest-err/ – beasts for riding and carrying goods, similar to horses. They have 8 legs, short curly hair, and a snout more similar to a cow.
Baldrian /bald-ree-an/ – soothing herb, similar to valerian.
Furutré /ˈfu.ɾa-tre:/ – tree found in Niflheim, similar to pine.
Örn /œrtn/ – a large bird, similar to an eagle, local to the Snaerfírar.
Fjall Mountains /fjatl/ – mountain range down the spine of the continent.
Björn /pjœtn/ – bear.
Skogkatt /sku:gkAt/ – large, long-haired fairy cats who live in the mountains and climb rocks.
Valhnot /vahl-nut/ – tree nut local to Fýrifírar, medium brown in color.
Grautr /græʉt-er/ – grain like porridge served for first meal, usually sweetened with fruit and syrup.
Niflfýri - forest of mist that separates the Fýrifírar from the Snaerfírar.

Time

Dagr /ˈdɑgr̩/ – day.
Vika /ˈvika/ – week.
Mánuthur /ˈmauːnʏðʏr/ – month.
Ár /auːr/ – year.
Áratugur /auːr aˈtʰʏːɣʏr/ – decade.

ACKNOWLEDGMENTS

I was tempted to publish *Agnarr's Teacher* without acknowledgements. It seemed too daunting to sit and think of all the people that have helped me along the way. But, I am not the same person I was when I started this journey eighteen months ago, and there are people who deserve my unending gratitude.

In January of 2022 I decided to attempt to read for pleasure again—something I hadn't done since I'd started college. I had spent so much time in graduate school and raising my children that I no longer had a safe space in my own head. I fell down a rabbit hole of reading and have never looked back.

It wasn't long into my journey that I discovered Ruby Dixon and *Ice Planet Barbarians*. I unabashedly love Ruby and the worlds she has created.

Ruby's books led me to the book community, without which this book would not exist. It is filled with magical (mostly) women cheering each other on and encouraging other women to do things only a mediocre white man would dream of. Without the book community I would never have met the authors, editors, and readers who now make up some of my closest friends.

Out of the book community came my Trash Cat Coven, Carlotta Hughes, Jersey Konlyn and Rob Ford—the creators of our little slice of the internet, the Smut Tea Stories Podcast. You have been my therapists, mentors, and cheerleaders more times than I care to admit. Without you, I would still be trying to write my first blow job.

To Sara Ivy Hill, Ami Wright, and and Krista Luna. You three trusted me with my first ever ARC reads. I didn't even know what an ARC read was. It pulled back the curtain on the world of writing and helped me take my first steps.

To every single author that has sprinted with me on Discord or patiently explained how to create a newsletter, strong women raise strong women.

And lastly, to my therapist, who has tried harder than anyone to get me to stop telling myself I can't.

ABOUT THE AUTHOR

Jen has been reading for as long as she can remember. She used to get in trouble for reading *Little House on the Prairie* under her desk in elementary school.

Jen is married to a very polite Englishman she brought back as a souvenir from her college study abroad trip. She has identical twin mutants who make her question her sanity daily. She enjoys reading about alien peens, napping, and watching soothing cooking shows.

She is a goth kid at heart and truly wishes she could wear platform combat boots and black nail polish on all occasions.

* * *

www.authorjeniferwood.com

www.ingramcontent.com/pod-product-compliance
Lightning Source LLC
Chambersburg PA
CBHW020134310726
48970CB00006B/1865